Greg tightened his hold, wanting her closer still

Then suddenly the contact was broken. She shrank back, pushing against his chest, her eyes wild with shock.

"Father!" she gasped. "No!"

Greg stared at her dazedly. Her words made no sense to him. He'd forgotten his part in the masquerade, forgotten everything but Julie.

"Father, please," she whispered desperately, "let me go. We . . . we can't. It's . . . wrong."

"It's right," he said hoarsely, and bent to kiss her again.

"Please, we'll both regret this. Your vows—"

"Julie, things aren't always what they seem. Believe me."

"No." She struggled out of his arms and stood, trembling, a few inches away.

It's over, Greg told himself. *Enough of this disguise. I can tell her. Now.* As she watched in shock, he reached up to remove his collar. . . .

ABOUT THE AUTHOR

Texas native Lorna Michaels decided she would be a writer when she was three years old, and with the publication of *Blessing in Disguise*, her first work of fiction, she is proud to have achieved that goal. A speech pathologist with a busy private practice, Lorna still finds time for her writing and is hard at work on her next book. She is married and the mother of three grown children.

Blessing in Disguise

LORNA MICHAELS

Harlequin Books

TORONTO • NEW YORK • LONDON
AMSTERDAM • PARIS • SYDNEY • HAMBURG
STOCKHOLM • ATHENS • TOKYO • MILAN

Published July 1990

ISBN 0-373-70412-7

CHAPTER ONE

"I PROMISE YOU, Allen. There's a Pulitzer with your name on it for this one."

Greg Allen leaned back in his chair and raised a skeptical brow. Accustomed to his senior editor's hard sell prior to any new assignment, he folded his arms across his chest and prepared to listen. "Okay, Lowrey, spell it out. If it's a short assignment and it's here in Washington, I might be interested."

Tom Lowrey brushed aside the clutter of papers on his overcrowded desk and leaned forward, cigarette in hand. "I want you to go to Houston to get a story on illegal aliens—"

"No chance. In case you've forgotten, my vacation's long overdue. Give this one to Skinner."

"Skinner doesn't speak Spanish."

"Someone else then. Brad Duncan."

"Duncan's good, but he doesn't have your experience. He's never gone undercover."

"There's always a first time. Look, I've got a ticket to Aspen. My suitcase is packed."

Lowrey stubbed out his cigarette in the heaping ashtray and immediately lit another. "At least hear me out. We've gotten wind of something unusual going on. Disappearances in the Hispanic community...people picked off street corners."

"Probably the INS."

Lowrey shook his head. "We've checked. The Immigration and Naturalization Service isn't responsible. And some of the people who disappeared aren't aliens. Hispanics, but not illegals."

"Interesting," Greg agreed, "but not good enough. Worldwide Press has people in Houston. Give it to one of them."

"Don't think the Houston bureau hasn't tried. So far we've come up against a blank wall. You know how aliens are with the press—they shut up like clams. Not a word, even though over thirty people have disappeared. We want to set someone up in the community, gain the people's confidence. We're sure something big's going on there."

In spite of himself, Greg felt his adrenaline begin to pump. If he uncovered the reason behind the disappearances, it would be a real scoop for himself and for Worldwide Press. "Well—"

"Got your attention, hmm?" Lowrey grinned. "Look, Greg. Put off your vacation, do the story, and I'll see if I can wangle you an extra week off afterward. No one could handle this story as well as you."

Greg smiled at the rare compliment. "Thanks," he said quietly, then got down to business. "We'll need information about who's disappeared, where they came from, their legal status. But how do I get it—move into the neighborhood and impersonate a Hispanic?"

"Hardly. We might darken your skin a shade or dye your hair." His eyes traveled to Greg's wavy blond hair. "But, short of special contact lenses, I doubt we could do anything about those eyes."

Greg nodded. "They're definitely blue. So," he said, his mind toying with the possibilities of the story, "what's my cover? I hope you've dreamed up something better than the last time I went undercover. Working on the docks in Miami to investigate smuggling was not my idea of a good time."

"You'll have it easier this go-round. You're going to be a priest in an inner-city church."

Greg shook his head as if to clear it. "Run that by me again, Lowrey. I must be losing my hearing. For a minute, I thought I heard you say something about a priest."

"You know damn well you heard me, Allen, and that's exactly what I said."

"How in hell did you dream that one up?"

"Simple. You're Catholic, aren't you?"

"I was brought up Catholic," Greg admitted. "I sing in the shower, too, but that doesn't mean I can impersonate Pavarotti."

"That's all been taken care of. I've arranged an instant seminary course for you."

"Instant seminary!" A peal of laughter burst from him. "The man is crazy."

Lowery shot him an injured look. "My cousin, Jim Donnelly, is a priest at St. Cecilia's here in Washington. He's agreed to give you some pointers."

"You can't be serious about this, Tom. The Catholic church would never agree to someone impersonating a priest. Who dreamed this up?"

"Two priests."

"Two— You *are* serious."

"Damn right."

"How'd you get in contact with these priests?"

"Conner in the Houston bureau has been in touch with them for some time, monitoring the situation. Last week they told him they're willing to do anything, even put their careers on the line, to get to the bottom of this. So far, no one who could help has shown any interest."

"That means the police."

"Yeah. Chasing down illegal aliens isn't high on their priority list."

"So what do the priests want from Worldwide?" Greg asked.

"They'll take the risk of putting someone in their church. As a priest, he'll automatically gain the community's trust *and* have access to information. They want someone who can ask the right questions, who'll be discreet—"

"But who can put the situation on Page One when the time's right," Greg finished.

"Exactly—the one thing they can't do themselves. And you're the guy to do it."

"I don't like it," Greg muttered. "Disguising me as a priest will slow the investigation to a crawl. I'll be there till August."

"So you'll scuba instead of ski when it's over."

"Dammit! I'm not concerned about my vacation but about my ability to dig out a story. Maybe illegals will talk to a priest, but what about the police? What'll they say when I show up with my little notebook and my collar?"

"We'll worry about the police later. Your first job is to concentrate on the Hispanics…as a priest. Now, take a few days to get some background on illegal aliens, then we'll arrange for you to meet with Father Donnelly. And after that you'll be on your way to Houston."

Greg sighed. The discussion about his cover was over…for today. If this didn't sound like such a good story, he'd be tempted to tell Lowrey to forget it. At least the location was a plus, he thought, glancing out the window at streets covered with late January slush. "Houston," he said aloud. "Sounds like a good place to be in the dead of winter."

Lowrey looked smug. "I'll take that to mean a yes."

Greg gave him a full grin then. "Why not? Some time in a warm climate—and it's certainly safer than my last trip south." His hand automatically went to his shoulder and rubbed the spot where the Nicaraguan bullet had entered.

Lowrey rose and walked Greg to the door. "At any rate, Allen, the priesthood will be a nice change for you. A month or so of celibacy will do you good."

Greg chuckled. "You married men have a distorted picture of the single life. You think it's all wine and women."

"Isn't it?"

"Nah. It's TV dinners and fantasies."

Lowrey opened his office door. "Get outta here, Allen," he said. "Go home and heat up a *Le Menu*."

With a grin and a wave over his shoulder, Greg left.

TWO WEEKS LATER Greg was on a plane bound for Houston. The last fourteen days had been busy. He'd read everything he could find on illegal aliens and followed up by interviewing the director of the Immigration and Naturalization Service.

He'd met with Tom Lowrey twice, each time trying unsuccessfully to convince him to scrap the priest idea. Greg had a healthy respect for Tom's instincts about news stories—they were usually correct—but this disguise was, in his opinion, absurd. Still, Tom was set on having him go as a priest, so a priest he would be. Nevertheless, Greg decided, he'd have no compunction about doffing his clerical identity if it hampered his ability to get his story.

Not that he hadn't enjoyed his crash course in the priesthood. Father Donnelly had been an excellent tutor, with a quick wit and a keen grasp of the problems that might be encountered by a "pseudo priest" as he had dubbed Greg.

The evening before his departure for Houston, Stephanie Barrett had thrown a party for Greg. Steph, fellow reporter for Worldwide Press, had done everything with her usual enthusiasm and flair. There was plenty to eat, and the liquor flowed freely. Greg took the expected jokes about sexual abstinence in good humor.

When the guests left, Greg sprawled on the couch and Stephanie curled up beside him. "How do you feel about this assignment, Greg?" Clear green eyes met his.

"It has definite possibilities."

"If it does, you'll find them. You're one of the best."

Greg grinned at her. "My fan club."

"I'll miss you, Allen," Stephanie said.

"I'll miss you, too." He meant it. He liked Stephanie. She was lively and intelligent, a friend as well as a colleague. There'd been a time when he'd thought she might be more. But it hadn't worked out. Both of them were too committed to their careers.

He'd always planned to settle down "someday," to have the kind of home he'd grown up in, but the challenge and excitement of his job had fascinated him more than any woman had. Not that he didn't like women. He did, very much. He liked them as friends, confidantes, lovers—and considered his relations with the opposite sex an important part of his life. But he'd never met a woman who'd captured his mind and heart, and lately he'd begun doubting he ever would.

The pilot's voice interrupted his reverie. "We're beginning our descent to Houston Intercontinental airport. The temperature is forty-seven, and skies are cloudy."

Immediately Greg turned his attention to the window. Below, the twinkling lights of the South's largest city came into view.

Houston! He felt the excitement and anticipation that always came at the start of an assignment. The challenge of digging out information and presenting it in a way that enlightened the public was irresistible.

The plane's wing dipped. The lights came closer, and a few minutes later he felt the bump of wheels touching the ground.

Phil Barnes, head of Worldwide's Houston office, was waiting in the terminal. Phil was a genial middle-aged man with a friendly handshake. Some forty pounds overweight, he reminded Greg of a balding Santa Claus.

"You look at home in your 'uniform,'" Phil remarked as they headed toward Baggage Claim.

Greg tugged at the collar that felt out of place around his neck. "I'm trying to get used to it."

"What are you calling yourself?"

"Father Gregory."

"Sounds good. Let's pick up you bags, Father, and head for the church. On the way I'll fill you in on the people you'll be working with."

When they pulled out of the airport parking lot, Phil continued the conversation "The priests have thought this out carefully. St. Martha's Church is a few blocks from the Port of Houston, smack in the middle of the area where these disappearances have occurred. You'll have access to a lot of people."

"How?"

"St. Martha's has a strong community-service program run by a social worker. Information about the community usually comes in that way. You'll be working with her."

Greg grimaced. "Great. First I'm a priest, now I'm a social worker, too."

Phil gave a wheezy, fat man's laugh. "You'll enjoy it. It'll be a new experience."

"What about the disappearances?" Greg asked. "How much have you learned?"

"Three months ago a young Mexican vanished. The family went to the police—"

"Illegal aliens called the police? Unbelievable!" Greg said.

"This family are citizens," Phil explained, "so they weren't afraid to call the authorities. But the boy's never been found. Later, we began hearing of other disappearances, some citizens, but mostly aliens."

"What's the word from the police?"

"Nothing," Phil replied. "They say the aliens are the INS's problem. The INS says they're not in the missing persons business—everyone's passing the buck. Your job's to come up with some hard facts."

"I'll start by talking to the family of the first young man who disappeared, and to the police."

"Uh-uh, not this time. You're a priest, remember, and you have to act like one."

"So I'll leave the collar at home."

"And blow your cover on the first day? No way. Besides, we have to think about the priests. They'd be in deep trouble if this got out. So you'll have to be subtle—gain the people's confidence. Then the information will come to you."

"I think it's a damn waste of time to do it this way," Greg grumbled.

"The direct approach hasn't worked so far. Just keep in character. No direct confrontations," Phil said.

They rode on in silence as Greg mulled over the facts Phil had given him. Again he reminded himself that his bosses usually knew what they were doing. Worldwide Press hadn't become the second largest news service in the country by making mistakes. He'd try to keep that in mind while he waited for the information that everyone assured him would come to him.

After a long ride down a freeway bounded by endless strip centers, billboards, and lounges with garish signs, Greg had his first view of Houston's skyline—imposing modern skyscrapers laced with lights against the night sky. "Awesome," he said.

Phil nodded. "The city of the future, all glass and steel. But wait until you see the contrast." Ten minutes later he turned off the freeway. "Welcome to the *barrio*," he said.

The change was almost immediate. No sleek modern buildings now. Instead Greg saw warehouses and small factories. Signs were in Spanish as well as English—*restaurante major, el super mercado, joyería*. Off the main thoroughfare he caught glimpses of small frame houses on tiny plots of ground. "Quite a difference," he agreed.

Within a few minutes Phil stopped the car. "Here we are."

Greg turned. Even in the darkness, which partially obscured the building, the church seemed to reach out to him. He saw a graceful steeple and windows of stained glass set in plaster. He smiled, surprised at his immediate reaction to the building. "I like it."

They walked around the corner to the rectory where Phil introduced Greg to the two priests and then left. The priests invited Greg into the parlor, furnished austerely with a sofa and several chairs of an indeterminate period, upholstered in a muted shade of gray.

Father Rudolfo was in his mid-thirties, Greg's own age, and Father Curry slightly older. Though they welcomed him and offered him tea at the dining-room table, Greg sensed their tension and wondered if they'd had second thoughts about the project. "You're taking a chance by doing this," he said, deciding to voice their concerns.

Almost inadvertently, Father Curry looked over his shoulder. "We are," he said, lowering his voice. "I don't mind telling you I was opposed to the idea at first, but Rudy convinced me we had to do it.''

Greg glanced at Father Rudolfo, the more soft-spoken of the two men, in some surprise. The priest responded with a rakish grin. *Lord, I hope he isn't into playing cops and robbers,* Greg thought, but Father Rudolfo's next words dispelled Greg's concerns about his motives.

"Our people are frightened, we are frightened, and we are getting no help from the police," he said in his softly accented voice. "The only ones who have shown any interest are from your news bureau. So I decided, why not bring in someone from the news service, someone who wants a good story and will work to get it. I thought long and hard about this and prayed for guidance, and it seemed the only way. I know we risk much, but I am not afraid."

Greg nodded. "I respect your courage. I'll do everything I can to cooperate."

"Of course," Father Curry said, "you will function as a priest in name only. You will not say Mass, hear confession, or administer any of the sacraments."

"Of course," Greg agreed.

Father Curry continued, "We ask that you do nothing to violate our parishioners' confidences. In working with the social worker, you will hear details of their lives that should go no further." Greg heard the strain in the older man's voice.

"Our social worker is Julie Whitaker," Father Curry added. The mention of the woman's name seemed to have a calming effect, for the tension left his voice. "You'll find her very knowledgeable about the people and the community."

Father Rudolfo agreed. "We are fortunate to have her here. She began part-time after her husband died, and within a few months she was so busy that we needed her full-time. She does the work of two. I think St. Martha had our people's welfare in mind and sent her to us.

"We have one other person on our staff," he went on. "Grace Matheson, our secretary and also a widow. Of course, neither of them have been told your true identity. We have simply said that a new priest is arriving."

"Let's keep it that way," Greg decided.

"Good. We have your agreement then, not to discuss who you are without our permission?"

"You have it," Greg said firmly and listened to Father Curry exhale a sigh of relief.

"And now," Father Rudolfo continued, "I will show you to your room. I will apologize for it ahead of time. It is very plain, but you must understand that we priests do not lead very luxurious lives." He led Greg upstairs to a small room furnished with a single bed, a desk, and a chair. "Make yourself at home," he said.

Greg thanked him, unpacked quickly and was soon sleeping soundly.

Greg spent the weekend learning about St. Martha's and its environs. Seen in the daylight, the small church charmed him. The tan brick structure, flanked by crape myrtle and magnolia, seemed curiously at home despite its drab surroundings. It exuded an aura of tranquillity and warmth that contrasted sharply with the run-down neighborhood.

Enjoying the February sunshine, Greg strolled across the small, neatly manicured churchyard and wandered through the nearby streets. The air was crisp and fresh, just cool enough for a light jacket.

Small, shabby houses with peeling paint lined the cracked sidewalks. Cars and pickups, old but carefully maintained, were parked alongside. A scruffy yellow dog barked at him from behind a chain-link fence; in another yard a gray tabby cat dozed in the sunshine. Despite the dilapidated appear-

ance of most of the homes, the sagging porches were filled
with a profusion of plants in terra-cotta pots. Through open
windows Greg could hear the cadence of Spanish conversation and smell the aroma of chili peppers.

Most of the people he passed were Hispanics. They eyed
him with curious interest and responded with deference to
his friendly greetings. Greg was surprised to find himself
enjoying his role as the new priest.

Across the street from the church he found a tiny, scrupulously clean bakery advertising *pan dulce*. Greg introduced himself to the young Mexican girl behind the counter.
She smiled shyly, and when he ordered, politely refused to
let him pay. Greg felt a twinge of guilt. After all, he wasn't
what he appeared to be. Yet he knew he'd hurt the girl's
feelings if he refused her offer, so he smiled and said, "I'll
accept this in the name of St. Martha's." When she nodded, he saw that he had done the right thing. He left,
munching a chunk of biscuitlike bread with sugary topping, and headed back to the church.

On Sunday Greg sat at the side of the altar as the priests
said Mass. The sounds, sights, and smells—the clicking of
rosary beads, the congregants' bowed heads, the odor of
candle wax—recalled boyhood Sundays in a small adobe
church in Arizona. He had grown away from organized religion in adulthood, but the familiar rituals evoked a feeling of nostalgia for his childhood.

By Sunday night he felt very much at home. The Spartan
atmosphere of his room pleased him. There would be no
distractions there. He anticipated none in his daily routine,
either. He sat quietly, making methodical notes in his neat
script. Again, that sense of anticipation he had experienced
on the plane surfaced. He looked forward to the days ahead.

Later, as he drifted toward sleep, the thought came to him
that Lowrey just might have been right. This assignment

would be special for him. He didn't know in what way, but the feeling was there, strong and sure.

JULIE WHITAKER was in a hurry this morning. The new priest would be at St. Martha's today, and she was anxious to meet him. Nevertheless, as she made her turn a few blocks from the church, her attention was arrested by a man. Dressed in shorts and T-shirt, he was running toward her along the sidewalk. She was immediately curious. He certainly didn't live in this Hispanic neighborhood—he was too blond—so what was he doing here, out for a morning run along the Ship Channel?

She studied him as he came closer and felt the pull of attraction...and the stirring of something more elemental. Tall and lean, with muscles that bunched rhythmically as he ran, he was the kind of man any woman would look at twice. Julie slowed the car and let herself enjoy him as he passed. She got a good look at his face and found it as attractive as the rest of him. His brows were furrowed in concentration on his running, his nose was straight, his mouth just short of sensuous. She continued to watch him in her rearview mirror, noting the way his damp hair curled at the back of his neck.

In the eighteen months since Dirk had died she'd rarely noticed a man. Perhaps her interest was a tribute to this stranger's virile good looks, or perhaps, like the first tiny cracks in a frozen pond, the ice around her heart was cracking, too.

Guiding her car into St. Martha's small parking lot, Julie focused on the coming day. She had several letters to write and some filing to do, and she wanted to get that out of the way before she met with the new priest. Thank goodness she was early.

She got out of her car and hurried to the door, but before she opened it, she glanced back at the street. No, he wasn't there, but she wondered, just wondered, if she came early tomorrow, whether she might see him again.

GREG SPENT A PLEASANT HALF HOUR getting acquainted with Grace Matheson, an energetic gray-haired woman in her mid-fifties who told him she had been working at the church for the six years since her husband died. She graciously offered to help him any way she could. Now it was time to seek out the other widow, the social worker, Mrs....Whitaker, was that her name? Her office, Grace told him, was next to the parlor, which functioned as her waiting room.

He located the parlor without difficulty and stepped inside. Couches with faded upholstery and straight-backed wooden chairs were grouped around the large room. Scarred wooded tables held Spanish newspapers and frayed Spanish translations of *Ladies Home Journal*, *Time* and *Newsweek*.

At first Greg thought the room was unoccupied, but then his eyes were drawn to someone standing on a chair beside a large file cabinet in a corner. He had a view of slim legs tanned to a healthy gold, and a blue wool skirt that fitted over gently flaring hips. The woman's upper body was hidden behind the open file drawer and her face was obscured by the large folder she held, but he caught a glimpse of rich brown hair with glints of auburn, highlighted by the sun shining through the window behind her. He stared. He couldn't help it. Forgetting his assignment, forgetting his role, he simply stood there for a moment feasting his eyes on this unexpected delight.

She put down the file, and he heard her startled, "Oh," as she saw him staring at her. He cleared his throat. "I was...uh...looking for Mrs. Whitaker."

Her lips curved. "I'm Mrs. Whitaker," she said. "And you must be Father—"

"Uh...Gregory." Why was he stammering like a schoolboy, he asked himself irritably. He'd seen his share of women, prettier ones even. It was just the surprise of finding someone so young when he'd been expecting an elderly widow.

The woman stepped gracefully off the chair and started across the room. Suddenly she halted, and her eyes widened with something like shock. Then, as if forcing herself to go on, she continued toward him. But Greg was too absorbed in watching her to pay attention to her behavior.

Her shoulder-length hair framed a face that was serene rather than beautiful—high cheekbones, straight nose, soft, enticing lips. She moved easily, like a dancer, her hips swaying slightly. The soft rounding of her breasts was visible beneath a fleecy blue angora sweater.

"I'm so glad to meet you," she said, extending her hand. "We've been looking forward to having you here."

Greg took her hand. It was small and soft, but her handshake was firm. He wanted to keep her hand in his, exploring the smooth skin and delicate bone structure, but he knew he couldn't. He dropped it abruptly and searched for something to say. "I...I was expecting an older person."

"Oh?" Her wide brown eyes sparkled with amusement.

"I was told you were a widow."

The sparks faded. "I *am* a widow. It can happen at any age. I was twenty-seven."

"I'm sorry."

"It's all right." Then she added briskly, "You said you were looking for me. Would you like to step into my office?"

Greg nodded and followed her across the room, again noticing her graceful carriage. "No distractions, huh?" he muttered under his breath. He would have to be careful, or Mrs. Whitaker could prove to be very distracting indeed.

CHAPTER TWO

THANKFUL FOR THE FEW SECONDS she had to collect herself, Julie led Father Gregory into her office. When she'd turned and glanced at him, he'd seemed vaguely familiar, but as she'd started across the room and gotten a closer look, she knew why. He was the runner.

That beautiful, sexy man she'd seen on the street this morning was a...a priest! Well, she'd certainly be seeing him again...but in a different role than she'd imagined.

For a moment, she was unreasonably angry at him...for destroying the fantasy she had been building since she first saw him. Then she directed the anger at herself. *You're a competent professional, Julie Whitaker. Now act like one.*

Taking her own advice, she turned and said pleasantly, "Coffee, Father?"

"Thanks. Black."

She poured a cup from the pot she kept on the table, sat down behind her desk, and looked at him thoughtfully. Her profession had accustomed her to sizing up people quickly. The man before her was even more handsome up close. From her car window she'd seen his even features and thick crop of sandy-blond hair. Now she could feel the full impact of his deep blue eyes with tiny laugh lines crinkling at the corners. His posture, as he sat across from her, was relaxed, his smile friendly, but she had the unmistakable feeling that, like a lazy tiger, he could spring into action instantly. There was power here. And confidence. The man radiated self-assurance.

Now she forced herself to see him in his professional capacity. His mission, she'd been told, was to work with her, helping parishioners with everyday problems. She'd been awaiting his arrival eagerly. She never seemed to have enough time to do everything that was needed. She was eager to have someone to work alongside her, someone who knew what he was doing. She hoped Father Gregory did, but she'd reserve judgment until she saw him in action.

"I'll be working directly with our parishioners," the priest began, "but first I want to get a feel for the community. You know the people. You know their situations. I want to be your shadow for the next few days—see what you do, go where you go."

"I'd like that," she said. "We're a small parish, but the problems are enormous. Most of the people here are from Mexico. Some were here long enough to be eligible for amnesty, and we're helping them through the legalization process. But even with legalization, they still need help finding jobs, filling out forms—" she leaned forward, warming to her topic. "They need help getting their children into the right school programs, getting medical care, dealing with employers—the list is endless.

"And the others—those who didn't get here early enough for amnesty. Are there many?" He withdrew a small yellow pad from his pocket and began to make notes.

Julie shrugged. "We don't know exactly how many. Most of them don't admit to being illegal, even to us. They're shadow people, living in fear, keeping out of sight." She sighed and her eyes clouded. "And of course, they come and go."

"Meaning?"

"Some of them go back to Mexico, some get picked up and deported, some just disappear."

"Disappear?" The priest's tone sharpened almost imperceptibly, but Julie heard it.

"Yes," she said slowly. "Lately there've been rumors of people vanishing."

He nodded. "I heard about that this weekend."

"I thought at first they were exaggerations," Julie continued, "but I've been hearing too many of these tales recently. The people in the Hispanic community are becoming alarmed, and so am I. The police haven't turned up anything. It's frustrating."

"Perhaps you could help."

She saw his hand tighten on the pencil as he fixed her with a piercing blue gaze. Surprised, she stared at the clear sapphire eyes that seemed to bore straight into her. "What could I do?"

"Ask questions, look for patterns."

"The police have done that."

"Oh, I suspect you could learn a lot more than they have," the priest said. "People tell you things they'd never divulge to the authorities. Just do what your profession is best at—listen and probe a bit."

"And then?"

"When you learn something, talk it over with me."

"I don't mean to be impertinent, Father, but wouldn't it be more appropriate to talk it over with the police?"

Father Gregory responded with an annoyed grimace. "Let me be the judge of that."

"I'm afraid I'm used to making my own decisions."

She saw a flash of anger, quickly masked. Then he said mildly, "I'm interested in anything that might cause unrest in the parish. Father Rudolfo and Father Curry mentioned these disappearances to me when I got here. Being a new arrival in the community, perhaps I can see things more objectively. I'm here to help. I'd like your cooperation.''

Julie felt a surge of annoyance. Perhaps *he* could see things more objectively? More objectively than she could, he obviously thought. Perhaps he'd never worked with a woman before, or maybe he hadn't had much experience with social workers. Objectivity was essential in her profession. She frowned but told herself to keep quiet. *After all, the best way to show him what an objective professional you are is to stay objective.*

So she nodded quietly and reminded herself that she wasn't one to lose her temper. It was just that the events of the morning—the surprise and, she admitted, the disappointment of seeing that he was a priest, had unsettled her. She'd give the man a chance, even though his intensity made her uncomfortable. She just hoped he wouldn't be the impulsive kind who created more problems than he solved.

Her first priority, after all, was the people of the community. She never thought of them as clients. That word was too cold to describe the relationship she had developed with the men and women she served. She felt a fierce protectiveness toward them, a deep commitment. For they had done as much for her as she had for them. Working at St. Martha's, becoming a part of this community, had been her salvation since Dirk's death. So, she decided, she'd cooperate with Father Gregory—as long as it was in the best interests of her people. "I'll do what I can," she murmured, amending that in her mind to *I'll do what I think best.*

A soft tap on the door interrupted them, and Julie rose to answer it. A dark-skinned middle-aged woman in an ill-fitting flowered dress stood outside.

"*Señora*, may I speak with you?" she said timidly in Spanish. Then, noticing the priest, she backed away. "Pardon me. I did not know you were busy."

"No, please come in." Julie led her to a chair. "This is Father Gregory, our new priest. Father, this is Sarita Gomez."

"Buenos dias, Sarita." Father Gregory held out his hand.

"Oh, Father. I'm so happy to meet you. If I am disturbing you—"

"No, not at all," he continued in Spanish. "I'm going to spend the morning watching Señora Whitaker work. Go ahead."

His warm smile and fluent Spanish put Sarita at ease. She sat down and turned to Julie.

Greg settled back in his chair and listened. Part of his mind registered the woman's concern about her grandson's vision problems, while the other part replayed his discussion with Julie Whitaker about the disappearances. He was relieved she'd mentioned the problem herself. That had given him the perfect opening to enlist her aid. He hoped she wasn't so rigid that she would insist on reporting everything they learned to the police—or worse yet, to the Galveston-Houston Diocese. If so, she could hamper his investigation—and endanger the priests as well. He'd just have to keep an eye on her.

He focused again on the women's conversation as Julie gave Sarita the address of a clinic that offered free vision testing.

"Oh, gracias, señora. I knew you could help. This one is an angel, Father."

FOR THE REST OF THE MORNING Greg watched and listened as Julie met with one person after another, always sympathetic, never impatient.

He was a conscientious reporter. He made careful notes about the parishioners' concerns, including all the pertinent details. Such information would add interest to his story.

But he was, above all, a writer who used all his senses to make a story come alive. And through his senses now, he absorbed the scene around him. The musty odor of books on the shelves along the wall. The faint hum of traffic on the street outside. Dust motes playing in the shaft of sunlight shining through the blinds that covered the room's only window. The room itself, which could have been drab, was brightened by posters in sunny yellows, cool greens, and vibrant reds. Throw pillows in the same cheerful colors stood out against the faded beige of the couch and chairs.

The variegated leaves of ivy trailed from a white porcelain pot across a tabletop, and a grinning china cat occupied one corner of Julie Whitaker's neatly organized desk. Altogether a warm, inviting ambience that seemed to say, "Come in. Here you'll find compassion without censure, help without obligation."

But most of all, the message emanated from the slender woman seated behind the desk. For a few moments Greg let his pencil still and watched her.

Her voice flowed over him like warm honey. The lilt of her Spanish reminded him of sultry nights under tropical stars. When she raised a hand to brush a stray lock from her face, he imagined his own fingers sliding through the silkiness of her hair. From his vantage point, he caught a glimpse of her legs—long, slim legs, made for wrapping around a man's body.

Damn, he thought, mentally kicking himself. What was he doing daydreaming about a woman when he was here to do a job? He picked up his pencil and began to write.

He was so engrossed that, when the phone rang, he was startled.

Julie picked it up. "Julie Whitaker."

Greg noted her surprised tones as she said, "Jack, how are you?" She listened for a moment, then said, "I'm sorry. Your company dinner sounds lovely, but my hours are so long I wouldn't be able to make it in time."

She was turned slightly away from him so Greg couldn't see her face. Was that regret in her voice? He wondered who Jack was and what Julie Whitaker's relationship was with him . . . and was annoyed with himself for caring.

By twelve-thirty the crowd of people waiting to see Julie had thinned. She turned to Greg with a smile and suggested that they break for lunch and meet again at one-thirty. Her smile, he noticed, was no different than the one she'd given to each person she'd seen that morning. But why should he expect anything else? He was a priest, after all, and women didn't respond to priests as they did to other men. He found his disguise, which he had been enjoying only a few hours ago, now seemed an unwanted encumbrance.

He wandered over to the rectory and found the priests seated at the large wooden kitchen table, already having lunch. The warm kitchen smelled of thyme, garlic, and the rich odor of browned meat.

"How was your morning? Any problems?" Father Curry inquired.

Obviously Father Curry was a worrier. "No. It went well," Greg said reassuringly as he sat down and helped himself to a hearty stew of fresh vegetables and thick chunks of beef.

"What do you think of our Mrs. Whitaker?" Father Rudolfo asked.

Great legs. "She seemed very competent."

"Ah, she is a jewel," Father Rudolfo smiled. "The people adore her."

"So I noticed. She's concerned about the disappear-ances. I've enlisted her cooperation in digging out infor-mation."

"I imagine she knows very little, no more than any of us, but I'm sure she'll do what she can to help," Father Curry said. "Rudy and I have come up with some information you might find helpful, too. At first the disappearances seemed to us to be isolated incidents, but when they began occur-ring more frequently, we started keeping records—of who disappeared, where, and when."

"The record keeping was Tim's idea," Father Rudolfo remarked. "He is our organizer, our human computer. He likes to deal with facts and numbers, put everything down in black-and-white."

"It's fortunate that he does," Greg commented. "It'll save me a lot of time." He turned to Father Curry. "What have you learned?"

"It seems that all the disappearances involved men."

"Interesting," Greg said. "No women at all?"

"None that we know of," Father Curry replied. "That's significant, don't you agree?"

"Could be," Greg said thoughtfully. "I'll give Phil Barnes a call after and see if his information agrees with yours. If it does, we could be on to something."

WHEN JULIE LEFT FATHER GREGORY, she headed for Grace Matheson's office. The two women usually lunched to-gether and today, having eaten only a hurried breakfast, Julie was hungry. When she arrived at Grace's office, the older woman had already spread out cheese, crackers, and fresh vegetables and was beginning her meal. Julie poured herself a cup of coffee and sank onto a chair.

"Whew, I'm beat. That was some morning." She opened her lunch bag and took out a tuna sandwich.

"New priest causing problems?" Grace inquired.

"No, we were just unusually busy. Father Gregory didn't cause any of it. He just sat and watched."

"What did you think of him?" Grace asked.

Beautiful eyes. "He seemed very competent."

"He's different from other priests I've known," Grace said thoughtfully.

Julie stared in surprise. So Grace had noticed it, too. She'd thought her own perception of Father Gregory was colored by the experience of seeing him on the street, but if Grace had the same impression... Interested in the other woman's view, she asked, "In what way?"

Grace frowned. "I can't put my finger on it. There's just something different about him. Didn't you notice?"

Julie shrugged. She wasn't about to tell Grace what she'd noticed—that Father Gregory wasn't *at all* like other priests. He seemed so... male. Maybe it was that aura of leashed power, or maybe it was his blond good looks. *And maybe, Julie Whitaker, you've been alone too long. Maybe if you'd had some normal contact with men, you wouldn't be reacting to a priest of all people, like a lovesick adolescent.*

"Well, pay attention and see what you think," Grace continued. "Will you be working with him again?"

"Mmm, for a few days. He's attached himself to me, says he wants to be my shadow."

"If you ask me, what you need is a real man as your shadow."

Julie sighed. She and Grace had had this conversation many times before. "I didn't ask you, you know," she said gently but firmly. "And what makes you think Father Gregory isn't a real man?"

"You know what I mean, dear. You need a man who can relate to you as a woman, who can bring some love into your life. It's not good for a young woman like you to be alone.

You should go out with Jack Benton. He's asked you enough times."

"Grace, I don't want to go out with Jack Benton. He's only asked me because he was a friend of my husband's."

"He'd be perfect for you. He's successful and so good-looking. I saw his picture in 'Around Houston' this morning. He was at the museum opening last night."

Julie rolled her eyes heavenward. Trust Grace to know that. The older woman was an avid reader of the local gossip columns and a virtual bloodhound at ferreting out tidbits of news in the parish.

"I think you're missing your chance," Grace went on. "Someone else will snap him up."

Despite what she had been telling herself only moments before, Julie answered, "Grace, I'm perfectly content being alone for now—and perhaps forever."

The older woman shook her head. "Julie Whitaker, someday I hope to see you eat those words, with as much gusto as you're eating that sandwich."

Julie laughed and took another bite. "I don't know about the future, but for now Father Gregory is the only man in my life."

AN HOUR LATER Greg strolled into Julie's office to find her pulling on her coat. "I'm going to a meeting of the Coalition of Latin American Organizations, Father. Would you like to come along?"

"As I said this morning, 'Whither thou goest . . .'"

Julie gave him a quick grin. "Follow me then."

Greg opened the door that led outside and stood back to let her pass. As she brushed by him, he caught a whiff of her perfume. A delicate floral. Annoyed at himself for noticing, he followed her across the parking lot.

To his surprise Julie halted beside a late-model silver Mercedes and unlocked the door. The automobile didn't fit his mental picture of her—a young widow who needed a job to make ends meet. He leaned an elbow against the car. "Mercedes?" he drawled, raising a brow.

She glanced up and he saw a flash of anger in her eyes. So there was temper beneath the placid exterior. Perhaps there was passion as well. He waited for her retort, but she only answered mildly, "Do you object to foreign cars, Father?" She opened her door and got inside without waiting for his answer.

Unable to resist the temptation to probe further for the emotion that simmered below the surface, he got in and said, "No. It just wasn't what I expected for a young widow working in an inner-city church. I had the impression you needed your job."

He saw her hands tighten on the steering wheel. "Oh, make no mistake about it, Father," she answered in a strained voice. "I needed this job...badly."

"I'm sorry."

She bent to lay her purse on the floor. Her hair fell forward, hiding her face, so Greg couldn't see her expression, but he heard the tremor in her voice as she murmured, "It's all right."

Contrite, he wished he hadn't felt compelled to push her so far. Later he'd ask one of the priests about her background. He was silent as she backed out of the parking lot and turned into the street.

Julie, meanwhile, glanced surreptitiously at Father Gregory. What was the "difference" about him that both she and Grace perceived?

His hair was sun streaked, his skin bronzed. Obviously he hadn't spent all his time inside a church. His priestly garb did nothing to hide the muscular physique she'd noticed this morning. He looked like a man comfortable with his body and himself.

She studied his hands, which lay relaxed in his lap. They were covered with a sprinkling of fine blond hair that disappeared into his sleeves. Though the cloth reached his wrists now, she remembered that his bare arms looked strong. Strong arms, gentle hands— *Enough of this foolishness,* she ordered herself. If she kept this up, she'd begin spinning daydreams about Father Gregory. Grace was right. She needed a "real man" to concentrate on. And right now, she'd better concentrate on getting to the Coalition meeting on time.

When they arrived at the drab brick building where the Coalition, habitually short of funds, maintained a three-room office, Julie led the priest up the stairs to the second floor. She opened the door to a sparsely furnished reception room, waved to the secretary, who responded with a cheery *"Buenas tardes,"* and entered the conference room. There the dozen or so representatives of various organizations involved with Hispanics were taking their seats around a conference table. Julie caught the attention of the Coalition director, a portly Mexican-American with a drooping mustache, and said, "This is Father Gregory, St. Martha's new priest."

"Welcome, Father," the gentleman said warmly, and the others chimed in.

The first item on the agenda was the discussion of a city-wide program to combat hunger. Julie was concerned about illegals' access to food programs. There had been talk of limiting donations to people who could prove legality. "I disapprove," Julie said firmly. "Legal or not, everyone is entitled to food."

"There are those who disagree," pointed out a well-dressed man across the table. "Some people feel that aliens who have no right to be here have no right to services."

"Not even to satisfy basic needs?" Julie argued.

"Not even that. Many people feel it would be best for the Hispanic community if these people simply disappeared."

"They may get that wish," remarked a heavyset man. "With this wave of disappearances, it appears that many of the illegals are vanishing."

"I've heard something about disappearances, but I've only been here a few days," Father Gregory remarked. "What's been going on?"

Julie glanced at him in surprise. This was the second time he'd asked about disappearances. Not only was it off the subject at hand, but there were certainly enough other problems in the community to worry about; yet he had zeroed in on this one. Perhaps Father Gregory was the kind of person who was compulsive about a subject once he got interested.

The man who had spoken before answered the priest's question. "All we know is that Hispanics have been picked up off the street, never to be seen again. Why, or what happens to them, we have no idea."

"The Hispanic community is becoming anxious," another member commented. "There's been talk of organizing lookout squads. We're advising people in our area to go out only in groups."

"Have you seen any pattern to these incidents?" Father Gregory inquired.

No one seemed aware of one, and the discussion returned to the subject of food distribution. Julie suggested the Coalition make a plea for illegals to be included. "We send food to Africans when there's a famine. Why deny it to people in our own community?"

Greg was impressed by her calm yet forceful argument, and apparently so were the others. The committee voted to send a representative to the Hunger Prevention Committee to present their views.

The discussion turned to other topics—black marketeering of green cards, job banks, medical needs. When they adjourned at five-thirty, several members of the group cornered Julie for a private discussion. Glad to have some time to talk to people on his own, Greg started a conversation with the man who had spoken about missing persons.

"You mentioned these disappearances I've been hearing about," Greg began. "What do you think is going on?"

"A smuggling ring perhaps," the gentleman replied.

Several other people joined them and gave their opinions. One woman suggested that the scarcity of jobs in Houston sent people back across the Rio Grande; an intense-looking young man in horn-rimmed glasses thought the Ku Klux Klan was responsible. *All conjecture,* Greg decided. He wasn't getting any useful information, but at least he was establishing contacts.

He hadn't realized how long they'd stood talking until he noticed that Julie had moved to the fringe of their group and was listening intently. It was time to end the discussion, Greg decided, sensing that she wanted to leave. She'd put in a full day and probably had a long drive home after she dropped him off. "I'd better not keep Mrs. Whitaker waiting," he said to the man with whom he'd been talking.

"Of course. You're fortunate to have her working in your church, Father. She's done so much good for the community."

Another testimonial to this paragon of virtue. He'd lay odds she'd been teacher's pet in grade school, too. Everyone seemed to adore her. And damned if he, too, wasn't falling under her spell, he thought as he followed her out.

THAT EVENING Greg called Phil Barnes at home and related the information he'd received about the disappearances. "Check your files for the sex of those who are missing," he suggested, and Phil promised to do it first thing in the morning.

"How are you getting along at the church?" Phil asked.

"Fine. The priests are most cooperative."

"And the rest of the staff? Have they accepted you?"

"I think so. I've spent most of my time with Julie Whitaker, the social worker."

"Whitaker," Phil said thoughtfully. "So that's who the social worker is. She must be Dirk Whitaker's widow. I'd heard she was involved in some kind of social program."

"You know her?"

"I've met her once or twice. Do I detect a note of male interest?"

"Purely professional interest."

"Keep it that way."

"Barnes, you don't even have to mention it. Who was Dirk Whitaker, by the way?"

"Whitaker was a self-made millionaire. He made a bundle in the oil business and was smart enough to invest his money elsewhere before oil prices dropped."

"That explains the Mercedes then. What happened to him?"

"He died not long ago." Phil yawned. "I've got to turn in. I'll call you tomorrow."

Greg agreed. In his room he began organizing his notes, but thoughts of Julie intruded. There was more to her than his first impression had led him to believe, more than just a pretty face and a sweet smile. She was an enticing blend of sweetness and steel. Given the opportunity, he'd like to dig deeper, but in his present situation he doubted he'd have the chance. Too bad. She'd be an interesting puzzle to solve, as interesting as the disappearances he'd been sent to investigate, and every bit as appealing.

CHAPTER THREE

FOG HUNG OVER THE CITY, turning the dingy neighborhood into a softly muted landscape. Dampness seeped through Julie's jacket as she stepped out of her car and started across the church parking lot. In the distance she saw a dim figure running toward her. She knew immediately it was Father Gregory. As he approached, he raised an arm in greeting.

She waited, studying him as he came closer. He was dressed in tan shorts, a worn blue T-shirt, and scuffed Adidas running shoes. His blond hair was tousled from the winds, and his cheeks were ruddy. He reached her side and gave her an engaging smile, his eyes crinkling.

She smiled back and searched for something to say. The sight of his tanned, muscular legs was doing odd things to her brain and to her voice. "You're out early, Father," she managed over the lump in her throat. "Did you go far?"

"About five miles."

And he wasn't even breathing hard. He hadn't been out for a casual jog this morning. Or yesterday, either, she guessed. He must be a serious runner. So that was how he kept in shape.

"Do you run?" he asked.

"I prefer tennis, but once in a while I do some halfhearted jogging."

He started to say something, then apparently changed his mind. For a moment Julie had the wildly improbable no-tion that he was going to ask her to run with him some morning. *Ridiculous thought.* For a moment, she'd responded to him as she had yesterday morning and almost forgotten who he was. Without his clerical garb, he appeared less formidable than he had yesterday... and more dangerous. He seemed to possess an innate sensuality that belied his role in life. The casual stance. The easy smile. The clear blue eyes that studied her thoroughly, as if he could see right through her clothes.

Nervously she moved a few steps back. "I'd better get to work."

"See you later."

She nodded and started toward the church but couldn't resist turning back to watch him as he moved off at an easy lope.

In her office she tried to put the disturbing thoughts out of her mind. But they kept intruding, interfering with her concentration. She'd started a report over for the third time when she heard a knock and the object of her musings appeared at her door, his hair damp and wavy from a shower, his eyes alight, but now, to her relief, dressed in somber black with his collar in place.

He dropped onto a chair and grinned at her. "Keep right on with what you're doing. I'll just fade into the woodwork."

If only it were that easy, Julie thought as her shaky fingers jammed the keys of her ancient typewriter.

"Problem?" the priest inquired. He rose from his chair and, to Julie's dismay, leaned over her shoulder to look.

Entirely too close, she thought. She had an intimate view of his thick golden fringe of lashes, his freshly shaved cheeks, even a tiny nick from his razor. The scent of his after-shave penetrated her nostrils, and his breath tickled her cheek.

He spent only a few seconds untangling the typewriter keys, but that was long enough for Julie's pulse to speed up alarmingly. She'd have to see that this didn't happen again, she told herself as he sat down. Maybe she'd donate a new typewriter to the church—they were long overdue for one. She rarely donated anything for her personal use, preferring to contribute items that could benefit people in the community, but in this case, she'd make an exception. She fought the urge to giggle hysterically. Of course, it wasn't the typewriter that was at fault. It was her response—her *juvenile* response, she admonished herself—to the man now seated casually on the chair behind her.

Julie was relieved when she heard voices from the parlor. Now she'd have something to concentrate on. Even when she'd just come to St. Martha's, in the first terrible months after Dirk died, her ability to shut out everything but the people who needed her help had been unaffected. This morning, though, it wasn't so easy. She had to force herself to focus on the endless succession of visitors to her office. Despite her efforts, she was always aware at some level of Father Gregory sitting quietly beside her, making notes on his yellow pad.

Midway through the morning Julie opened her door to find a young woman with tear-streaked cheeks sitting on the edge of a chair. "Teresa," she said, with concern. "Come in. What's the matter?"

Teresa only shook her head as tears welled up in her eyes.

Julie took Teresa's hand. "I can't help you if you don't tell me," she said gently, switching to Spanish.

"Mario, my baby," Teresa whispered.

"Yes?"

"He is sick. Very sick."

"Then we'll take him to the doctor."

"*Sí, sí,* I want to take him, but it is so far and the wait is so long."

"We'll go in my car."

Julie reached for her purse, but Teresa's hand closed on her wrist. In such rapid Spanish that Julie could hardly follow, she burst out, "The *señora* where you got me the job, Señora Mellon, she says no. She says if I am not at work this afternoon I will lose my job. She says she is having a party, a big one, and I must be there today to help get ready and tomorrow to work. I say to her I will send my sister in my place, but she will not hear of it. *Señora,* I must get help for my baby, but I cannot lose my job. With no job, I cannot pay for food. Arturo, my husband, does not make much money. What can I do?" She put her head in her hands and sobbed afresh.

"What were you to do at Mrs. Mellon's party?"

"I help in the kitchen, *señora.*"

"Listen to me, Teresa. We will take your baby to the doctor. And you will not lose your job. I will see to it."

Teresa raised her head and stared at Julie. She sniffed. "I believe you."

"Good. Now go and wash your face, and by the time you get back, everything will be taken care of. I will call Señora Mellon." She reached for the phone.

When it was answered, she said brightly, "Claire, it's Julie Whitaker. How are you?"

Claire's voice was impatient. "Terribly rushed just now."

"Yes, I know you must be busy. I hear you're entertaining Andre Cherbourg after the symphony. I won't keep you long, but one of your maids came by my office. Teresa Sanchez. Her baby is ill, and it sounds contagious. She insists on going to work, but I was sure you wouldn't want her to come and spread germs all over your kitchen." Julie glanced at Father Gregory, who was chuckling softly.

"Of course I don't want germs, but this is so upsetting," Claire said petulantly.

"Yes, it's a shame when you need her so badly," Julie continued, "but I think I have someone to take her place. This woman would be perfect. She's worked for a caterer in San Antonio for three years, knows everything about the kitchen." Julie gave Father Gregory a conspiratorial grin. "You won't have to tell Rosa a thing," she added.

"Really? If she's that good, I'll let the other one go and keep her."

"No, you won't be able to keep her," Julie said quickly. "She's going back to Mexico. I'll see that she gets to your house this afternoon to clean, and tomorrow she'll be ready for the party."

"Darling, you're a lifesaver."

"Glad to help," Julie said sweetly. "I know your evening'll be a great success."

She hung up and saw Teresa standing hesitantly in the doorway. "Rosa will take your place," Julie told her. "Now, let's go get Mario."

"Coming, Father?" she asked over her shoulder. He moved to her side as Teresa hurried down the hall ahead of them.

"Pretty slick," he said in a low tone.

Julie laughed. "Yeah," she agreed. "The catering experience was an inspiration. I'll come in early tomorrow and tell Rosa what to do. She's pretty sharp. I think she can pull it off. Besides, Claire will be too busy showing off Andre Cherbourg to pay attention."

"One of the world's greatest violinists. A real social coup," Father Gregory said. Then he grinned at her. "You did an admirable job of keeping your temper."

"I don't let myself get angry at Claire," Julie replied. "Besides, she'd not deliberately mean. She just doesn't see her household help as people. She doesn't 'see' them at all. Actually, Claire's a good person to know. She's into 'causes.' I'm hoping to interest her in chairing a benefit to raise money for this parish.''

''A woman who doesn't view her maids as people?''

''Oh, Father,'' Julie laughed. ''To Claire, those are two different concepts. Teresa is Household Help. St. Martha's is Charity. It would never occur to her that they're related.''

Father Gregory shook his head. ''Let's not tell her then.''

They stepped out into the parking lot and hurried to the car. The wind had picked up; the weather was raw now. Julie turned the key in the ignition. The engine turned over, but the car didn't start. Irritated, she turned off the engine. ''It's been cranky since yesterday. Must be the cold weather.''

''Get your battery terminals checked,'' the priest advised.

''Mmm.'' Men always thought they were experts on auto mechanics. Obviously Father Gregory was no exception. Julie turned the key again. This time the engine caught. She pulled out of the parking lot and put his suggestion out of her mind.

Teresa directed Julie to a small house a few blocks from the church. Julie went inside and waited in the living room while Teresa went to get the baby.

The room was almost bare of furniture. A sagging couch. One chair. In the corner by the window a group of carefully tended plants. In another corner, below a mirror, stood a rickety table covered with a square of lacy cloth. On it was a small china statue of Our Lady of Guadalupe and several half-burned candles.

Probably a dozen people lived in this house. Julie shivered. The room was ice-cold. She'd have to see about picking up some heaters for the Sanchez family and others who were facing the winter cold.

Julie heard the baby fretting at being awakened. In a few moments Teresa came in with him, wrapped in a blanket. Rosa, Teresa's younger sister, followed her and stood, nodding silently, while Julie gave her directions to the Mellon's house and promised to meet her at the church early the next morning.

Julie glanced anxiously at Mario as she spoke to Rosa. The infant's cheeks were flushed, his breathing labored. She touched the tiny forehead. It was burning. "We'd better hurry," she said. With a last nod to Rosa, Julie pulled the blanket up over the baby's face and led Teresa outside.

A half hour later they arrived at Ben Taub Hospital and made their way to the Pediatric Clinic. Teresa signed in, and they sat down.

Julie had been here many times, but the county hospital never failed to shock her. People sat in stoic anonymity on row after row of pewlike wooden benches. Squalling babies sat in their mothers' laps or crawled around on the cold floor. Older children sat beside their parents, clinging to their arms. Two rows over a little girl moaned, "How much longer, Mama?" Julie knew it would be a lot longer. She settled back to wait.

After an hour she took Mario from Teresa's arms and sent her to get something to eat. She peered at the infant's flushed face and glanced at the desk in the front of the room. Bored-looking clerks sat behind it, shuffling papers.

The baby began to whimper, and Julie held him against her, rocking him gently, murmuring to him. Father Gregory reached over to touch the baby's forehead, frowned, and asked, "What's taking so long?"

"This is typical," Julie replied. "We could wait all day."

The priest's mouth turned grim. "Maybe I should go up there and hurry them along," he suggested.

"Won't help," Julie said, shushing the baby gently. "They do things in their own good time."

Father Gregory lapsed into silence, staring steadily at the desk, as if he could will the clerks to call Teresa's name.

Teresa returned, took the baby, and paced with him until he quieted.

Father Gregory wandered off, returned with a newspaper, and began to read. Though he glanced up occasionally, an hour later he was still reading. Julie wondered if he always read the newspaper so thoroughly.

At last Teresa's name was called, and they were directed to a small cubicle where a harried-looking doctor examined the child. "Looks like strep throat," he told Julie. "We'll do a culture to be sure." Efficiently he swabbed the baby's throat. "I'm going to give you a prescription for antibiotics. Tell her to give him plenty of fluids. He's dehydrated. If he won't drink, she can try powdered Gatorade. Bring him back next week."

Julie translated for Teresa. "Don't worry," she assured the young woman. "We'll get him back next week if I have to bring him myself."

They waited for the prescription, stopped, at Julie's insistence, to buy a heater, and drove back to Teresa's house through the afternoon traffic. Father Gregory offered to carry the heater inside, and Julie was glad to let him. She was bone tired. She shut her eyes and leaned against the steering wheel. A few minutes later she felt a rush of cold air and looked up to see the priest getting in beside her.

"You're exhausted," he said gently.

She nodded "And hungry."

"Do you have a long drive home?"

"An hour."

"There must be someplace to eat between here and St. Martha's. Let's get a bite before you have to hit the road again."

"All right. There's a little café, Mi Cocina, about two blocks from here." She started the engine without incident, and in a few minutes pulled up in front of a small, cheerful looking café.

They chose a booth near the back. The waitress brought a coffeepot along with the menus, and Julie felt her energy returning as the caffeine hit her system.

She recommended tamales, and when the waitress had gone, smiled at Father Gregory. "Eating their tamales is one of the fringe benefits of my job. Grace and I have lunch here at least once a week."

"A Mexican food addict, hmm?"

"Yes. Tex-Mex isn't like the food in the interior of Mexico, but it's close enough for me. I lived in Mexico for three years when I was a teenager, and I've never lost my taste for spicy food."

"Why were you in Mexico?"

"My father was an executive with Tri-Co Oil. They have a big Mexican operation."

"Is your father still in the oil business?"

"No, he retired a few years ago. He and Mother bought a home near Vail. It's beautiful country, and the skiing is great. I was there for Christmas."

Greg thought of his unused skis and his wasted ticket. He wondered if he'd be finished with this assignment before spring. He'd like to be out on the slopes now, filled with exhilaration as he faced a challenging run. And then in the evening, snug by a cozy fire, a woman in his arms. As he pictured the scene, the face of the amorphous woman became Julie Whitaker's, her hair spread on the pillow, her eyes dark . . .

The rattling of dishes interrupted his thoughts. The waitress had arrived with their orders. As they unwrapped the cornhusks that covered the spicy tamales, Greg gave Julie an easy smile. "So you like Mexican food and skiing. And I can see you enjoy your work. How did you choose social work? Something you always wanted to do?"

"No, I fell into it by chance. I took a couple of electives in college—psychology and sociology, and before I knew it, I was hooked. I went right on through the Masters program."

"And the job at St. Martha's? Was that by chance, too?"

He watched a look of pain cross her face as she shook her head. "I was doing some volunteer work with the Coalition. Then my husband died."

"Was he ill?"

"He was killed in a plane crash. He was on his way back from West Texas in the company plane when the engine gave out. I was leaving for the airport to pick him up when his associate called to tell me there'd been an accident. He was only thirty-five."

Greg saw her eyes cloud with grief. He wanted to take her hand in his, but of course he couldn't. He could only sit across from her and watch in silent commiseration.

She was quiet for a moment, then she continued. "I had just found out I was pregnant. I was planning to tell him that evening. The champagne was chilling...someone threw it away, I guess. Two weeks later I miscarried. They said it was the shock and the stress. Anyway, after I recovered from the worst of the trauma and finished taking care of all the things you have to do after someone dies, I needed to do something with my time. I found this job through the Coalition. If I hadn't, I think I'd have gone mad.

"Julie," Greg said softly, "I'm sorry."

"Thank you." She sat still for another moment, then squared her shoulders and forced a smile. "What about you, Father? Where are you from?"

Greg realized she needed to change the subject. He obliged her. "Arizona," he answered.

"Sun, sand, and cactus. Do they teach Spanish in school there? You speak it very well."

He nodded. "I took some Spanish in school, but I learned to speak it in Mexico and Central America. My father is an archaeology professor who specializes in pre-Columbian cultures. I spent a couple of summers on digs with him."

"That must have been exciting."

"Yeah. They were still uncovering the ruins of Tikal when we went. The jungle was at our doorsteps—steamy heat, tangled vines—and under those vines, the remnants of an ancient civilization. It gave me a taste for adventure and taught me patience, too. Archaeology is a painstaking science. Every shard of pottery, every kernel of grain has to be studied and cataloged." He was silent for a moment, thinking how much of his father's character he had absorbed during those long-ago summers.

Julie interrupted his reverie. "But you didn't become an archaeologist. How did you choose your profession?"

Greg took a bite of his tamale. "In high school a buddy of mine talked me in to becoming a reporter for the school newspaper, and—" He glanced up to find Julie looking at him with a puzzled frown. *Damn!* He'd been about to say, "And I never wanted to do anything else." He'd been so engrossed in their conversation he'd totally forgotten who he was supposed to be. *Not smart, Allen.*

He improvised quickly. "And during Brotherhood Week we interviewed clergymen of different religions. Since I was Catholic, I interviewed the priest. I was fascinated with his work."

"And you found your niche. Do you," she hesitated for a moment, "ever regret your decision?"

Greg supposed everyone wanted to ask that of a priest but few had the courage. He'd wanted to ask that himself when he'd been with Father Donnelly. He'd wondered if the priest missed having a "normal" life, with wife and children. He considered his own answer carefully. "It's a little confining at times, but, no, I don't regret it."

"What did you do before you came to St. Martha's?"

He was on safer ground here. He gave her a description of Father Donnelly's work in Washington. As he talked, the murmur of conversation from other tables, the movements of the waitress as she hurried back and forth, the clatter of dishes in the kitchen became a muted background. He felt their booth was a private haven for just the two of them.

When he finished, he glanced at the windows and was surprised to see that it was almost dusk. "We'd better go," he said. "I don't want you getting home after dark."

When Julie dropped him off at the rectory, Greg walked slowly inside, his mind crowded with thoughts of her. She'd won his respect for her courage in dealing with double tragedies. She could as easily have decided to drown her sorrow in frivolous pursuits. Instead she'd pulled herself together and given to others. He suspected that no one who really knew Julie Whitaker would have been surprised at the path she'd taken.

He greeted Father Rudolfo, who was in the living room reading the evening paper. "Hungry?" the priest inquired.

Greg shook his head. "I had a bite with Mrs. Whitaker. She told me a little bit about herself at dinner. Yesterday I wondered why a woman in her circumstances was working here. Now I think I understand."

"I think we have helped her," the priest said. "And she has helped us. Through her efforts, influential people in the community are becoming aware of Hispanics and their problems. As for her personal circumstances, I believe much of what she inherited is tied up in trust. She does have an income and, therefore accepts a lower salary than we would have to pay someone else . . . certainly lower than she is worth.''

The two men turned as Father Curry appeared in the doorway. ''Phil Barnes has been trying to reach you,'' he said to Greg.

When Greg reached him, Phil wasted no time on social amenities. ''Dammit, Allen. I've been trying to get you all day. Where in hell have you been?''

''Sitting in the Pediatric Clinic at the county hospital.''

Phil uttered a short, pungent oath.

''That's my job, Barnes. You wanted it that way.''

Another oath. ''Did you learn anything while you were there?''

''Yeah, Houston is having a chicken pox epidemic.''

This time he was rewarded with a string of four-letter words. ''Well, Phil,'' Greg interrupted. ''I know you didn't call to show off your vocabulary, impressive though it is. What did you want?''

''There was another incident this morning. Witnesses said a green van pulled over to the side of the road. Two men got out, grabbed a fellow off the street and pushed him in.''

''Where did it happen?''

''Not far from your church. Corner of 78th and Canal Street.''

''Damn. If you'd let me out of this crazy disguise, I could go out and get some information.''

''Sorry. Not a chance, Allen. Orders from higher up.''

''Did you check your records?''

''Yeah,'' Phil replied, ''and the priests were right. Every disappearance involved a man. I've got a list of approximate locations of kidnapping, too.'' He read them off while Greg scribbled quickly.

''What do you think, Phil? A smuggling ring for farm workers?''

''Maybe.''

''What I have to do is get to the men in this community.''

''Father Gregory could start a men's group of some sort—help them with job-related problems.''

''Good idea. I'll get that underway. Any more suggestions?''

''Yeah. Have you had chicken pox?''

''What? No, I haven't.''

''Keep away from kids then, Allen. It itches like hell.'' Greg heard Phil's laugh, and the line went dead.

CHAPTER FOUR

JULIE RAN EASILY along the jogging trail. The fresh air was filled with the scent of pine, the sky blue. Birds twittered in the trees; gravel crunched under her feet. Her companion's powerful legs were made for a faster pace, but he matched his stride to hers. Side by side they ran, enjoying the movement. As if at a prearranged signal, they veered off the track and stopped at the foot of a giant oak. They stood for a few moments, letting their breathing slow, then sank to the lush carpet of green beneath the tree. As he reached toward her, Julie's eyes half closed, leaving his face a blur. No longer relying on sight, she experienced him through touch. Hands, strong but gentle, cupped her face. Fingertips tenderly traced her lips. He bent to taste them, softly at first, then more greedily with his tongue. He pulled her closer until she could feel his heart pounding in his chest and hers beating in tandem. She heard him moan and opened her eyes to gaze into the deep blue ones above her. Unable to tear herself away from his compelling gaze, she stared for endless moments. Then, with an effort, she forced herself to pull back and focus on his face. It came into view...

Father Gregory!

With a start, Julie shut her eyes and jerked upright. A cry tore from her throat. She opened her eyes and stared...into darkness. Disoriented, she looked around her. She was in her bed, her hands clutching the sheet, her heart pounding madly. A dream. It was only a dream. She'd had such dreams many times since Dirk had died, dreams in which he'd come to her...but not tonight. Tonight the dream was different. The man who had held her, caressed her, moaned against her mouth was Father Gregory.

With a groan, she dropped back on the pillow. What crazy daytime thoughts had prompted such a dream? That was easy, she thought, remembering her response on seeing Father Gregory in running clothes that morning. The memory, coupled with her reactions in the vivid dream, caused her pulse to jump and her cheeks to flush. Erotic dreams about a priest! How...shameful?

No, of course not, she told herself. Women often fantasized about men who were unattainable—their doctors, their college professors, even movie stars. A friend of hers had once confessed to indulging in wildly erotic daydreams about her butcher. Julie felt a bubble of laughter. She tried imagining Father Gregory as a butcher. No, he definitely was not the type to stand behind a meat counter. A tennis pro—that was more like it. She pictured him moving over the court, easy grace combined with raw power, his tennis whites a perfect contrast to his bronzed skin. God, the women would be lined up for blocks to have tennis lessons...and other, more intimate lessons. And she'd be right there in line with the rest.

What a prize idiot you are, Julie Whitaker. A twenty-eight-year-old woman developing a schoolgirl crush on a priest, of all people. Go back to sleep. You have to be at work early. Work. Where she'd see Father Gregory. It was lucky he couldn't see into her mind. She just hoped she didn't blush when he came into her office. With a half laugh, she plumped up her pillow, turned on her side, and shut her eyes.

Julie arrived at St. Martha's early, half hoping she'd run into Father Gregory again, half relieved when she didn't.

She spent an hour in the church kitchen working with Teresa's sister Rosa. When she was satisfied that the girl could manage her job that evening, she sent her off to the bus stop. Then she headed for her office, stopping on the way to pop her head into Grace Matheson's office. As usual, she found Grace poring over the morning newspaper.

"Hi," Julie said. "What's the latest with Houston's jet set?"

"Senator McMahan from Utah is in town. It's rumored he's seeing a Houston divorcee. Know anything about that?"

"Haven't heard a word."

"Oh, before I forget, Father Gregory stopped by a few minutes ago and said to tell you he wants to see you in his office."

"Oh." Was her voice a bit breathless? Julie hoped Grace didn't notice. "I'd better see what he wants."

When she reached Father Gregory's office, she heard the murmur of his voice from behind the closed door. He was on the phone, she realized, and not wanting to interrupt him, she paused in the hallway. She listened to the cadence of his voice but couldn't hear his words. Then he laughed. A low, husky laugh that set her nerves tingling. "Take it easy, Barrett," she heard him say clearly, in a voice that hinted of...of *intimacy*. That was the only word Julie could think of to describe what she'd heard.

Now there was silence. Julie took a shaky breath and knocked. In a moment, Father Gregory opened the door. "Good morning," he said in such a perfectly normal voice that Julie decided her mind was playing tricks on her.

"Good morning, Father. Did you want me?" The bland words suddenly seemed to Julie to convey a deeper meaning. She bit her lip, but apparently he didn't notice her remark.

"Come in and sit down." He gave her one of his engaging smiles. "I appreciate the time you've spent with me the last two days, but I think it's time I began working on my own."

Julie nodded. That made sense. She should be pleased that he was going to relieve her of some of her duties. She *was* pleased. But she couldn't help feeling a twinge of disappointment. In just two days, she'd gotten used to his presence in her office. On the other hand, last night's dream told her that presence was evoking too many feelings—feelings she didn't want to name. Yes, it was best that he work alone from now on.

"We'll have to decide how to divide the caseload," she said thoughtfully. "Perhaps you could take the new people."

"Good idea. But that still leaves you with a heavy load. Father Curry and I discussed this last night. We decided that I should work with the men in the community while you continue with the women."

Julie stiffened. *Without consulting me?* She was, after all, the professional in this area. She should have a say in what happened to her clients.

"That may present some problems," she said, keeping her voice level. Her tone betrayed none of her irritation. But she knew there was a glint in her eyes that someone who was well acquainted with her would notice.

"Surely nothing we can't work out," the priest said.

"Let me think." Quickly Julie thought over her list of clients. "I'm seeing perhaps thirty men. I could hand most of them over to you . . . they're routine cases. But there are four or five I feel I should retain—people with more complicated problems, people I've established relationships with over a long period."

She'd spoken firmly. She didn't expect Father Gregory to challenge her. But she was mistaken.

The priest went on pleasantly, "Tell me about them."

"There's Felipe Valdez. He was injured in a construction accident when a tilt-up concrete wall fell. He had multiple fractures, was hospitalized for some time, and was released a few weeks ago. He needs ongoing physical therapy. I'm setting that up and finding financial help while his wife gets vocational training, and I'm also discussing future occupational possibilities with Felipe."

"Why don't you keep that one? Tell me about the rest."

Did he expect her to justify keeping every one of these critical cases? Julie's irritation level rose a notch. Still she kept her voice calm.

"And I have Mr. Salazar. A real tragedy. He's an old man in poor health. Esteban, his son, came to Houston about eight years ago and found a good job in the shipyards. He sent for his father six months ago. The old man had a long, grueling trip from the mountains in western Mexico and a difficult time adjusting to the city, so Esteban brought him to me. He needed medical attention, but mostly he needed someone to talk to. He began making progress, adjusting to the new environment. Then about a month ago Esteban disappeared. He'd gone through the legalization process, so we thought he'd been picked up by mistake. We checked with the INS. Nothing. No one knows where Esteban is or what's happened to him."

"I'll take that one."

He'll take that one? Hadn't he heard a word she'd said? "Father, I don't think Mr. Salazar would adjust well to a new counselor."

"Perhaps you underestimate the old man," Father Gregory said lightly.

Damn, this man was stubborn. Well, he was not going to intimidate her. He might be in charge in the church, but her professional opinion ought to count for something. "I don't think I'm underestimating him. He's in serious distress." Her voice stayed steady, but she clenched her fingers.

"Don't worry. I'll handle it." His voice remained low and easy, but something flickered in his eyes, something that told Julie he meant to have his way. Abruptly she remembered her first impression of him. The tiger. Lazy but powerful. Instinctively she shivered, then squared her shoulders.

"I'd really prefer—"

"I'll look at his file this afternoon. Next one?"

Julie's professional training had taught her to be direct, to verbalize feelings. She applied it in her personal life as well. "Father," she said quietly, "I feel we're involved in a tug-of-war over this man. Perhaps we can compromise."

The priest studied her through narrowed eyes as he seemed to weigh various alternatives. Julie's muscles tensed. Tug-of-war was too mild for what they were experiencing, she thought. For all their polite words, they were more like two dogs snarling over the same bone. Why? Why was Father Gregory so set on adding poor Mr. Salazar to his own caseload? She started to ask, but the priest spoke first.

"A compromise then. We'll work on this one together, until he's ready to make the transition."

And who'll decide that? she thought. *If you think it's going to be you, Father, you're in for a surprise.* Aloud, she simply said, "All right. After all, Mr. Salazar's welfare is our main concern." Then, determined to keep her temper in check, she rose. "I have to get to my office. Perhaps we can discuss the other cases later."

The priest got up and walked her to the door. He took the knob before she could reach it and stood staring down at her, trapping her between the doorway and his body. All traces of anger had vanished from his eyes, replaced by something infinitely more dangerous.

Julie's body heated, but no longer from anger. Like a helpless rabbit stunned in the glare of headlights, she felt herself held prisoner by those eyes. She couldn't move, couldn't reach around him for the door. How long they stood there she wasn't sure, but at last the priest broke the spell.

"We'll go over your other cases this afternoon," he said softly. Without taking his eyes from her face, he pushed the door open.

Like a sleepwalker, Julie moved down the hall. Her hands were trembling when she opened her office door. She shut it behind her, opened her desk drawer and, in an unaccustomed show of emotion, threw her purse into it and slammed it closed. She sank onto her chair and covered her face with her hands.

She felt as if she'd been put through a wringer. What was going on between her and this priest? First their politely phrased argument with its angry undertones. Then that soul-stirring look that had passed between them. What had it meant? Was this Father Gregory's modus operandi—intimidate people one minute, mesmerize them the next? Keep them off balance? If so, it was working. He'd been here three days and he'd even invaded her dreams.

Unable to sit still, Julie jumped up and began to pace her small office. Deliberately she changed the direction of her thoughts. It was safer to dwell on the argument, safer to focus on her anger. Father Gregory was a formidable opponent, she admitted. If he was going to be so pigheaded over one case, their professional association would surely suffer. But no, she wouldn't let it. Her job and the people of the parish were too important to her. This round may have ended in a draw, but she promised herself their next encounter would have a different conclusion.

"Enough of this," she told herself aloud. She'd always been able to manage her emotions. She'd manage them now, too. No problem. No problem at all.

To Julie's disappointment, there were few people who required her services this morning. Working had always calmed her nerves. But by ten-thirty the parlor was deserted. She took out some of her files with the idea of deciding which men should go to Father Gregory, but she didn't want to think about that now. She returned them to the drawer.

She glanced out the window. In typical Houston fashion, the weather had changed from raw and gray to sunshiny, the kind of day that beckoned one outside. That was an idea. She'd take a walk to Teresa's house and see how the baby was doing. She called Grace's extension to inform her, grabbed her coat, and headed down the hall.

As she turned the corner, she almost collided with Father Gregory. With a gasp, she halted and dropped her purse. The priest bent to pick it up. "Sorry I startled you. Are you on your way out?"

Julie took the purse from him, her hands not quite steady. "Yes, I'm going to walk over and check on the Sanchez baby."

"I'm headed that way, too. I'll walk with you. I'd like to see how little Mario is coming along." He motioned her down the hall.

Damn, she had planned this walk to keep from thinking about Father Gregory, and now here he was strolling along beside her. *Well,* she thought as they stepped outside, *might as well make the best of it.* "Nice day," she murmured.

He nodded absently. He was, Julie noticed, studying the neighborhood. "Interesting area," he observed as they crossed the street. "Little houses here, and then a grocery store and a couple of bars."

"Houston has no zoning laws," Julie explained. "You can build anything just about anywhere you choose."

"Must be rough living next door to a bar on Saturday nights."

"Or paydays," Julie agreed.

"Do you always walk around alone in this neighborhood?" the priest asked suddenly, his tone sharp.

"Usually. Why?"

"I don't like the idea." He frowned down at her. "This is a rough area."

Julie shrugged. "I've never had any trouble."

"That doesn't mean you never will. If you have to go out again, come and get me. I'll go with you."

"That's kind of you, Father, but—"

"Not kind," he interrupted. "Sensible. Promise me."

"All right." Julie smiled inwardly. She was touched by Father Gregory's concern. It had been a long time since someone had offered to watch out for her. Though she valued her independence, she realized she rather liked Father Gregory's male protectiveness. She liked walking with him, too, now that her anger had subsided and her emotions were on their usual even keel.

This was one of those perfect winter days, the air cool with just a hint of warmth. The sun glinted off Father Gregory's hair, shooting golden highlights through the darker ash blond. *He's beautiful,* Julie thought. In past centuries he might have been a Norman knight, or an American cowboy. Strong, sure, proud. Yet he had chosen a vocation that demanded that his harsher qualities be tempered by gentleness. And she could see the gentleness, too. He was a paradox, she decided.

They passed a small park, a tiny pocket of green. Julie glanced at the rusty slide and creaking swings shaded by oak trees. She wondered, if the park were on the other side of town, whether the run-down equipment would be replaced. Then her eye was captured by a large oak tree standing apart from the others, and she forgot the playground. How similar this tree was to the one in last night's dream. The memory of that dream, coupled with Father Gregory's nearness, brought a blush to her cheeks. Eyes straight ahead, she increased her pace, avoiding conversation.

They arrived at Teresa's house a few minutes later. Julie knocked at the door, but no one answered. She waited and knocked again. Now she noticed a movement at the window. Still no one came to the door.

Puzzled, she said, "I know there's someone home. I saw the curtains move."

"So did I." Father Gregory reached around her and knocked, louder this time.

The door opened a crack, but a heavy metal chain prevented entrance. The opening was wide enough for Julie to see a pair of suspicious black eyes in a wizened face, thin white hair pulled into a bun, and an unsmiling mouth.

"¿Qué?" the woman asked.

"I'm Julie Whitaker," she said in Spanish. "We've come to visit Teresa."

At Julie's Spanish words, the door opened a bit farther, but the chain remained in place. "Teresa is busy. Her baby is sick."

"Yes, I know. We took her to the hospital yesterday. We're from St. Martha's. We came to see how Mario is getting along."

At this point Father Gregory stepped in front of Julie. "I'm the new priest from St. Martha's. May we talk to Teresa?"

The woman looked him up and down. Her eyes remained wary, but she reached a wrinkled hand toward the chain. She unfastened it and opened the door just wide enough for them to enter. Without a word, she turned and went into the other room, leaving Julie and Father Gregory in the doorway.

"Hospitable soul," the priest remarked in an undertone.

Before Julie could answer, the old woman returned, followed by Teresa, who was wiping her hands on a checkered apron.

"Father, Señora Whitaker. How kind of you to come. This is my mother-in-law, Carmela Sanchez."

"Señora Sanchez." Father Gregory said pleasantly and held out his hand.

The woman took it, inclined her head, but said nothing.

Julie turned to Teresa. "How is Mario?" she inquired.

"Not well yet, but better. Would you like to see him?"

They followed Teresa into the back bedroom, now warmed by the heater Julie had provided, and found the baby in a makeshift crib. Teresa picked him up, and Julie touched the tiny forehead. It was still warm, but no longer burning. His eyes were clearer today; he focused on Julie's face and his tiny lips curved into a dimpled smile.

Father Gregory came up beside her. He, too, looked at the small face. Then, to Julie's surprise, he took the baby from Teresa's arms. Julie watched as he held Mario against his shoulder, one large hand patting the baby's back. After a few moments, he put Mario back in the crib and bent to smooth the child's shock of black hair with a gentle hand.

Julie bent over the crib, murmuring to the child. A tiny fist grasped her finger. She felt a sudden pang. Her own child would have been about Mario's age if it had lived. She glanced up and met Father Gregory's eyes. They were filled with understanding, compassion. He had guessed her thoughts.

Forcing back tears that threatened to spill over, Julie turned to Teresa. While the women chatted about Mario, Father Gregory wandered off. Soon Julie heard the murmur of voices.

When she and Teresa reentered the living room, Julie stopped in surprise. Her mouth nearly dropped open as she stared at Father Gregory. He and Carmela were seated companionably on the sofa, engaged in animated conversation.

"Señora Sanchez is telling me how she came from Mexico to the United States," the priest said. His eyes sparkled with laughter as they met Julie's.

"I'd like to hear your story," Julie said to the old woman, marveling at her demeanor. Her air of hostility had disappeared, and her face now wore an amiable smile.

"Sí." Carmela nodded, gestured for Julie to take a seat, and continued in rapid Spanish. "My husband, Ramon, and my son came first to the United States. I stayed with my daughters and their families in Torreon. But I was lonely. So I decided to leave and go to my husband. My daughters tried to talk me out of it, but my mind was made up. I tied up my money in an apron, went to the bus station and bought a ticket to Neuvo Laredo. There I followed a group of men who were heading for the river. We sat in a little park until dark. I bought some tamales and ate them. I thought to myself this might be my last meal. It is dangerous to cross the river, even for a young person, and I—I was nearly sixty. But I wanted to go. When darkness fell, I walked to the river. The water was waist high, the current was strong—too strong for an old woman like me to wade across. But there

is always someone to take you—if you pay. I found a young man—young and strong—and—'' she gave a cackling laugh ''—I rode across the Rio Grande on his shoulders.''

"You must have been terrified," Julie said.

"Scared out of my wits. But I thought of Ramon and held on tight. The young man—I never found out his name— slipped in the middle of the river. The water was above his waist and up to my ankles. I felt the current pulling at us. I shut my eyes and prayed. The man steadied himself, and we went on. When we reached the other side and he put me down, there were welts on his neck where my nails had dug in.

"I didn't have time to thank him. There was noise all around, people running this way and that, lights and sirens."

"Immigration," said Father Gregory.

"*Sí, la migra.* I ran until I saw a little house. I hurried around the back, took my money out of my apron and stuffed it in my shoes. Then I put on the apron and walked around to the front of the house. No one noticed a little old lady in an apron sitting on the porch steps." She cackled again. "*La migra* went right by me. I sat on the porch for two hours." She winked. "My feet were sore from the money in my shoes, but I was safe."

"You are a brave lady, Señora Sanchez," Father Gregory said.

"Ah, no. It was not bravery but the thought of my Ramon that saved me."

"And you still had a long way to go."

"*Sí,* Laredo to Houston. But that is another story for another day."

"Yes," Julie said regretfully. "We must go. I'm glad Mario is better. I'll take him back to the doctor next week."

"Gracias, Señora. You have been so kind." Teresa walked them to the door.

When the door had shut behind them, Julie grinned at Father Gregory. "That was incredible. How did you do it?"

"What?" His expression was deadpan.

"You know what. Win her over. The woman had a complete change of personality in five minutes."

"Ah, Señora Sanchez is a marvelous lady."

"Said with a straight face."

"No, really. She didn't recognize you. When she saw you, she thought you were conducting a house search for the INS."

"Me?" Julie's voice rose in a squeak.

"Sure. These people can't be too careful. Even though this family has papers, they have some illegals living in the house, so they're always suspicious of strangers. You, of all people, should know that."

Julie nodded. "You're right, but," she laughed, "I've never been taken for an agent before."

They reached the corner and Father Gregory turned. "Let's walk back a different way," he suggested. "I want to see more of the neighborhood."

They walked along quietly, Julie thinking about the incident she had just witnessed. Father Gregory certainly had a knack for drawing people out, she thought. Today Señora Sanchez, practically a miracle. Yesterday he'd done the same with her. She'd told him more about herself than she usually shared with a stranger. She was impressed, too, by his gentleness with little Mario.

"You seemed at home with the baby," she remarked.

"Mmm, I've had lots of practice."

"Really?" She raised a brow.

"Being a priest doesn't preclude acquaintance with infants. As a matter of fact, both my brother and sister are happily married and are busy producing heirs in record numbers. I'm an experienced baby-sitter, giver of piggy-back rides, and even diaper changer.''

"And you enjoy it."

"Yeah, except for the diapers, I confess, I love the little devils."

They walked briskly until they reached Canal Street, one of the neighborhood's main thoroughfares. Here Father Gregory slowed his pace. He studied the area as if searching for something. Julie saw nothing unusual. Behind a chain-link fence was a gravel covered area filled with old car parts. An old house now converted to a taco café stood next door, then a vacant lot overgrown with weeds, and finally a modern service station. Across the street were several nondescript buildings housing a hardware store, a barbershop, and on the corner, a small grocery. In front of the grocery was a wooden bench used by people waiting for buses.

"Not an attractive neighborhood," Julie remarked.

"Mmm," Father Gregory murmured absently. He walked to the corner and looked both ways. Julie watched, perplexed, as he surveyed the cross street. What on earth was he looking at, or looking for?

Suddenly he said, "Let's go to the grocery. I need some razor blades."

Razor blades? Was that what was on his mind? *How strange,* Julie thought as he strode across the street and she followed at a jog.

She followed him into the store and stopped, letting her eyes accustom themselves to the dim light. Father Gregory picked up his razor blades at the front of the store, where the proprietor, an aging Hispanic in an old-fashioned white grocer's apron, stood behind the counter. The priest paid for his purchase at a rusty cash register that opened with a squeak, but now, to Julie's surprise, he no longer seemed in a hurry. He introduced himself to the owner and began a rambling conversation in Spanish.

Well, as long as there was no rush, Julie thought, she'd take a look around. She enjoyed browsing through these little markets, looking at foods that reminded her of the years she'd spent in Mexico. She started down the aisle, eyeing the shelves with interest. Compared to the upscale supermarket she usually frequented, this store was an anachronism, but a delightful one. Julie meandered past the spice rack, redolent with chili, and made her way to the old-fashioned produce bins where she amused herself by identifying the exotic vegetables.

When she returned to the front of the store, ten minutes had passed, and Father Gregory, still chatting with the grocer, seemed to have forgotten all about her. Julie leaned against the counter a few feet away from the priest. Obviously this was "man talk" and her intrusion into the conversation would not be welcomed. She stood quietly, listening, then suddenly tensed as she picked up the thread of the discussion."

"—and there were three of them, an old man and two younger ones, sitting on that bench out there, waiting for a bus."

"How did it happen?" the priest asked.

"So fast, it was like a scene in a TV show. A big van parked in front of them, two men jumped out, and—excuse me, Father—all hell broke loose. They grabbed one young man. He struggled, but they pushed him into the truck. The other young man ran—ran right through my store, yelling 'Help!' He knocked over cans and boxes and broke a whole display of peanut butter jars."

"Did the kidnappers catch him?"

"Didn't even try. They had one man, and that must have been enough because they got in the van and drove away.

And, Father, you know what was the strangest thing? The third man at the bus stop—the old one—he never moved from the bench. Just sat there the whole time—in shock, I guess—and they never laid a finger on him."

"Strange," agreed the priest thoughtfully. Then he asked, "Did you write down the license number of the van?"

The grocer shook his head. "I couldn't see it." He paused and scratched his head. "You know, Father, I'd seen that van before. Several times."

"Oh?" Though Father Gregory's relaxed posture didn't change, his voice betrayed tension.

"Yes. A couple of months ago I saw it pull up to the bus stop. A man—an anglo—got out and came over to the bench. He spent a few minutes talking to the men waiting there, and one of them got into the van with him. That happened twice in the same week. I supposed the van belonged to a company looking for workers. That happens all the time. But *this* time... this time, there was no friendly talking. They just jumped out and hauled someone away... just hauled him away."

"Are you certain it was the same van?" the priest asked, his voice sharper now.

"I'd stake my life on it."

Father Gregory said nothing for a moment, then inquired, "Did you call the police?"

"Oh, yes, and do you know how long it took before they got here, Father? Nearly an hour. I had my store cleaned up long before they arrived. But that's typical. What do they care for poor Mexicans?"

Father Gregory nodded his head in acknowledgment. "Did anyone else see what happened?"

"Of course. Everyone on the block."

"I'd like to talk to some of them."

"Come back this afternoon, and I'll go with you."

"Thank you." Then Father Gregory turned and noticed Julie. "Ready?" he asked.

She nodded automatically, walked out, and fell into step beside him. She couldn't believe what she had just heard! *There he goes again,* she thought, *fixating on those disappearances.* As if there weren't a hundred other problems ... problems they at least had a chance of solving. Did the man fancy himself an amateur detective ... Father Sherlock? Wasting his energy and that of the church on ... on police matters. It made her blood boil.

Then, another thought occurred to her. As if the pieces of a puzzle had suddenly fallen into place, Julie had the answer to the question that had nagged her earlier. Why did Father Gregory want to work with Mr. Salazar? Because she'd told him the old man's son had disappeared. The priest wanted to find out about Esteban's disappearance.

Her impulse was to confront Father Gregory immediately, to tell him how she felt about the matter. But that would only cause dissension. No, she'd proceed cautiously. Like a detective herself, she'd gather her evidence. First order of business would be to go over the other folders with Father Gregory. None of the other men she had considered keeping on her own caseload had any connections with disappearances. If her hunch was correct, Father Gregory would suggest she continue working with them. Then she'd steer the conversation back to Mr. Salazar. She was skilled at probing for answers. She'd do a little probing with this ... this infuriating man.

"Why don't we go over my other cases when we get back to the church?" she suggested.

"Good idea."

When they reached St. Martha's, he followed her into the office. Julie went through her files, picked out four folders, and stacked them on her desk. "Now this first one—" she began.

A knock at the door interrupted her. "Come in," she called and looked up. Her eyes widened in amazement at the tall, broad-shouldered man who filled the doorway. "Jack," she murmured, "what are you doing here?"

Impeccably attired in a three-piece gray pin-striped suit, his dark hair perfectly styled, the man leaned against the doorframe and surveyed the room with cool gray eyes, then gave her an easy smile. "The mountain has come to Mohammed."

"Wh-what?"

"I've come to take you to lunch. You've turned me down on the phone so many times I decided to ask you in person."

"But, we were just—oh, excuse me, this is Father Gregory. Jack Benton." Benton crossed the room and put out his hand. Julie thought Father Gregory hesitated just a moment before he rose and took it. He gave Benton an appraising look.

"You've caught me at a busy time, Jack," Julie said.

"Come on, no excuses," Jack said smoothly. "You have to eat, and it's—" he consulted a slim gold Rolex "—twelve-thirty already." He turned to the priest. "You don't mind if I kidnap Mrs. Whitaker for lunch, do you, Father?"

Was the priest annoyed by Jack's arrogant tone? Probably her imagination, Julie thought. Or wishful thinking. She wanted him to say he minded, to get her out of this situation. But he did no such thing. He simply murmured, "Not at all."

Well, she chided herself, Jack had come all this way and she shouldn't be rude. Jack had been a good friend of Dirk's, had been kind to her after the funeral, and didn't deserve a rebuff just because she wasn't ready for dating—

or because she wanted to spend more time with a...a priest,
for goodness sake. With an inward sigh of resignation, Julie stood and made herself smile at Jack. "Let's go," she
said.

GREG WATCHED as Julie and Benton left the room. Did he
mind if she went to lunch with Benton? He did. He had no
right to, but he'd hoped he and Julie could share lunch together. She hadn't wanted to go, either. That much was
clear. So why hadn't he said something? Something like,
"Mrs. Whitaker and I are conducting church business."

He went into his office and glanced out the window.
Mistake. He looked out just in time to see Benton helping
Julie into a low-slung black Porsche.

Greg dropped into his chair and stared in the direction the
car had taken. He'd wondered about Julie's relationship
with Benton when she'd gotten the phone call the other
morning. Obviously Benton wasn't her lover. She didn't
even look particularly pleased to see him. But he had looked
at her with the gaze of a predatory wolf. Though he wasn't
her lover now, he meant to be.

Maybe he was her type. Smooth. Perfect, male-model
features. Projecting wealth, from his expensively tailored
three-piece suit to his French cuffs fitted with gold cuff
links.

Greg frowned. Jealousy was a new experience for him,
and he didn't like it. But he couldn't escape the feeling of
envy that it was Benton who was having lunch with Julie and
not he. "And what have you got to say about it, 'Father?'" he muttered. "Face it. You're not even in the race."

Not now anyway. But perhaps after his job here was over,
he's see what Julie thought of an easygoing reporter with a
low-key style.

He opened his desk drawer and took out a sheet of typing paper. Instead of wasting his time mooning over a woman he couldn't have, he should be making notes about his conversation with the grocer. That could be his first real lead in the story.

Earlier that morning he'd made up a flyer announcing his men's group and given it to Grace Matheson to duplicate. After he finished his notes, he'd pick up the copies and distribute them around the neighborhood. That would give him an opportunity to talk to more people. And he'd go back to the grocery store and do some more digging into what happened yesterday. With any luck he'd crack this story and be out of here in a couple of weeks.

JULIE SAT ACROSS THE TABLE from Jack Benton and tried to convince herself she was having a good time. The restaurant he had chosen, Charley's 517, was elegant and expensive. The antique brick walls with softly lit oil paintings, the waiters hovering attentively in the background, the extensive menu, the muted conversations of people anxious to see and be seen in a chic downtown spot spelled sophistication, Houston style. She should enjoy herself, Julie thought. She didn't lunch in such surroundings often. "This is a treat for me," she made herself say to Jack.

"You're working too hard," he replied. "Why? Surely you don't need the money."

"Money isn't the point," Julie said. He responded with a skeptical look. Like most people, he didn't understand. She tried to explain. "Working fills my time, but more than that, it gives me a purpose."

"You could spend your time managing your money," he suggested.

The trust took care of that. Besides, it was Dirk's money. But what she made at the church was her own...something she'd accomplished by herself. But Jack wouldn't understand that, either, so she said nothing.

He turned away to nod to several acquaintances—the vice president of a major oil company, an investment banker, and the owner of a commercial real-estate firm.

When he turned back to Julie, he changed the subject. His conversation was light, ranging from improvements he was making on his beach house to news of mutual friends. Julie found it hard to keep her mind on what he was saying, though. She was still puzzling over Father Gregory's strange behavior that morning. She wished Jack hadn't interrupted their meeting. His timing couldn't have been worse. If her suspicions were correct and Father Gregory was becoming overinvolved with the disappearances, what was her next move? Should she—

"What do you think?" Jack asked.

"Hmm?" Oh, darn, he'd asked her a question, and she hadn't the faintest idea what it was. "Well, I'm not sure," she hedged.

"Think about it. How about coffee?"

"I don't think so, Jack. I really have to get back."

"All right," he said reluctantly. "But next time we'll see to it that you don't have to rush."

Julie didn't answer. She wasn't sure there would be a next time, she thought as Jack took her arm and led her toward the exit. They had almost reached it when she heard a familiar voice calling her name. *Oh, no,* she thought. With a sinking heart, she turned. Miranda Niles, gossip columnist for the Houston *Star,* was seated at a table near the door.

Julie couldn't ignore her. "Hello, Miranda."

They halted by Miranda's table, and Jack bent to kiss the reporter's cheek. "Jack, you handsome devil," Miranda cooed. "And Julie Whitaker. How wonderful to see you out again, and to see you two together."

"Oh, Miranda—" Julie began, but Jack interrupted her.

"Now don't go reaching for your little notebook, 'Randa love. We're not an item...yet." He winked at Miranda and slipped an arm around Julie's shoulder. "We'll see you around." He urged Julie on toward the exit, but she gave Miranda a quick glance over her shoulder and saw that the reporter had indeed pulled out her little notebook and was scribbling furiously.

Julie seethed all the way back to the church. She wasn't fond of Miranda Niles nor of her chatty little column. She hoped Miranda had more interesting news to print than speculation about her and Jack Benton. She herself certainly had plenty of other things, more important things, to think about.

She was tempted to say something to Jack about Miranda, but she decided anything she would say would sound petulant. After all, Jack could rightly point out that he hadn't *done* anything to give Miranda a story. If Miranda chose to read something into his innocent remarks, that was her business. *Best to let it go,* Julie told herself. She reminded herself how close Jack had been to her husband. He and Dirk had known each other since college, had both fought the same battle for success. But when they'd reached the top, their paths had diverged, Jack opting for a faster, more glamorous life-style. Only with Dirk did he show his best side. For that, if nothing else, Julie decided, she'd put up with Jack.

As soon as Jack left her at the church door, she hurried to Grace's office. She'd let the secretary know she was here and then get to work.

But Grace wasn't about to let her get away so easily. "Tell me everything," she said, her eyes sparkling with anticipation.

Julie couldn't help but laugh. "Sorry. There's nothing to tell."

"You just spent two hours with the most gorgeous man this side of Tom Selleck, and you have nothing to tell? Come on. Cater to my sense of romance."

"Okay. I had shrimp remoulade. He had chicken dijon. Neither of us had dessert—"

Grace rolled her eyes. "Julie, Julie. What is wrong with you?"

"Nothing's wrong with me. I'm just not interested in Jack Benton."

"Give me one good reason why a woman wouldn't be interested in a man who looks like a fantasy come true."

Julie paused a moment. What was the reason? "Well," she said thoughtfully, "I don't find him very stimulating."

"My dear, any woman who doesn't find Jack Benton stimulating is practically dead. If I were twenty years younger—"

"You don't have to subtract the twenty years. I'd be happy to step aside and let you have him," Julie mumbled. "Now, where is Father Gregory?"

"Out distributing his flyers."

"Flyers?"

"Yes, about the men's group he's starting. I told him one of the high-school boys who works here in the afternoon could do it, but he insisted on taking them out himself. I wonder why?"

I know why. He's going back to talk to those people about the kidnapping. "If you see him, tell him I'd like to talk to him." Julie left before Grace could ask any more questions about Jack Benton. Enough was enough.

Julie spent an hour making phone calls and writing letters. She had just stopped for a cup of coffee when Father

Gregory poked his head around the door. "Hi. Were you looking for me?"

She stared at him for a moment without speaking. He wasn't nearly as good-looking as Jack Benton, but there was something infinitely more appealing about him—the way his eyes gleamed, the stray lock of hair that seemed perpetually out of place—and even though she was about to do battle with him, she found his company much more stimulating than Jack's. It didn't make sense, but—

"Am I disturbing you?" the priest inquired, obviously puzzled by her silence.

"Oh, no," she said, coloring as she realized she'd let her thoughts get away from her. "I wondered if we could go over those folders."

"Fine." He sat down across from her. They made quick work of the four cases Julie had selected. She summarized each one, and as she had predicted, he agreed to her continuing with all of them. *Now,* she thought, *let's get to the bottom line.* "Father, why are you so concerned about taking over Mr. Salazar? How is he different from the others?"

The priest hesitated.

He couldn't think of a reason, could he? Julie waited.

He seemed to be debating what to say. Then he gave her a smile and a direct look. "I'm interested in his son's disappearance."

At least he was honest. "But why, Father?"

"I don't think the police are giving the matter the attention it warrants."

"I agree with you, but what can you accomplish by talking to Mr. Salazar? After all, he doesn't know anything. He's an old man and—"

"Maybe Mr. Salazar won't tell us anything, but I have a gut feeling that if we continue to delve into this, we'll turn up something that *will* be important." He rose, indicating the conversation was over. At the door, he turned and looked back at Julie. "Trust me on this," he said, then was gone.

Julie sighed in exasperation. Sherlock Holmes again. Trust him? She thought of their encounter in his office that morning, then murmured aloud, "I'm afraid, Father, you're one of the last people I trust, about this matter and a few others."

CHAPTER FIVE

THE FLOWERS ARRIVED the next morning—a dozen perfect red roses. The card, signed with a flourish, read simply "Jack." Grace *oh'd* and *ah'd* over the romantic gesture, and Father Rudolfo gave Julie a knowing wink. But Father Gregory's reaction puzzled her. He'd stopped by her office to ask a question, and his eyes were drawn immediately to the vase, which Julie had placed on a table.

"Birthday?" he inquired.

She shook her head.

"Benton?"

"Yes."

"Enjoy them," he murmured, but she had the feeling he disapproved. Of the flowers? Or of Jack? Father Gregory was certainly a confusing man.

"Hothouse roses," Greg scoffed, walking down the hall. Benton had no imagination. *If I were sending her flowers,* he thought, *they'd be wildflowers.* Light and delicate, but strong enough to endure no matter what storms might buffet them. Wildflowers reminded him of Julie.

Well, he wasn't sending her flowers, he told himself as he entered his office and sat down at the typewriter. He needed to organize the information he'd gathered yesterday afternoon. He typed a few lines, but the scent of roses lingered in his nostrils and the surprising surge of jealousy he'd experienced on seeing the flowers refused to disappear. It wasn't often that a woman interfered with his concentration this way. Journalism had always been his passion; the story of the moment, the current adventure, his focus. Now, he was spending as much time thinking about Julie Whitaker as he was about his assignment. This was new, unexpected.

Was it just that Julie was off limits? Because, like a little boy with his nose pressed against a candy store window, he could only look but not touch? Perhaps, when he could remove his collar, when they could meet as man and woman, perhaps then he could put things into perspective. For now, he'd better get back to work.

He mulled over the information he'd collected the previous day, and the additional data he'd received from Phil Barnes. A pattern was emerging. Not only were all the kidnapping victims men, but all were young—somewhere between twenty and thirty-five.

"That has to mean something," Greg said aloud. He stopped typing and stared out the window.

Someone needed workers. For something that required strength and endurance. But what? Farm work was the logical answer. But why pick men up off the streets? Smugglers of men, *coyotes* they were called, could bring plenty of workers across the border, men who would be only too willing to work the fields. But not now. This wasn't planting season or harvest time. No, farm work was out.

Who else needed workers? Factories, restaurants, construction projects.

"Could be anything, anywhere." He needed to talk this over with someone, Greg decided. He dialed Phil Barnes.

"Can we get together?" he asked Phil. "I have some ideas I want to kick around."

"Sure. I'll come over tomorrow night."

"Good. By then I may have more information. Father Gregory's first men's group meeting is tonight."

"What time tomorrow?"

"Make it around six, late enough for the staff to be gone. We can meet at the rectory."

"Okay. See you then."

Greg leaned back in his chair. He was optimistic that together he and Barnes would come up with something. Then he could wind this up and make it to Aspen before the season was over. But lately Aspen hadn't seemed so appealing . . . not nearly as attractive as the idea of staying in Houston and spending time with Julie.

What kind of lover would she be? Giving. He was certain of that. Passionate. He'd seen hints of that beneath her serene facade. He suddenly recalled his flippant remark to Tom Lowrey about the single man's life. "Bring on the TV dinners," he muttered. He certainly wasn't lacking for fantasies.

He resumed his typing, the clattering of the old machine so loud he almost missed hearing the knock on his office door. He rose and started across the room to open the door, then turned, went back to his desk, and pulled the paper from the typewriter. It wouldn't do to leave the notes he was typing in plain sight. He slipped the sheet into his desk, turned over his legal pad, then went to the door and found Julie waiting in the hallway.

"Come in." He wondered how she'd react if she knew the fantasies he'd been having about her. Shocked out of her mind, that's what she'd be. Suppressing a smile, he said pleasantly, "What is it?"

"A problem, Father."

"Come and sit down, and let's discuss it." He motioned her to take a chair, noticing the way one stocking-clad knee was revealed when she crossed her legs. Did she wear perfume behind her knees? He'd like to ease those panty hose down . . . ever so slowly . . . and find out.

Tearing his gaze away from her legs, he looked at her face. Her eyes were troubled. "What's wrong?" he asked.

"It's Anna Valdez. She's nineteen years old, and she's planning to be married soon, but...well, it seems she's pregnant. I know you disapprove, but—"

"I understand passion."

As her eyes widened, he hastened to add, "Theoretically," and wondered what she'd think if she knew that his body was experiencing quite a passionate response to the sight of her legs. He dropped his legal pad into his lap.

Julie was clearly unaware of his discomfiture. "Anna wants to make confession," she went on, "and I thought perhaps she could come to you."

"I...ah..." *Think fast, Allen.*

"I know you're here principally to act as counselor—"

Greg seized the opening she'd inadvertently given him. "Right. I'm not hearing confessions at the moment."

Julie's brows knitted, then she flushed. "I'm sorry, Father. I realize I've overstepped my bounds."

Damn, now she was embarrassed, uncomfortable...and what could he say?

A rap at the door caught his attention. *A reprieve.* "Come in," he called and was relieved to see Father Rudolfo.

"Am I interrupting something?" Father Rudolfo inquired.

"No, as a matter of fact, you should hear this, too," Greg said, giving him a pointed look. He quickly filled Father Rudolfo in on Anna Valdez's situation.

"Ah," the priest said, nodding. "I think we should attack this from two sides—confession and counseling. Yes, it would be best for one of us to hear her confession and the other to be responsible for face-to-face counseling. I know this family, and I would like to help them. I'll hear Anna's confession."

Greg telegraphed a message of thanks to the priest. "Good idea."

Julie nodded. "Yes, I guess that makes sense." She thanked them both, and left the room.

In unison, Greg and Father Rudolfo sighed with relief.

"A close call," Father Rudolfo said, dropping his head to his hands.

"Thank goodness you happened to walk in. What did you need?" Greg asked.

"To tell the truth, I don't remember. Right now I think I need a drink," the priest admitted.

"I'm with you on that," Greg said. "Let's go."

THE NEXT DAY Father Curry was called away. His father had a mild heart attack, and his family asked that he come home for a week or so.

Julie had helped him with some of his rushed preparations to leave and had gotten behind on work in her office. She glanced at her watch. Six o'clock, already later than her usual workday, and no one else was likely to come in, especially on a Friday. She got up from her chair and stretched. Tomorrow she was meeting friends for lunch and shopping, but tonight she'd go home, warm up whatever her housekeeper had cooked, and curl up in bed with a mystery novel.

A sound in the hall startled her. No one should be in the building now. Heavy footsteps were moving down the hall toward the parlor, toward her office. Alarmed, Julie reached for the phone. She'd call the rectory. She'd seen Father Gregory heading over there when she'd glanced out the window a few minutes earlier.

She lifted the receiver, tensing as the steps came nearer, then let out a gasp when Jack Benton appeared in her doorway. The easing of tension left her weak, and she sat down abruptly. "My God, Jack, you scared me to death!" she croaked.

"Sorry." He looked at her sharply, then sat down beside her desk, reached for her hands, and began to rub them briskly. "Your fingers are like ice. You really were frightened, weren't you?"

"Of course I was frightened," she answered irritably, "I thought you were a prowler, or... or one of those kidnappers we've been hearing about."

"You shouldn't be working in a neighborhood like this." The rubbing of her hands softened to a caress.

"Jack—"

"You were going to walk out of here into a dark parking lot. You shouldn't be doing that alone."

"I can take care of myself," Julie said coolly. Funny. When Father Gregory had said almost the same thing the other day, she'd found it endearing. From Jack, it sounded patronizing.

"Surely you didn't come all the way over here to lecture me about my work schedule." She kept her voice light, but she pulled her hands out of his grasp.

"I've made reservations for us for dinner at Maxim's."

"You've *what?*"

"A group of us are meeting there to plan a gala for the Contemporary Arts Museum. I want you to come along."

Just like that! "Why didn't you call first and ask?" she said.

"And give you a chance to say no? Uh-uh, sweetheart. I decided to come in person and sweep you off your feet."

"Railroad is more like it," Julie mumbled. "Really, Jack. You should have called. I'm not dressed for Maxim's, I'm tired, and my car is sitting in the parking lot."

"Number one, your dress is fine. You look beautiful. Number two, dinner out will energize you. You need to have a little fun. Number three, I thought about your car. I brought two of my foremen along. One of them will drive your car home while the other follows. Then they'll drop the keys off at the restaurant.'' He gave her a smug smile and crossed his arms over his chest.

"You've certainly thought of all the answers...and gone to a lot of trouble." Julie couldn't keep the sarcasm from her voice.

He ignored her tone. "No trouble at all." He reached for her arm and urged her out of her chair. "Come on."

Julie disengaged her arm, and stood in front of him. *Patience,* she told herself. "Look, Jack," she said in a slow, distinct voice, "I'll go with you this time because you're already here, but next time—"

"Next time?" he repeated, lowering his voice to a seductive purr.

"There won't be a next time," Julie said firmly, "not without a call."

"Ah, sweetheart, you're adorable." He bent to place a light kiss on her cheek, commandeered her arm again, and propelled her out the door.

As they started down the hall, Julie considered planting her feet firmly in place and refusing to move. The arrogance of the man! Waltzing in here as if he owned the place, ignoring her irritation, talking to her as if she were an empty-headed imbecile who could be jollied into anything he came up with.

They passed Father Gregory's office. The door was ajar, and Julie glanced in, picturing him at his desk. She almost fancied she could smell his after-shave. A wave of embarrassment washed over her, followed by a stab of guilt. What was she doing, fantasizing again about a man who was forbidden to her?

Abruptly she turned and looked at Jack. Here was the "real man" that Grace had prescribed, perhaps not the one she'd choose but an evening with Jack was certainly safer and saner than letting her mind run on its present course. Taking a deep breath, she forced a smile. "Tell me who'll be there this evening," she said.

"IT HAS TO BE SOMEONE who needs workers and needs them fast. I think—" Greg broke off, tensing as he glanced out the window of his room.

"What is it?" Phil asked.

"There's a man getting into Julie Whitaker's car." He rose and went quickly to the window. "I'd better—no, never mind."

"Everything all right?" Phil came up behind him to peer down at the parking lot.

"Yes, there she comes, with Jack Benton. They must be going out."

"Ah, Benton."

"You know him?" Greg turned and fixed Phil with a piercing glance.

"Sure. Big business tycoon—land development. Pillar of the community. Patron of the arts. Member of the jet set."

"That covers everything," Greg said dryly. "Not married, I suppose?"

"He's been married several times. He divorced his last wife six months ago."

"I don't like him."

Phil laughed and sat down again. "You're turning a fetching shade of green."

"Jealous. Me? Don't be an ass, Phil."

"Don't *you* be an ass, Allen. All we need is for you to get involved with a woman and blow this whole thing sky high."

"I haven't forgotten," Greg replied irritably. "Let's get back to work."

They got down to business, and by the end of the evening they'd come up with two possible motives for the kidnappings. One was a factory of some kind that needed workers, the other a construction company. "With the economy the way it is in Texas, a company could have laid off men to save money and then replaced them with illegals who would work for next to nothing."

"But they wouldn't have to resort to kidnapping," Greg argued. "And, if they were located in Houston, someone would get wind of it."

"True."

"Okay. So they're outside of Houston," Greg said. "They don't want cheap labor, they want free labor. They pick up these men, transport them to their site, and nobody's the wiser, because—"

"Because the Houston police aren't interested in tracking them down, and the local cops, whoever they are, don't give a damn, either," Phil finished.

"Well, that leaves all of Texas, the Southwest, or possibly the United States to check on," Greg said.

"You can scratch off areas where unions are strong. They'd give plenty of grief to anyone who brought in a bunch of non-union laborers."

"That still leaves Texas," Greg said.

"Good. That'll keep you busy. Keep your mind off…other things." Phil clapped Greg on the shoulder, and, laughing wheezily, told him good-night and headed for the door.

ON THE WAY TO MAXIM'S Julie lectured herself sternly, *You will enjoy the evening. You will forget work. You will for-*

get Father Gregory. You will concentrate on Jack. You will . . . you will . . . you will.

At the restaurant Jack led her to a long table where most of the group was already assembled.

She accepted the greetings of "nice to see you out again" but wasn't pleased with Jack's, "You'll be seeing more of her from now on." Nor was she happy with his possessive air. He angled his body toward her, touched her at every opportunity, and gave everyone around them the unmistakable message that he was staking a claim.

Julie tried her best to ignore him and concentrate on the conversation. She had been active in the arts during her marriage and still served on the board of the Museum of Natural Science, but she was more interested now in raising money for St. Martha's or the Coalition. Perhaps when the current gala was over, this group would consider another. She decided to put this evening to good use by planting that idea.

Halfway through the meal she noticed Jack turn and wave to someone at another table. A few seconds later she felt a hand on her shoulder. She turned to see Miranda Niles standing behind her.

The reporter gave her a knowing look. "Well, Julie and Jack again. Is this serious?"

"Now, Miranda, don't get any ideas in your pretty little head. We're just . . . good friends," Jack told her in a tone that implied the opposite.

Miranda wagged her finger at him. "Jack, you sly fellow. I'm going to keep an eye on you two."

Julie gave Miranda a direct look. "Really, Miranda, we *are* just friends. Jack and Dirk knew each other well, and Jack was very kind to me after Dirk died."

Miranda patted Julie's shoulder. "Okay. I'll keep this under wraps for now."

When Miranda moved off to greet other members of their party, Julie turned to Jack. "Jack, please," she told him in a low, angry tone. "You deliberately let her think we were seeing each other."

Jack smiled and took her hand. Bending his head close to hers, he said, "I suppose so. But it was because I wanted it to be true."

Julie pulled her hand away. "I'm not ready for a relationship."

"All right. I'll take it slow. I just want to be with you. I won't ask you for anything more . . . for now."

Noticing that others at their table were watching them with undisguised interest, Julie didn't reply. There was no point in continuing this conversation. Since Jack seemed unwilling to accept what she said, she'd show him by her actions that nothing could come of this. Nothing at all.

"TYPICAL MONDAY," Julie muttered as she looked at the folders piled on her desk. There were even several telephone messages, and it wasn't nine o'clock yet. Still, she was glad to be back at work. The weekend had been difficult. Though Jack had assured her he would honor her desire to remain "just friends," he had called Saturday to ask her to dinner. When she had refused, he's suggested Sunday brunch. Again, Julie turned him down, prompting him to say, "It seems the only way I can get you to go out is to turn up on your doorstep."

"No, Jack," she'd said hastily, afraid he would do that. "I have plans." Those "plans" had included writing a long letter to her sister, taking her dog for a walk, and puttering around the house. However, as soon as Jack hung up, she called a friend and scheduled an afternoon movie followed by dinner. Sunday she'd take the dog to the park. If Jack showed up, he'd be disappointed.

At least he wouldn't turn up on her doorstep at St. Martha's, she thought with relief. He had flown down to South Padre Island to check the progress of a condominium development and would be gone most of the week.

Julie began leafing through her messages, then looked up as Grace came into the room. The secretary shut the door quietly behind her and, with an air of suppressed excitement, sat down by Julie's desk.

"Something wrong?" Julie asked.

"Not wrong exactly. Just odd."

"Well, out with it. I can see you're bursting to tell me."

"Father Rudolfo has the flu. Did you know that?"

"No, I'm sorry to hear it, but that doesn't sound strange to me."

"The strange thing is he called Father McLaughlin from St. Sebastian's to come over here and say Mass this morning."

"And?"

"And that doesn't strike you as odd?"

"No. Should it?"

"Think about it, Julie. Father Rudolfo is sick, Father Curry's out of town, but *Father Gregory* is here. Why didn't *he* say Mass?"

Julie was silent. Why indeed?

Grace continued, "I was thinking. What would keep a priest from saying Mass?"

"And?"

Grace lowered her voice. "Maybe he's in some kind of trouble. Maybe he's on probation for something—"

"Grace, don't be absurd. For what?"

"I don't know. Some infraction of conduct, something serious enough to keep him from participating in religious affairs. He *is* supposed to be just a counselor here, isn't he?"

"Yes," Julie said slowly, suddenly remembering Father Gregory's discomfort when she'd asked him to hear Anna Valdez's confession. No, that was just a coincidence. There was a reasonable explanation for this. "Grace, I'm sure there's a good reason for all this. Father Gregory is probably busy with something else—"

"Too busy for *Mass*? Now *you're* not making sense."

"Grace, I—"

A commotion in the parlor stopped her in midsentence. "What on earth?" She could hear sobs—long, keening sobs as if someone were in pain. She ran across the room and opened the door.

Two women stood in the middle of the parlor, looking lost. The smaller of the two, young and pregnant, leaned against her companion, her eyes shut, lost in an agony of grief. She seemed unaware of Julie moving toward her, unaware of anything but whatever it was that tore through her with such desperation.

The taller woman, whose arms encircled her companion protectively, fastened her eyes on Julie. "Are you Señora Whitaker?" she asked, her words barely audible above the anguished sobs.

"Yes. What's wrong? Is she ill?"

The young woman stopped wailing long enough to shake her head and moan, *"No, no. Mi esposo."*

"Her husband," the second woman explained, though Julie needed no translation. She motioned toward her office.

"Come, Nanda. The *señora* will help you. I am Cecilia Guererro, her sister," the taller woman said to Julie.

Julie nodded and quickly urged the women into her room. Grace slipped out, shutting the door behind her as Julie guided the two women to the couch.

She sat down beside Nanda and took her hands. The young woman couldn't have been more than eighteen. Knowing that she was too upset and self-absorbed to understand English now, Julie switched to Spanish. "Is your husband hurt . . . sick?"

"No, no, *señora*. Taken," She sobbed louder.

Puzzled, Julie looked to Cecilia for an explanation.

"He was kidnapped."

Julie's heart lurched. "Tell me how it happened," she said in a calm voice. But inside, she was far from calm. Her heart was pounding. Another kidnapping. Another young wife torn with grief. What in God's name was going on?

Cecilia took a handkerchief from her pocket and tried to dry Nanda's tears. Still they poured from her eyes, staining her cheeks and dampening the front of her faded cotton smock. "Shh," Cecilia said, stroking the young woman's tangled hair. "Tell the *señora*. She will help you."

At last Nanda's cries faded to occasional hiccuping gasps. She took a shaky breath and began. "We were walking, just walking. It was early. There was no one on the street."

"Where were you going?"

"To the bus stop. Carlos was going to work. He had a job for today with a company that sends men to work on buildings."

"Temporary work," Cecilia interjected.

"*Sí*. We'd almost gotten to the bus stop when this . . . this truck pulled up. A man jumped out. He ran to Carlos and grabbed his arm. Carlos hit him. He kicked the man and punched him. I tried to help. I screamed . . . I pulled at the man, but he . . . he was big and strong and he knocked me away like I was a . . . a mosquito." She lifted her arm for Julie's inspection, showing a torn sleeve and an ugly purple bruise.

Julie couldn't contain her horrified gasp. "Go on," she said.

"Go on? There is nothing more. The man...he pushed Carlos into the truck. There was another man inside. He grabbed Carlos around the neck. Then they...they drove away." She began to sob again, her shoulders shaking uncontrollably. "I will never see him again...never again."

"Listen to me, Nanda." Julie's voice was firm. "Have you gone to the police?"

"¿Policía? No, señora. We are...I am...I have no papers." This last was said in whisper.

"No matter. You must still go. I will go with you."

Nanda gripped Julie's hand. "You will help me?"

"Of course."

"And the police? They will find him?" Her grasp tightened until pain wrenched through Julie's fingers.

"I can't promise. They will try."

Nanda's grip relaxed. Again, her eyes filled with tears. "They will call *la migra*. They will send me back to Mexico."

"No. They will not ask about your papers. They will want to hear about your husband, and that's all." Rising, Julie helped Nanda to her feet. "Did anyone else see what happened?"

"No...I...I don't think so. No one came. No one tried to help us."

Damn, Julie thought. *No other witnesses. The police won't be able to do anything.*

Perhaps she should go get Father Gregory. Maybe he could do something.

No, she decided. She wasn't comfortable with Father Gregory's fixation on the kidnappings. For all she knew, he was planning to organize a vigilante squad. No, she'd keep this to herself.

Sure in her judgment on the matter, she took Nanda and Cecilia through the parlor and down the hall. She slowed as she approached Father Gregory's office. The door stood open, the room empty. Breathing a sigh of relief, Julie led the women to Grace's office where she stopped to tell the secretary she would be gone for a while.

She noticed, as they walked out to her car, that Father Curry's car, which he had left for Father Gregory's use, was gone. Good. Father Gregory was out of the building and with any luck, she'd be back from the police station before he returned.

Completing their business took all morning. First there was the trip to the police station and the wait until someone took Nanda's statement. Then Julie insisted on taking the young woman to the nearest health clinic, which involved another long wait. Fortunately, except for the bruised arm, Nanda was uninjured. Relieved, Julie drove the two women to their home, a squat concrete structure in a row of six identical cottages.

Inside, the tiny house was cold and barren. Julie sighed as she left, again reminding herself that she must get some heaters. She drove slowly back to the church, wanting to cry. So much misery, so much pain. Poor Nanda was very possibly correct. She might never see her husband again.

Julie pulled into St. Martha's parking lot and got out of the car. She was starving, she realized, and glancing at her watch, saw that it was almost two o'clock. No wonder she was hungry.

She didn't feel like going inside and eating the sack lunch she'd brought this morning. She'd give herself a treat, she decided, and headed around the corner to *Mi Cocina*.

She took a booth near the front and picked up the menu. Maybe she'd have a full meal instead of just tamales. She studied the entrées, then sensing someone beside her, she glanced up. Father Gregory was standing by the table.

"Care for some company?" he asked.

"Certainly. Sit down."

He sat down and picked up the menu. "I was looking for you a while ago," he remarked. "Where've you been?"

Julie felt a twinge of discomfort. She was sure she was right in not telling him about Nanda, yet she felt inexplicably guilty, as if she'd broken some implicit rule of conduct. No, that was crazy. She'd done what she thought was right; she had no reason to feel remorse.

"I took a woman to the health clinic for prenatal care."

That much was true. Julie was glad Grace hadn't heard her conversation with Nanda. For all the secretary knew, the young woman was having trouble in her pregnancy. If Grace had heard about the kidnapping, Julie would have had to ask her not to tell Father Gregory. That would certainly have fueled Grace's suspicions about the priest. *God knows, she has suspicions enough.*

"You've been out, too," she observed. "Grace said you weren't at Mass this morning." She'd find out where he'd been and put the secretary's mind to rest.

Greg kept his eyes on the menu. So they'd missed him at Mass. He was distinctly uncomfortable and had been since Rudy had stumbled into his room at dawn, his eyes fever-bright.

"You have to leave the building," Rudy had whispered urgently. "I'm too sick to say Mass, and I've called someone to substitute. He mustn't see you."

"I'll stay in my room," Greg offered.

"No! You have to be away. There mustn't be any question that you were out of the building and couldn't say Mass yourself."

The priest was right. Greg sent him back to his room and pulled on his clothes. Damn, this would never work. He'd be found out for sure. His story would suffer, but far worse, the lives of the two priests would be ruined. He grabbed his jacket and sprinted down the stairs in double-time, straightening his collar as he ran.

Greg knew Julie was expecting an answer to her question. "I've been on an errand...church business," he said, knowing she had no right to question him further.

The waitress appeared, they ordered lunch, and when it arrived, ate silently.

Julie concentrated on her plate, avoiding Father Gregory's eyes.

Greg concentrated on his lunch, hoping fervently that Father Rudolfo would be well enough to say Mass tomorrow.

WHEN JULIE RETURNED to St. Martha's, she went immediately to Grace's office. "I had lunch with Father Gregory," she announced.

"Mmm."

"I found out where he was this morning."

Grace gave her skeptical look. "And where was that?"

"Taking care of church business."

"Humph." The secretary turned back to her typewriter.

"Why humph? That's a perfectly reasonable explanation."

"Maybe to you. *He* says he's taking care of church business, but I don't buy it. *I* say the business of the church is Mass. There's something fishy going on here," she muttered.

Julie laughed. "What's your theory?"

"He's in some kind of trouble with the Church."

"Right," Julie said. "A scandal. What do you think he did? Steal from the collection basket?"

"Maybe he's involved in some radical movement."

That gave Julie pause. Maybe he was! Something to do with immigration. She was glad she hadn't given in to her momentary guilt and told him about Nanda.

Watching the expression on Julie's face, Grace nodded sagely. "You think I'm right, don't you?"

"I think you're too used to scandal sheets. You read intrigue into everything," Julie said, keeping her tone light. But a few minutes later, when she left Grace, she wondered if the secretary might have hit on something.

THAT AFTERNOON Julie had an appointment with Mr. Salazar. With misgivings, she informed Father Gregory, and he joined her. Julie expected Father Gregory to approach the old man with the same intensity with which he had spoken to her about the kidnappings, but she was pleasantly surprised. Instead, the priest was kind and sympathetic. He probed gently for details of Esteban's disappearance and did nothing to upset the frail old man who sat before him. In fact, Mr. Salazar seemed pleased by the priest's interest and thanked him profusely when the appointment ended.

Still, the conversation with Grace preyed on Julie's mind. She didn't want to distrust Father Gregory, but the incidents of the past few days made it difficult to accept his interest in the kidnappings at face value. She glanced at the priest. He was lost in thought.

Nothing new, Greg thought in disappointment as he stared into space. The old man's story differed little from any others he'd heard. *Poor fellow,* Greg thought, fingering his collar. His son had been due home from work and had never arrived. Someone reported seeing him dragged into a van but what van or who owned it, no one seemed to know. Didn't anyone ever write down a license number? He'd bring that up at his next group meeting.

The ringing of the phone interrupted his thoughts. Julie picked it up. "Jack," she said, "I thought you were out of town."

He should leave, Greg thought but, perversely, he chose to remain where he was. Maybe he wanted to make Julie uncomfortable enough to sound cool to Benton. Maybe he just wanted to reassure himself that she didn't care for the guy. Whatever the motive, he found that he didn't enjoy listening to her talk to another man, but he couldn't make himself leave.

"How is your development at Padre going?" Julie was asking. Her voice was no different than it had been when she was talking to Mr. Salazar. Perhaps, Greg decided, there was nothing between them after all.

"What can you bring me? Why, nothing. Please don't being me anything... unless... unless you'd like to get me a heater or two.

"Yes, I did say a heater. I'm planning to distribute some in the parish. Most of the houses here have no heat, or if they do, it's inadequate. So if you want to give me something, make it that." She ended the conversation quickly.

Greg couldn't pretend he hadn't been listening. "Having a heater drive?" he inquired.

"Yes."

"And you're donating some of them yourself?"

"A few. I'd like to do more—the needs are so great. But I learned from a few mistakes when I began here that bringing my own money into the picture changes my relationship with the people and interferes with objectivity. So I give my time and training, and limit financial contribution to occasional small ones, like the heaters. Usually I try to get people I know to donate, but that's not efficient. If we can get an organized effort, like the benefit I mentioned to you, then we'd be on our way."

"You care a great deal, don't you?" he said softly.

She nodded. "Don't you?"

"Yes," he said, aware that it was true. He was beginning to care . . . for St. Martha's parishioners . . . and for Julie.

THE NEXT DAY at lunch Grace again brought up her suspicions about Father Gregory. "Maybe he's running an underground network for political refugees," she suggested.

"On the other hand," Julie suggested, deciding to make light of it, "he could be feeding information to the INS. Yeah, that's it. He's some sort of spy."

"Mmm," Grace said seriously. "Maybe he's an agent of theirs, not a priest at all."

"An imposter," Julie intoned dramatically.

"You're making fun of this," Grace grumbled, "but it could be true."

"No, it couldn't. The whole idea is bizarre. He was—"

She broke off abruptly as Father Gregory appeared in the doorway. He strolled into Grace's office, put some papers on her desk, and said pleasantly, "I'd like these typed as soon as you have a chance."

Grace eyed the papers warily, as if she thought they might be written with a poison pen. Julie noticed Grace's eyes skimming a page. Did the secretary think it was a secret message? Julie's lips twitched.

"Is this all, Father?" Grace said.

"That's it."

"Really? You've been so busy—"

What's she driving at? Julie wondered.

"—We missed you at Mass yesterday." Julie nearly choked on her coffee. She glanced at Father Gregory.

"I was on an errand for the church," he said abruptly, his tone suggesting that she'd better not ask any more questions.

Julie stared at him, noticing a hint of color in his cheeks. Grace seemed to notice it, too. As Father Gregory turned to leave, she gave Julie a pointed glance. Julie pursed her lips and shook her head. As soon as Father Gregory was out of earshot, she'd give Grace a scolding. She had to get off this silly idea that Father Gregory was in trouble.

The priest stopped at the door as a delivery boy appeared in the hall. "This St. Martha's Church?" the young man asked.

"Yes," Father Gregory replied.

"Delivery for—" the youth glanced at a sheet of paper "—Mrs. Whitaker."

"For me?" Julie was surprised.

"Yes, Ma'am. Twelve boxes. Sign here." He held out his clipboard, then began lugging boxes into the room.

"What in the world?" Julie asked as she began unpacking a box. Father Gregory came back into the room to watch, and Grace started on a second carton. "It's...it's a heater," Julie cried. "But I didn't order a—oh, wait a minute. Jack must've sent them."

"Jack Benton?" Grace inquired.

"Yes, I asked him for heaters when he called me yesterday."

"I told you," Grace said. "Handsome, rich and generous, too. I could fall in love with him myself."

Julie glanced up in time to see Father Gregory's disgusted look, but Grace paid no attention, continuing to exclaim over Jack's thoughtfulness. "Julie," she gushed, "aren't you thrilled?"

"I...of course I'm pleased," Julie said but, though she was glad to have the heaters, she wasn't at all certain how she felt about the gesture. She had a strong feeling that Jack never did anything on impulse. He'd probably expect a payoff, and she had a pretty good idea what that was. "I'd better call Jack," She said distractedly. She picked up Grace's phone, called Jack's office and found out where to reach him. When he answered, she said, "Jack, thank you. It was very kind of you to send the heaters."

"Anything to please a lady. I did please you?"

"Yes, of course."

"Then I think you should return the favor."

I knew it. "What did you have in mind?"

His voice deepened. "Have dinner with me Friday night."

Julie sighed inwardly. How could she turn him down after his grand gesture...and of course he knew very well that she wouldn't. "All right," she said. "Friday night."

"Good. See you then."

Julie hung up the phone and looked up in time to catch Father Gregory's scowl as he turned and strode from the room. "What's gotten into him, I wonder?" she muttered.

Greg marched down the hall, still frowning. Frustration gnawed at him. *Score one for Benton,* he thought. *The way to this lady's heart is definitely through her clients.*

CHAPTER SIX

ON THURSDAY Julie's car gave out. It began sputtering a few blocks from the church. She managed to keep the engine alive just long enough to chug into the parking lot; then it gave a final weak gasp and died. "A Mercedes isn't supposed to do this," she muttered. At least it never had before. She opened the hood and stared at the engine, but she might as well have been looking at the inside of a spaceship for all the sense it made to her. Auto mechanics, she thought, was definitely not for her.

"Problems again?" called a deep voice from her left.

Julie turned to see Father Gregory coming back from his morning run. Today, since the weather was cooler, he wore faded gray sweats. But he still projected the lean, rugged power she'd noticed when he was in shorts.

"Again?" Julie said blankly. Oh, darn, she'd forgotten the trouble she'd had starting it the other day.

Father Gregory stopped and looked over her shoulder. The odors of fresh air and male sweat mingled with the smell of the engine.

"What's the problem?" he asked.

"It started jerking and making strange noises, then it just gave out."

He moved closer and peered into the engine, then began jiggling various things. "See anything?" she asked.

"You're not out of gas, are you?"

"Of course not," she answered peevishly. She didn't know much about cars, but she could certainly read a gas gauge.

"Did you get the battery terminals checked?"

"Ah . . . no, I forgot."

"Is the battery dead now?" he asked patiently.

"I don't think so." She frowned when she saw Father Gregory stifling a laugh. For all her independence, she knew she was acting like a bewildered and totally helpless female. But that's the way she felt when confronted with the intricacies of an automobile engine.

"Let me look inside," the priest said. He opened the door and got in, turned the key, and checked various dials, then got out again. "I think it's the alternator," he said. "Do you have a mechanic?"

"Near my home."

"You'd better call him. This car isn't going anywhere."

He followed her into her office and waited while she placed the call.

"He says he'll call a tow truck and have the car towed over there," Julie reported. "If it's the alternator, he can have it fixed and back at my house by the end of the day. Now my only problem is getting home this evening."

"No problem. I'll drive you."

"Oh, Father," she said. "I don't want to impose on you. I'll call a taxi."

"Nonsense," he said firmly. "I'll meet you here at five-thirty."

JULIE HATED TO ADMIT that she'd spent the day looking forward to spending time with Father Gregory. It was just that they'd have an opportunity to discuss church affairs, she told herself. Still, her pulse rate didn't speed up when she met with the other priests.

Feeling rather foolish, she fluffed up her hair and repaired her makeup before she put on her coat and went to meet him.

"Why don't I drive since I know the way?" she suggested as they headed for Father Curry's old Pontiac.

"All right." She noticed the slow, secret smile as he said this and wondered what he was thinking.

Greg decided that the arrangement she'd suggested suited him just fine. Now he could sit and look at her. He flipped on the radio, found an easy-listening station, and settled back, stretching out his legs and throwing one arm across the seat. The rays of the setting sun highlighted the auburn in Julie's hair, turning it to a cloud of flame. Another inch and he could touch it, Greg thought, knowing it would be soft as a baby's. He curled his fingers into a ball.

"Busy day?" he asked.

Julie maneuvered the car into traffic. "They're all busy. Yesterday I took little Mario to the hospital for his checkup."

"How is he?"

"Much better. His temperature's normal and his appetite is returning. I think he's out of the woods."

"And Teresa?" he inquired. "Is she back at work?"

"Yes. She was working yesterday so Carmela went with me to the hospital. She kept me entertained."

He chuckled. "I imagine she did. She's apparently decided you can be trusted."

"Thanks to you," she said, glancing at him as the car sat idling at a stoplight. "It isn't surprising that these people become so suspicious, is it? How do they know who's there to help and who's going to turn them in?" She sighed. "I wish them so much more than what they have."

"What?"

"A little peace, a little comfort after all their hardships. A life of dignity."

"That seems little enough." He studied her expression—the concern, the love written on her face. "You said you weren't working when your husband died. Had you worked with Hispanics before, though?" he asked.

"No, I worked at a hospital for a year after graduation. Then I got married and quit."

"Why didn't you work while you were married?"

"I couldn't."

"Didn't need to?" he countered.

She gave him a wry smile. "No...couldn't."

When she didn't volunteer anything further, he decided to probe. Priests were allowed to ask personal questions. "Was your husband opposed to your working?"

"Yes and no. He wouldn't have argued if I'd decided to work, but I knew how he felt inside."

"How was that?"

"He thought if his wife worked, people wouldn't see him as successful...even though he'd made his first million well before we were married."

He wanted to keep her talking, to listen to the sound of her voice, to learn more about her. "Tell me about him. I'm a good listener."

She smiled suddenly. "Yes, you are. You certainly got Carmela to tell her story."

"Now it's your turn."

"All right," she said. "Dirk came from a family that just got by. He put himself through college working in the oil fields every summer, got a degree in geology, and then talked a couple of guys he'd played football with into staking him on an oil lease."

"It must have been a profitable one."

"Oh, yes. That lease paid off many times over. Dirk's friends got their money back...and Dirk became one of the most successful oil operators in the state. People said he could just sniff out oil. He never hit a dry hole." She paused and added softly, "Too bad he couldn't have lived to enjoy his success fully. He deserved it."

Greg resisted the urge to put his hand on her shoulder. "Sounds like an exceptional man."

Julie nodded. "He was a hard-driving, charismatic man...but he still had his insecurities about working wives. His mother had to work, and he'd been ashamed of that."

"So you gave up your career for him."

She shrugged. "Don't make it sound like such a sacrifice, Father. Marriage is always a compromise. It was worth it."

"You must have loved him very much," he said softly.

She nodded. "We had three wonderful years. A few months after his death I went back to work. At first it was a lifeline, something to cling to. Then it became important for itself. I care for people. And I needed to—"

"Accomplish something on your own," he finished.

Julie glanced at him. "You understand," she murmured. "So few people do. They think since I inherited some money, I should be traveling, shopping, playing all day. Not that I'm averse to those things," she added lightly. "It's just that I wouldn't find them fulfilling as full-time occupations."

Greg laughed. No, he couldn't see her spending her days frequenting boutiques or lounging around a pool. "Will you marry again?" he asked.

"Marry again?" She sounded surprised.

"You're a warm, nurturing person. I'd imagine you'll want a home and family."

She shrugged. "Remarriage isn't part of my plans."

"Isn't there anyone...special? He found himself holding his breath as he waited for her answer.

"No," she said promptly. "A relationship is the farthest thing from my mind right now. Work is the focus of my life."

He was conscious of a vast feeling of relief. So Benton wasn't in the picture. At least not yet. "If you do marry again," he asked, "will you continue to work?"

"You're determined to marry me off, Father," she laughed. "Yes, I'm sure I would work." She narrowed her eyes and glanced at him briefly. "Don't you approve of working wives?"

"Very much. My sister is a wife, mother of three and a successful tax attorney. I'm not sure how she manages all of it, but I applaud her."

"Good for her. You said you had a brother, too. Does his wife work?"

"Part-time, in an art gallery."

"And your brother?"

"Is a gynecologist. You'd like my family," he added suddenly, surprising himself. When had he ever thought of introducing a woman to his family? "We're a lively bunch."

She smiled. "I miss having family around. My sister and her husband live in Minnesota."

"We're scattered, too. It's funny how we miss each other. When we were kids, we did everything possible to drive one another crazy. I remember the year my sister was in love with a basketball player and I devised a system to amplify her phone calls. My friends and I would tune in on their drippy conversations. She didn't realize what was happening for several weeks. Then she almost broke my nose."

"You deserved it." Her laughter flowed through the car, warm and free. He liked hearing it, and seeing the sparkle in her eyes.

He continued watching her and talking desultorily as they drove on through the gathering dusk. To the west, the sky was still tinged with pink and gold, but twilight surrounded them, closing them in, making the car seem more intimate. The scent of her perfume filled the small space. The radio played soft, soothing music. Greg felt . . . what was it? Contentment, he supposed, and was surprised.

When they turned down a gravel driveway, he leaned forward, eager to see Julie's home. Trees lined either side of the drive, their branches a canopy above it. In the dusky twilight he could see the lawn, filled with shrubs and flowers scattered randomly. He liked the naturalness; planned formality didn't appeal to him.

The house came into view—a two-story redbrick Georgian, elegant but warm. Julie pulled up in front of the door. "Here we are. And there's my car," she said, pointing to the Mercedes, which was parked in front of the closed garage. "I imagine my mechanic left a note saying what was wrong."

"Let's see if my diagnosis was correct," Greg said. He followed her to the car, checked the invoice, and nodded smugly. "Alternator, just as I thought. I'll walk you in," he added, and accompanied her to the front door.

She unlocked the door, and Greg followed her inside, glancing at the entry hall. A seascape hung above a small marble table near the door. The colors were soft, serene— pale aquamarine water beneath a summer sky. The painting fitted his image of Julie. He glanced past the entry hall, toward the partially visible family room with furnishings in the same aquamarine and cream. Again serenity. His eyes wandered to a cobalt-blue vase on the coffee table. In summer there'd be flowers in it. Jasmine perhaps, white and delicate. On winter evenings there'd be a fire in the grate he noticed across the room. There'd be warmth and laughter. Home.

He turned back to the painting and studied it thoughtfully, then started as he heard a sound from upstairs.

Was there an intruder in the house? Instinctively Greg reached for Julie's arm to pull her back outside. Before he could act, though, he heard a deep bark and turned to see a russet-colored dog bounding down the hall, tail wagging frantically. There was his intruder, he thought with relief.

The animal launched itself at Julie, whimpering with delight. "Down, boy," she laughed, then remarked over her shoulder, "This is Rett."

"As in Rhett Butler?" Greg asked, watching her scratch the animal behind the ears.

"As in Birraporetti's. It's an Italian restaurant."

"Strange name for a . . . isn't that an Irish setter?"

"Yes, well, he likes spaghetti—he's been known to polish off a whole plate. And, Birraporetti's advertises itself as 'a great Italian restaurant with a heck of an Irish bar,' so the name fits."

She nudged the dog's paws down from her waist and turned to Greg, her eyes filled with laughter.

Desire shot through him like an electric current. Shocked at its intensity, he stared at her.

Not seeming to notice, she smiled and said, "Will you stay for dinner, Father?"

"What . . . oh, no . . . thank you. I'd better get back."

"Well, thank you for bringing me home." Automatically she reached out to touch his arm.

He stepped back. If she touched him, he'd be lost.

At his movement, she dropped her hand awkwardly. Both of them stood in the doorway, uncertain of what to do next.

Greg took another step back. "I'll see you in the morning," he said, turned, and headed for the car.

Hands gripping the wheel like vises, he made it to the end of the driveway. There he stopped, shut his eyes, and drew a long breath. Had he ever wanted a woman this much? He wanted . . . no, he *ached*. Seeing her in the hallway with the light of humor in her eyes, he'd known if he took one step toward her, if he spent one more minute with her, he'd have pulled her into his arms.

He dropped his head to the steering wheel. Father Donnelly had gone over a thousand things he'd have to know, but this was one scenario he'd omitted. Had James Donnelly ever felt these needs? Had he ever spent his nights longing for a woman, for one certain woman? Greg sighed raggedly. He supposed not. A real priest made a commitment to serve God above all things, and what he gave up was worth the sacrifice. But *he* wasn't a real priest, just a man forced into a charade he'd never wanted, and right now he'd give anything to toss it away. To turn the car around. To tell her who he was and how he felt. . . .

A beam of light shining into the car jerked him from his reverie. Confused, Greg stared into the eyes of a police officer. A white squad car was parked a few feet away. He hadn't even noticed. He rolled down the window.

"Are you all right, Father? I saw you sitting there and thought you might be sick."

"Just a . . . muscle cramp. I'm fine now, officer. Thanks."

"Okay. Have a good evening."

Greg nodded and pulled out of the driveway. *Thought I was sick? He was close. Lovesick is what I was. Damn!*

JULIE STOOD at the kitchen counter, staring into space. The image of Father Gregory retreating from her touch was frozen in her mind. How could she have been such a fool? She was so accustomed to touching her clients—a pat on the shoulder, a squeeze of the hand—that she hadn't thought twice about reaching toward Father Gregory. Touching was automatic, as natural to her as breathing. But how could she have forgotten that he was a priest, that he was untouchable? He'd pulled away as if her fingers might sear him.

Perhaps he was...afraid. The first day they'd met, they'd shaken hands, she remembered. But things had changed since then. There was a magnetic force between them, a chemistry that could only make a priest feel uncomfortable, wary. She'd felt it in the long looks he sometimes gave her when he thought she wasn't watching, sensed it simmering just below the surface during their conversation in the car. Seconds before he'd pulled away from her in the hallway, he'd been staring at her as if...as if he were stunned. His eyes had darkened....

"Julie Whitaker, you moron," she told herself. "You're imagining something that could never happen." She picked up a sponge, wiped at the spotless counter, then marched into the family room.

"Adolescent!" she said aloud. The last time this had happened to her she'd been in junior high. Flopping down on the couch, she remembered. She'd been in the eighth grade, not quite old enough to date but anxious to begin. There'd been a new science teacher that year. Young, handsome. All the girls were giggling about him, and so was she. She and Tracy Adams, her best friend, had developed twin crushes on him. What was his name? She couldn't even remember now, but back then she'd vowed to love him all her life.

Oh, the hours she and Tracy had spent talking about him. "He *looked* at me today. Do you think it meant something? He never looks at anyone else that way." Oh, the dreams they'd woven. What would it be like to go to a movie with him? To dance with him? Kissing had been too scary; they'd never considered that.

Well, here she was again, having an imaginary love affair, but at an age when such things should no longer be
necessary. Here she was again, experiencing feelings that
would never be reciprocated and probably for the very same
reason. Back in junior high, real boys had been too fright-
ening so she and Tracy had conceived a substitute who was
totally safe because he was totally out of reach.

Wasn't that what she was doing now? Fantasizing about
a priest, a man she couldn't have, because "real men," as
Grace called them, were too darn terrifying.

Nothing made sense. Not her reactions to the priest nor
his to her. Because she knew he'd responded, too. What
she'd seen in his eyes was too real, too close to mirroring her
own feelings . . . and very terrifying in its own right.

A sound caught her attention. The dog was whining
plaintively. "Oh, Rett, I forgot your dinner." She got up
and went back into the kitchen.

JACK CALLED EARLY the next morning to inform her that he
would pick her up at her office. Again, his foreman would
drive her car home.

"That's not necessary," Julie protested. "I can leave my
car at the church."

"Two blocks from the Ship Channel? At night? By the
time we get back, it'll be stripped . . . or gone."

She couldn't argue with that. "I'll drive home after work
and you can pick me up there."

"How long would that take?"

"An hour or so if the traffic's moving."

"Too long. I made early dinner reservations so we'll be
finished in time for the eight o'clock curtain at the Alley."

She made one last try. "I could meet you downtown."

"I don't want you driving home alone later."

Julie gave up. She could have pointed out that she'd driven around Houston many times at night, but why bother? Jack was set on having his way. He could take her home, but she wasn't inviting him in for a nightcap, that was for sure.

Hurrying upstairs, she dressed in a mint-green knit suit. Later, she'd add gold loop earrings and dressy shoes, but for work she'd keep her outfit toned down.

Grace didn't miss it, though. "Going out with Jack?" she asked.

Julie sighed. "I could hardly turn him down after all those heaters."

"Well, maybe something else will heat up."

"Grace, for your age, you have amazing ideas."

"My dear Julie, you're never too old for romance," Grace said loftily.

Though she knew better, Julie wished fervently that romance was not what Jack had in mind. As the day wore on, she found herself increasingly nervous as she thought about what might happen—or rather what Jack might *want* to happen that evening. But he'd have to be content with friendship because that's all he was going to get.

She went into the parlor to wait for him and found Father Gregory leafing through a magazine. "Hi," she said.

"Hello," he responded. "You look nice."

Julie smiled. Perhaps the awkwardness she'd sensed last night had been her imagination. They stood talking easily, and then Jack arrived.

The atmosphere in the room changed subtly. There was nothing Julie could put her finger on, just a subliminal feeling of tension...on Father Gregory's part. Jack was his usual effusive self.

"Nice to see you again, Father," he said, then crossed to Julie and put his arm around her with a proprietary air. "You look lovely," he said to her, "like a breath of spring."

The flowery compliment made Julie uncomfortable. *Strange how different people affect you in different ways.*

Father Gregory excused himself and left them alone.

"Your guardian angel doesn't seem too pleased about our relationship," Jack said in an amused tone.

"Don't be ridiculous, Jack. Why should he mind? And, anyway," she added in an attempt at a light tone, "you and I don't have a relationship." Then, to change the subject, she said, "I can't tell you how much I appreciate the heaters. There are twelve families who'll be eternally grateful to you."

"And you?" he asked, twining a strand of her hair around his finger. "Are you grateful, too?"

"Of course I am."

"Why don't you show me then?" He pulled her into his arms and covered her lips with his.

She'd keep the kiss friendly, Julie thought, but friendly wasn't what Jack had in mind. His tongue laid siege to her mouth, licking and teasing. Julie pushed against his chest. "Please, Jack. I meant what I said. I'm not ready for this."

"All right, but you can't blame me for trying, sweet. You're so enticing, it's hard for me to keep away from you."

"Try."

He laughed, then added, "Back to the heaters. They were a gift for the church. I brought you something more personal." He reached into his jacket pocket and removed a long narrow box. "Open it," he said, putting it into her hand.

"Oh, Jack, no."

"All right, I'll open it." He removed the silver foil paper to reveal a jeweler's box. Inside was a single strand of pearls.

"Jack!" she gasped.

"Let me put them on." He took them out and, before Julie could stop him, fastened them around her neck. "They're perfect," he said, standing back to look. "They reminded me of you—classic elegance."

"They're lovely, and it was sweet of you to bring them, but I can't accept them."

"Of course you can." He smiled confidently.

She put her hands on his chest. "No," she said firmly. "They're too personal. The thought was lovely, but please understand, Jack. I can't keep them."

"Wear them tonight at least."

She shook her head and reached for the clasp. When she put them in his hand, he raised a brow. "You're making me waste my money," he cajoled.

"Return them and buy some more heaters. Now those I would accept."

"You're a hard woman, Julie Whitaker," he sighed, giving her a hug. "Let's go."

As they went down the hall, Father Gregory came out of his office. He gave them only a brief nod, and then apparently absorbed in thought, continued to the door. Outside, Julie saw him hurrying to the rectory. She wondered if something was bothering him, then shrugged her shoulders. Not her problem. She had enough to worry about, dealing with Jack.

Once upstairs, Greg prowled the confines of his room like a caged tiger. He wished he could shed his disguise, leave the masquerade behind, if only for one night. He needed an evening out with friends, listening to music, trading jokes, just being himself. His usual patience had deserted him, replaced by tension. He'd been here two weeks, and he was no closer to breaking this story than the day he'd arrived.

And then there was Julie. Unfulfilled desire had plagued him all last night, and now there'd been the scene in the parlor. He hadn't been in the best of moods when he'd left Julie and Jack, but when he'd passed the room a few minutes later on his way back from his office, he'd glanced inside and seen Julie in Benton's arms. The two of them were so absorbed in each other they weren't even aware of the movement in the hallway.

Phil had been right the other day. He was jealous. Of the way Benton had walked over to Julie and put his arm around her, as though he were staking a claim. Of Benton's freedom to spend an evening with her, touch her. Jealousy was a new experience for him, and he didn't like it.

He pulled his notes out of the desk and tried to work. After twenty minutes he looked down at the paper and frowned. All he had accomplished were several crossed-out sentences and a handful of doodles, most of them sketches of a woman with long, dark hair. This was crazy! *He* was crazy! With a snort of self-disgust, he opened his door. Maybe he could talk Father Rudolfo into a game of gin rummy.

GREG ENTERED THE PARLOR on Monday evening for the second meeting of his men's group and was pleased to see that the attendance was double that of the first meeting. Good! This was the perfect evening to bring up the kidnappings.

After the group discussed jobs, services, and other matters, he introduced the topic. Immediately there was a clamor of voices. Men who hadn't witnessed a kidnapping firsthand had heard the stories. The group was adamant in their belief that the police had placed a low priority on the matter.

"They believe the fewer of us the better," said one man bitterly. "If these kidnappings keep up, soon they will be rid of all of us."

"What are we going to do?" someone asked.

"You can be cautious," Greg suggested.

Others chimed in.

"Stay together."

"Only go out in groups."

"Carry a weapon," said a voice from the back of the room.

Greg vetoed that idea. "Then you're asking for trouble. One thing you can do is get the license numbers of those vans. Do you realize that, with all the kidnappings, not one license number has been turned in? If the police had those—"

He was drowned out by cries of "Forget the police. They still wouldn't help."

"Okay," he agreed. "If the *church* had the license numbers, maybe we could help."

"What could you do, Father?" a serious young man asked.

"Find out who those vans belong to. Take the information to the right people. Push harder for help."

"He is right," said a tall, bearded man who seemed to be a leader. Murmurs of agreement followed his statement. The man turned to Greg. "We will do what you said, Father."

"Good. Tell your wives, your children. Everyone must work together."

The meeting ended after a few more minutes of discussion. Greg stood at the front of the room, talking with people as they left. He spoke with the man who had supported his ideas, with a handsome young man who introduced himself as Teresa Sanchez's husband, and with several others.

He felt cautiously optimistic about the meeting. Although he had learned nothing concrete, he had at least planted a seed. Perhaps it would bear fruit soon.

His upbeat mood continued the following morning. After lunch he strolled from the rectory to his office, whistling. When he opened the door to the building, he almost bumped into a man standing just inside. He was stooped and thin, with sparse black hair and eyes that darted from side to side.

"Buenos días," Greg said.

The man nodded and looked about uneasily. "Father," he said in a low voice. "May I speak with you?"

"Certainly. Come into my office."

Inside, Greg shut the door and motioned the man to a seat. "What is your name?" he inquired.

"I am Salvador Gutierrez."

Greg noticed that the man's nervousness had not dissipated. He hoped the fellow didn't want to make confession. If so, he was out of luck. "How can I help you?" he asked.

"I came to your meeting last night. You spoke of the kidnappings—Father, I have the license numbers you want."

Greg stared at the man in amazement. Here was the information he'd been seeking. His pulse speeded up. "Give them to me."

Salvador reached into the pocket of his faded jeans and took out two wrinkled scraps of paper.

Greg felt like he'd been handed two gold nuggets. "You saw two kidnappings?" he asked.

"Sí."

"Tell me about them." He reached for his pad and pen. Salvador eyed them warily. "Don't worry," Greg assured him. "I won't give your name to *la migra* or anyone else.

What you are telling me is important. I don't want to forget anything.''

His words seemed to calm Salvador, for without further hesitation, he began his story. ''The first kidnapping was quick, so quick, Father. The van pulled up, a man jumped out and spoke to a boy who was walking just in front of me.''

''What did he say?''

'''Can you tell me how to get downtown?' The boy stopped, the man took his arm and led him over to the van. I saw the boy lean down to talk to someone. Next thing I knew the man shoved him inside, and the van drove away. I have good eyes and a good memory, Father, and I knew the number on the license plate was important. I looked at it as the van drove away. When I got home, I wrote it down. Since then, I always take a pencil with me when I am on the streets.''

''Good thinking. And the second kidnapping?''

''That was by the park. Some men were sitting there, smoking and talking. A man walked up and asked one of them for a match. When he reached in his pocket, the man grabbed his arm and pulled him toward a van parked nearby. No one, Father, no one lifted a finger to help him. I didn't, either. I am like the others...afraid to bring attention to myself...afraid I will be picked up and sent back to Mexico...but I did write down the license number.''

Greg looked at the tattered bits of paper. Two different license numbers...two different vehicles. He looked up as Salvador rose. ''Why didn't you take this information to the police?''

The man shifted from one foot to the other, staring down at the floor. At last he lifted his head and looked into Greg's eyes. He lowered his voice. ''Father, I am an alien. I have no papers. I make my living cutting grass for people who ask no questions. If I go to the police, I fear they will send me away."

"I understand," Greg said gently. "You were brave to come to me. You have done your people a service." He shook Salvador's hand.

"I trust you, Father. Perhaps," he added almost as an afterthought, "I am wrong about the police. They did nothing to Nanda Morales, and she, too, is illegal. When the *señora* from the church took her to the police, she told her story and they sent her home."

"The *señora* from the church?" Greg asked, puzzled.

"*Sí.* Señora Whitaker. She went with Nanda after her husband was taken."

"And when was that? A long time ago?" Greg asked. He walked Salvador to the door.

"Only last week. I hope the license numbers will help you get her husband back. She is young, and she expects a child."

"I hope so, too. Thank you again," Greg said. He watched Salvador start down the hall, then shut his office door and started in the other direction. *Only last week, huh? Only last week!*

Anger building, he headed toward Julie's office. He needed to have a long talk with Señora Whitaker. But he promised himself he'd do it with finesse. Though he felt like marching into her office and throttling her, he'd remain in character. The kindly cleric. He rapped at her door.

When he entered the room, Julie gave him a cheerful smile. "Good morning, Father. What can I do for you?"

Explain yourself. Tell me what kind of game you're playing. He took the chair across from her desk and folded his hands in his lap. "We need to talk."

"Is something wrong?"

"I'm concerned," he replied. "I was just informed there was a kidnapping in the area last week, that a young woman came to you about it, that you took her to the police."

She looked uncomfortable. "Yes, that's true."

"Why didn't you come to me with the information? You knew I was interested in the kidnappings." He kept his voice even, calm, the way he imagined Father Donnelly would.

"Yes, Father, you made that clear. That's precisely why I didn't come."

He stared at her, puzzled. "Would you explain that?"

"Father, this community is a powder keg just waiting for a match. You seemed so...so intense about these kidnappings. I had no idea what you might be planning to do. I didn't feel I could take the chance."

Her explanation struck him as absurd, and he laughed mirthlessly. "What did you think I might do? Raise a posse? Start a riot?"

Julie spread her hands. "Of course not."

"What then?"

"I thought you might...cause unrest in the community."

She met his gaze unflinchingly. He had to admire her for that. Obviously she was sincere in what she was saying.

"I thought," he said at last, "we had come to an understanding...that you were going to discuss anything you found about the kidnappings with me."

"Father, I always reserve the right to do what I think is best for the people I work with." Her chin came up, daring him to challenge her.

"All right," he said. "I'll grant you that. But tell me what you thought I would do to cause this unrest you spoke of? Have you seen me do *anything* in the past two weeks to lead you to believe that?"

For the first time, Julie had to look away. She stared thoughtfully at the papers on her desk. *Had* he done anything to warrant the conclusions she'd drawn? He's asked a lot of questions, seemed almost obsessed with the disappearances. But had he actually *done* anything out of line? She had to admit he hadn't.

And she couldn't help but remember his gentleness with Teresa's baby, his sensitivity to Mr. Salazar when the old man spoke about his son. Had she made a mistake in assuming Father Gregory was a troublemaker? Perhaps. In the past two weeks he had done nothing to merit her distrust and much to earn her friendship and admiration.

Julie had always believed in standing by her principles, but she also believed in admitting when she was wrong. "You're right, of course, Father," she said softly. "I had no reason to assume you would cause trouble in the community. I apologize."

He looked at her with surprise and then with respect. With a smile that went straight to her heart, he said, "Well, then, shall we work together from now on?"

"Yes, Father," she agreed. She made a decision. She'd give him her cooperation, and as a first step, she began to tell him about Nanda.

He leaned forward, absorbed in her story, occasionally stopping her to ask a question or to make a comment. When she had finished, he sat tapping his fingers against her desk. "What was the attitude of the police?" he asked.

"They took her story down and said they'd look into it."

"The question is, will they? People around here say these kidnappings are very low on the police priority list."

"I suppose you could be right," Julie answered slowly.

"I know I'm right," he said intensely. "Don't you see, Julie? If we can find out more about these kidnappings, we can put pressure on the police and get them moving." He rose from his chair and moved toward the door.

Julie followed him, considering his statement. What he said made sense. "I'll do what I can, Father," she said. She smiled up at him, but this time she was careful not to reach for his hand.

GREG STOOD AT THE COUNTER in the Motor Vehicles Department. He'd signed the requisite affidavit that he would not use the information he'd requested for illegal purposes, and now all he had to do was wait until the department's computer came up with it. He ignored the curious stares of several of the clerks who were probably wondering what a priest would want with someone's license number.

The woman who'd waited on him returned. "License number 3927 RC is registered to Lone Star Development Company, and 4939 AH is registered to the same company," she told him.

Bingo! Now he had some hard facts. With a sense of elation, Greg thanked her, drove back to St. Martha's and dialed Phil's number.

When Barnes answered, Greg didn't waste time with preliminaries. "We're onto something," he said. "I was handed two license numbers this afternoon. I've just checked them out. Both vehicles are registered to Lone Star Development Company."

"How'd you get the license numbers?"

"Fellow in my men's group gave them to me. He's had them for weeks but he was afraid to go to the police."

"What'd we tell you? I knew Father Gregory would come up with something."

"Next step," Greg said, "is to find out who owns Lone Star Development. I'll get on that first thing tomorrow."

"No need," Phil said. "I can tell you right now."

"Okay. Shoot."

"All right. Lone Star Development Company is owned and operated by Jack Benton."

CHAPTER SEVEN

GREG WAS STUNNED. He hardly knew what to answer when Phil asked, "Well, what do you think? Could Benton be involved in this?"

"Hell, I don't know." He paused, then admitted, "The way I feel about Benton, it's hard for me to be objective."

"The green-eyed monster, huh?"

Greg grimaced. Trust Phil to hit it right on the nose. "You know more about Benton than I do," he countered. "What's your opinion?"

"Well, as I told you the other day, he's known as a pillar of the community."

"Yeah," Greg said wryly. "He even donated a dozen heaters to help the poor." He stared out the window for a moment, thinking, then said, "Just because his company owns the vans used in the kidnappings doesn't mean he's personally involved. Some of his employees could be 'borrowing' company vehicles and running a little business of their own. There's a lot of money to be made in smuggling aliens."

"True," Phil agreed. "But just to be sure...just to cover every angle, let's check into Benton's business affairs."

"Okay. If anything turns up, this could be one shocker of a story."

"Now," Phil said, "what about the woman?"

Greg felt his heart jump. This was a subject he didn't want to touch. "Woman?" he murmured.

Phil's voice was sharp. "Don't get coy, Allen. You know what woman. What's Julie Whitaker's role in all this?"

"No role whatever."

"Well, that was emphatic. Was that the objective reporter, the just-minded priest, or the besotted swain talking?"

"Knock it off, Phil. From what I've seen of Julie, she'd never get mixed up in kidnapping."

"She's in a perfect spot to hear what's going on in the community and feed that info to Benton."

"Maybe. But I doubt she'd do it. Look, let's leave her out of it for now. Give me a couple of days to check up on Benton and think this through. I'll get back to you."

"Do that. You're doing a good job, Allen. Don't lose your objectivity now."

There the conversation ended. But not Greg's anguished thoughts. Back and forth they went through the rest of the day and a long and sleepless night.

He rose early in the morning, put on his running clothes, and headed east toward the Ship Channel. His feet pounded on the pavement in rhythm with the name pounding in his brain. *Jack Benton. Jack Benton. Jack Benton.*

Breathing deeply, Greg caught the smell of brine as he turned to run along the docks. Tankers and freighters were berthed nearby, waiting to be loaded or unloaded. Dock workers in jeans and shirtsleeves shouted to one another, their raucous voices disturbing the early-morning hush. Dawn colors lit the sky with the promise of warmth, but now in the first hours of daylight, the breeze blew cold against his face. He welcomed it. Perhaps it would clear his head, help him make sense of the thoughts that had been battering him since his conversation with Phil Barnes. Ignoring the sights and sounds around him, Greg replayed those thoughts still another time.

Could Benton really be involved in anything so despicable as kidnapping? What possible motive would he have? As soon as he got back to his office, Greg promised himself, he'd begin digging into Benton's affairs, and if there was a motive, by damn he'd find it.

And what about Julie? She was seeing Benton regularly. She'd been uncooperative, damned uncooperative, with Father Gregory. All that crazy talk about being afraid of unrest in the community.

No, that was absurd. Julie Whitaker wasn't a kidnapper or a kidnapper's accomplice. Not Julie, with her tender heart and laughing eyes. Not Julie, who was as committed as anyone could be to the people of the community. She was firmly on their side and rock-solid in defending her principles. No, she wasn't involved. He'd stake his life on it.

Greg halted. He needed to head back to the church. He'd been out longer than usual. The sun had risen high enough to reflect off the channel, touching the brackish water with sparks of gold. He quickened his stride, still thinking of Julie.

Just yesterday she'd promised him her cooperation. Maybe he could find out more about Benton through her.

No! However important this story, whatever information Julie could supply, he wouldn't take that chance. He wouldn't risk Benton's finding out that Julie was involved, however innocently, in an investigation of him.

Best thing to do... *only* thing to do was to keep Julie out of this. He'd check on Benton, and meanwhile, he'd avoid Julie. That would keep her safe, and as a side effect, would curb his own overactive libido. He'd been finding it more and more difficult to keep away from her. Now, with her safety at stake, there would be no choice.

SEVERAL DAYS LATER Julie wandered into Grace's office, lunch bag in hand. She found Grace absorbed in *People Magazine*.

"What is it this time," Julie inquired, "a new engagement in the House of Windsor...a divorce in Hollywood?" She flopped down on a chair and waited, knowing she'd hear the story in detail and Grace would relish the telling of it.

"This is an article about Washington," Grace began.

"Oh. Who's the president seeing these days?"

"Don't be sassy. It says the Brazilian ambassador's daughter is dating the congressman from New Mexico. Interesting. Only last year she and the president's domestic advisor were an item."

Julie shook her head in amusement. "Grace, how do you remember all this stuff?"

"Gossip is my life, dear. Now," she said, her face lighting up with anticipation, "tell me your latest. I saw your name in Miranda's column the other day. What's going on with you and Jack?"

Julie grimaced. "Nothing. On my part anyway."

"And on his?"

Julie sighed. "He has other ideas. He calls every day—"

"I know. I answer the phone."

"I wish you'd tell him I'm out."

"I'm a *church* secretary. I cannot tell a lie."

"Make an exception. He's moving too fast for me. I tell him I only want friendship and *he* drops hints that he'd like something more. The other night he showed up at my house with a bottle of champagne, yesterday he sent me violets. Sunday he's having a party, and he wants me to act as his hostess."

"And?"

"I told him no. You know what he said? 'I'll be out of town till Friday. I'll call you when I get back. Think it over again.'" Agitated, she pushed her half-finished lunch away and got up to pace the room.

"And have you?"

"Yes, I'm going to tell him I don't want to see him again."

"You know, Julie, Dirk's been gone well over a year now. It's time for you to get on with your life."

Julie halted beside Grace's desk. "It isn't Dirk. I use him as an excuse when I talk to Jack, but honestly, if Jack were the right man for me, I'd welcome a relationship. But he isn't. He's changed too much since the old days when he and Dirk were friends. In fact, if I didn't keep remembering him as he used to be, I'd have ditched him already."

"I hope you're making the right decision, dear. He seems like such a nice man."

"I know I'm right, Grace. I don't want to talk about it anymore. Let's change the subject, okay? Do you still have suspicions about our notorious Father Gregory? Has he done anything unpriestlike lately?"

"Mmm, well, he's been at Mass every morning...but only as a spectator."

"Really, Grace. You shouldn't be wasting your time on gossip columns. You should be reading detective stories. Or writing them." She deepened her voice. "*The Riddle in the Rectory. The Priest's Confession. The—*"

Grace sniffed. "Laugh if you want to, but something's not right. I feel it . . . here," she said, placing her hand over her heart.

Realizing Grace was serious, Julie controlled the impulse to laugh. "Where is Father Gregory anyway?" she asked. "I haven't seen him lately, and I need to talk to him."

"He's in his office. He said he was going out later, but if you hurry, you can probably catch him."

Julie rose. "I'll go look for him now."

She hurried down the hall, all traces of humor gone. She wondered if Father Gregory had been deliberately avoiding her since their discussion about Nanda's husband. She'd thought they'd settled their differences, but perhaps he was angry. Previously he'd popped into her office for a daily chat, but he hadn't been by once in the past two days, and she missed him. She hated to admit it, but her feelings were hurt.

He looked up from his typewriter when she tapped on his open door and gave her an impersonal glance before returning to his work. He finished a line, then looked up again. "Yes?"

Julie swallowed. He acted as if he hardly knew her. What had happened to the easy camaraderie between them? She wanted to question him, but she had no right. Okay then . . . she could be just as cool as he was. "There's a Coalition meeting tomorrow," she said in a carefully controlled voice. "Are you coming?"

He considered for a moment. "I suppose so. Two o'clock, isn't it? I'll meet you in your office."

He turned back to his typing, dismissing her. Julie turned and walked slowly down the hall, feeling deflated, then irritated. Dammit, she'd admitted she was wrong the other day. How much did it take to get back in Father Gregory's good graces? She stalked into her office and slammed the door.

GREG RAKED HIS FINGERS through his hair. Keeping his distance from Julie wasn't proving as easy as he'd hoped. He missed her. As usual, her scent lingered in the room after she left. He breathed deeply and shut his eyes. The vision of her, clad in a soft rose wool dress that brought out the glow of her skin, remained in his mind's eye. He sighed. He'd wounded her just now, he knew, with his cold reception. Though she hid her feelings well, he'd seen a flash of hurt in her eyes. Well, he had no choice, especially now....

His investigation into Jack Benton's business affairs had turned up some disturbing facts. The puzzle was slowly coming together, and Greg didn't like the picture that was emerging. He'd been trying to get hold of Phil all morning to tell him what he'd learned.

He picked up the phone and called again. When Phil answered, Greg announced, "Jack Benton is on the verge of bankruptcy."

Phil whistled. "You do believe in dropping bombshells, don't you, Allen? How'd Benton get into this state?"

"Heavy investments in oil leases during Houston's boom days for one thing."

"Yeah," Phil agreed. "A lot of people here have seen that black gold turn to water. What else?"

"His divorce settlement was a whopper. It drained him of cash and other assets. And," Greg continued, "he's drastically overextended himself on a condominium development on ... South Padre Island, I think the place is called."

"Right. It's a barrier island that extends along the south Texas coast ... just a stones throw from the mainland. Padre's a hot resort area."

"Benton has a preconstruction loan, and if he defaults, the lender will foreclose. The due date is six weeks away. All he can hope for is to finish the construction and do a fast selling job on as many units as possible."

"And that's not likely," Phil put in, "given Texas' weak economy. So ... to save money, he could use illegals to complete the project. But ... kidnapping? Would he resort to that?"

"A desperate man might. And I get the feeling Benton's desperate," Greg answered.

"But using his own company vans?"

"From what I've seen of that arrogant bastard, it'd never occur to him that anyone would find out. Or, if they did, that he couldn't get out of it. After all, he's not driving the vans himself."

Phil was silent. "Assuming all this is true, sooner or later Benton will overplay his hand."

"Why wait?" Greg asked. "I could fly down to Padre Island today and check out his project."

"Hold off on that for a few days," Phil said. Before Greg could voice a protest, he continued, "let's see if we can catch someone in the act of kidnapping."

"Good idea," Greg agreed. "I think I'll have a talk with Father Curry and Father Rudolfo. It's time to make contact with the police."

Greg had anticipated problems in convincing the two priests they should go to the police. Predictably Father Curry was the more reluctant of the two. He came up with any number of reasons why Greg shouldn't go.

"You don't have enough information yet."

"I have more than anyone else," Greg argued.

"You're jumping to conclusions about Jack Benton on flimsy evidence."

Greg controlled his irritation. "I can substantiate all the information I have. It's true I can't say unequivocally that Benton is involved, but what I have will give the police something to go on."

"They'll never believe you," the priest said emphatically.

"Tim, at some point they'll simply have to make a leap of faith."

Father Curry grimaced at the religious connotation. "They might find out who you are," he argued.

Now they were getting to the priest's greatest concern, Greg thought. "Look," he said. "I gave you my word. As far as the police are concerned, I'll be just another priest. They're not likely to check me out with the Diocese."

Father Rudolfo, who had been listening quietly, said, "Tim, we knew at some point whoever was here would have to contact the authorities. It's time."

At last Father Curry agreed, but only if one of the priests accompanied Greg. Father Rudolfo volunteered, and they made an appointment to see the lieutenant at the nearest police substation immediately.

The appointment was a dismal failure. The young lieutenant listened to them with a bored expression on his face, took a few perfunctory notes, and thanked them for the information. "We'll get back to you," he said.

"The hell they will," Greg muttered as they left. "Let's go downtown."

They spent a frustrating afternoon at police headquarters, being shuffled from one office to another, telling their story until, as Father Rudolfo said, they had it down to a fine art. Nobody seemed to care.

The attitude they met was condescension. Greg felt like he was being patted on the head and told to run along. He was used to announcing his credentials and having people sit up and take notice of what he had to say. Was this what it was like to be a clergyman? No wonder the priests had wanted an outsider's help. But then, of course, they'd nullified that by restricting him to presenting himself as a priest in all situations. He felt his press card burning a hole in his pocket. Damn, he wished he could've tossed it on the desk of the last officer they'd seen and watched his mouth drop open in shock.

"I'm afraid we have accomplished nothing," Father Rudolfo said gloomily as they drove back to the church.

"Not yet, but we will," Greg said. "What was that other name we were given?"

"Ferris. Captain Steven Ferris."

"Tomorrow we go back and camp on his doorstep." Greg hadn't gotten where he was in his profession without a strong streak of determination and persistence. He'd go back to police headquarters tomorrow and the next day and the next, for as long as it took to get someone to listen.

Greg awoke on Friday to the sound of rain pelting against the window. Thunder growled ominously. "I hope this isn't an omen," he remarked to Father Rudolfo as they raced out to the car. Both of them were thoroughly soaked by the time they'd made another dash from the car to the police station.

Captain Ferris agreed to see them, chiefly through the efforts of his Catholic secretary, who convinced him to give the two priests a few minutes of his time. He ushered them into his office with an air of barely disguised impatience.

"We have information on this rash of kidnappings in the Hispanic community," Greg began.

"Oh, the disappearances."

"Kidnappings."

"Father," Ferris said, "our records show that, except for...let's see...two, all these recent disappearances involved undocumented workers. Now you and I both know these people move around a lot. They get picked up and sent home. They go back to Mexico to see their families. There's no way of tracing them. They don't have social security numbers or driver's licenses. It's not unusual for them to disappear."

"But not in this case," Greg persisted. "These people were kidnapped. They were shoved into vans...."

"Now, Father, most of the people who were supposedly abducted probably got into the vehicles of their own free will. Any day of the week a construction foreman who wants workers can get in his pickup, drive through the barrio, and pick up a dozen men, none of whom will even bother to ask where they're going. They just want a job. You could take 'em to Austin... hell, you could take 'em to Chicago... and they'd never say a word."

"But that's not what happened in the cases we're talking about," Greg said. "The men we're talking about never came back. And recently, they haven't been enticed into vehicles with offers of work. They've been forced in. Here's what we've learned."

For the next ten minutes he gave Ferris a succinct account of the information he'd acquired—witnesses' descriptions of kidnappings, license numbers of the vehicles involved, and background on Jack Benton's business affairs. As he talked, he saw Ferris's expression change from skeptical to interested... to incredulous.

There was a moment of silence when Greg finished, then Ferris spoke. "Unbelievable. I've heard Benton's name. He's a big businessman, a community leader—"

"And very possibly, a crook," Greg interjected.

"This information about Mr. Benton's business problems—how did you get it?" Ferris asked.

"We...ah, have some connections with Worldwide Press. Someone on their staff dug it up," Father Rudolfo replied.

Greg watched the expression on Ferris's face and knew exactly what the man was thinking. Ferris was envisioning a headline: Houston Police Drag Feet in Alien Kidnappings. Not the sort of publicity any big city police department desired.

Ferris cleared his throat. "Look. If you're telling me the truth, this is bigger than just a few missing persons. It could be a full-scale scandal. I'm going to have to put you on hold until I talk to my superiors."

"I understand," Greg replied, "but I suggest you take this up with them as soon as possible. Benton is running out of time, which means we are, too." Although he understood Ferris's unwillingness to proceed too quickly on the matter, he was disappointed. He was impatient to get things moving. They'd waited long enough.

"Monday," Ferris promised. "First thing Monday." He reached for the phone. Within a few minutes he had set up an appointment for eight-thirty Monday morning.

"Hallelujah," Greg said jubilantly as he and Father Rudolfo headed back to the car.

"Amen," murmured the priest.

"Ready to brave the storm?" Greg poked his head into Julie's office that afternoon and found her tying the belt on a trim London Fog raincoat.

"Soon as I find my umb—oh, here it is." She reached beneath her desk to get it, then tucked it jauntily under her arm as they started down the hall. "Don't you have an umbrella, Father?"

When he shook his head, she grinned. "You'd better get one if you're planning to stay in Houston. At least half our days will be rainy until summer . . . when we need it."

"Mmm," he murmured, enjoying the way she walked. He enjoyed everything about her—her voice, as soft as a caress; her hair falling softly over her shoulders; her expressive eyes that mirrored her every thought. *Whoa!* he told himself. This was not the time to wax poetic. This was the time to back off, for her protection. With any luck, in a few days, everything would be out in the open . . . the kidnappings, his identity, everything.

They emerged from the building into a dismal gray world. The rain, which had wakened the city in the early hours of morning with its intensity, had decreased to a monotonous drizzle, but the slate-colored skies held the ominous promise of more rain to come. They splashed across the parking lot and got into Julie's car.

Greg sensed her eyeing him as she drove. He supposed she was wondering why he was so quiet, but he was not inclined to talk. He'd promised himself he'd keep his distance, and conversation would make it harder.

Julie frowned as she slowed the car. Father Gregory had been silent all the way to the meeting, apparently lost in thought. She'd wanted to confront him, to ask him why he'd been avoiding her, but he seemed almost unaware of her presence. She decided to let the matter rest.

When they reached their destination, she parked the car and got out. He made no move to open his door. Didn't he realize they'd arrived? Julie slammed her door and noticed that the sound startled him. He blinked and reached for his door handle. Julie stared at him, perplexed. Whatever was going on in his mind, he wasn't going to discuss it with her. Annoyed, she hurried ahead of him into the building.

The meeting was long, as usual. Julie glanced at her watch as they rose to leave and saw that it was after five. The skies outside had darkened so that it appeared much later. Thunder rumbled in the distance.

She hoped they'd make it to church before the storm broke, but fate seemed against them. Traffic had slowed to a crawl, and she could do nothing but join the throng of cars and hope the rain would hold off awhile longer.

They were still a few blocks from St. Martha's when it began. Huge drops pelted the windows, the torrent making it almost impossible to see. Julie switched on her headlights and leaned forward, peering anxiously through the windshield.

It was still raining when they reached the church. She'd park as close to the door as she could, Julie decided, then muttered under her breath when she saw the truck. A delivery van was parked at the only entrance to the parking lot, blocking it completely.

"I'll have to park on the street," she said.

"That's all right. I'm a fast runner," the priest answered.

"I'll...oh, darn. I have to come in, too. I left some papers for Grace to type, and I have to put them in the mail tonight."

"Can't they wait?"

She shook her head. "They have to be postmarked today." She pulled up next to the sidewalk. "See, Father, I told you you needed an umbrella."

"Why don't we share yours?" he suggested, smiling at her for the first time.

When his eyes crinkled in that endearing way, how could she resist him? She smiled back at him and handed him the umbrella.

He got out and came around to her side of the car, holding the umbrella above them both. As they hurried along the sidewalk, he automatically put his hand on her waist. Julie started at the contact, her whole frame of consciousness suddenly riveted on the feel of his hand. *Crazy,* she thought. Crazy for the scent of a man's after-shave, the impersonal touch of his hand to affect her so strongly.

Then, with her thoughts focused on the priest, she failed to notice how slippery the sidewalk had become, until...until it was too late, and she felt her feet slide out from under her. Her arms flailed frantically at thin air, her purse fell with a splatter, and she readied herself for the slam of the pavement against her body.

But it never happened. Instead of falling, she found herself caught by a strong arm, pressed close against a hard male body, her eyes only inches from a pair of firm, sensuous lips. His mouth was so close she could feel his breath whisper in and out, his arms held her tightly against him, and his touch was no longer impersonal.

The chemical reaction that had been building between them exploded into life. Julie felt the blood roar like thunder through her veins, felt her heart stop for an instant, then pound at breakneck speed. She raised her eyes and stared into his, watching transfixed as they slowly darkened. She sensed his heart thudding against hers, felt the unmistakable arousal of his body. They stood unmoving, their bodies locked together. The umbrella he held was askew, but neither of them was aware of the rain pouring in sheets around them, soaking them. How long they stood there Julie was never certain, but at last Father Gregory drew away. "Are you all right?" he asked huskily.

She nodded mutely, and he straightened the umbrella, picked up her purse, and urged her along the walk. When they reached the door, he opened it and stood back to let her enter the building. He folded the umbrella and handed it to her along with her purse. "You'd better dry off before you leave," he murmured, then turned and headed through the rain toward the rectory.

Julie drew a long, shaky breath. For a moment, she leaned against the door, her legs too weak to carry her down the hall. Then she walked carefully to her office and picked up the papers she had come for. She went into the rest room, found a towel to dry her hair, and stared at herself in the mirror. She saw a wide-eyed stranger with flushed cheeks and pupils still dark with desire. She raised trembling fingers to her lips, then turned and headed back outside.

Greg strode down the hall to the rectory's communal bathroom and opened the shower door. "Ice-cold," he told himself. That was what he needed to slow the racing of his heart, the humming of all his senses from the contact with Julie. He could still feel her, warm and sweet against him, see her eyes wide with shocked desire, hear her shallow breathing even above the sound of the rain. He could still feel his own needs, warring with reason and common sense. He knew she'd been aware of how aroused he was; there was no hiding it. He reached for the faucet and turned the water on high, then stepped under the spray and stood there until his body was numb and desire was only a memory.

He dried off, knotted the towel around his waist and returned to his room where he threw himself on the bed. Arms behind his head, he lay staring at the ceiling. God, he wanted her. He wanted to spend the evening in one of those dark little clubs with smoke in the air and music pounding in his head. He wanted to drink wine with her, laugh with her, hold her close on the dance floor with the music throbbing around them, then take her home. He wanted to undress her slowly, with the lamp on low, and then make love to her while the rain still pattered against the window and the room was still and there was no one in the world but the two of them.

He'd almost done it, too. Then in the final seconds before he'd lost control, that last shred of reason had asserted itself and made him pull back while there was still time. With a groan, he got up and pulled on his clothes. He still had to call Phil Barnes and give him a rundown of the day's activities. Well, most of them. He left his room and went downstairs to make the call.

JULIE POURED HERSELF A GLASS of brandy. The trip to the post office and the drive home were a blur. Her car had been on automatic pilot, her thoughts a jumble. Even now, standing in her familiar living room, she could hardly manage a coherent thought.

The urge to flee was strong. She wanted to get in her car and drive away, to call an airline and buy a ticket to...to Tahiti or somewhere, anywhere far away from Father Gregory...and temptation. She'd almost kissed him! Another inch and their lips would have touched. She took a gulp of brandy, focusing on the liquid that burned her mouth. She didn't want to imagine kissing him. His mouth would burn hotter than brandy ever could.

Abruptly, she turned and started for the stairs. She'd run a bath, a hot one. Soaking in the tub would relax her...maybe.

Oh, damn, what was she going to do? Keep out of his way, she supposed. Pretend an aloofness she didn't feel. Bury herself in work.

Was that the answer? She could keep busy during the day and spend her nights in frustrated dreaming. Wasn't that the way she was headed now?

Or...she could run in another direction. Move out of her isolated world and into the company of other single people. There were plenty of "real men," as Grace would call them, around, men who would eventually replace Father Gregory in her dreams and in real life as well.

She stood poised at a turning point, not sure which way to go. But, before she could make a decision, the telephone rang.

She picked it up.

"Hi, sweetheart." It was Jack Benton.

Another time, his words might have irritated her. Tonight she welcomed them, welcomed the sound of a male voice. *Fate,* she thought.

"How are you, Jack?"

"Fine. About Sunday—"

"I'll be there."

Silence. She knew Jack was amazed that she had agreed without an argument. She wondered what kind of conclusion he would draw from her easy capitulation, but right now she didn't care. She wanted to go out, have fun, talk to people. Forget.

"You'll make a beautiful hostess."

"No, Jack. I won't come as your hostess. Please understand. I just want to be a guest this time."

"All right. As long as you're coming to the party, I won't insist. Shall I come over for a while?"

"I'd rather you didn't tonight. I got caught in the rain, and I need to get out of my wet clothes, take a hot bath, and go to bed."

"I could come and tuck you in."

Oh, please! Spare me from his innuendos tonight. "I don't think so. I'll see you Sunday."

Ten minutes later she was in the tub. The tranquilizing hum of the whirlpool droned in her ears, the warmth of the swirling water calmed her nerves. Now she could think, she decided as she leaned against the bath pillow and stared through the skylight at the now-clear night sky.

What she felt was mostly regret. Regret that the incident had happened, because it would destroy a relationship that had become important to her. She liked Father Gregory, respected him, and valued the friendship that had developed between them. Whatever silly romantic dreams she'd had about him had been harmless. The moment in his arms this evening had affected her strongly, but she would work through it. Eventually the feelings would fade and her life would go on as before.

But how would such an incident affect a priest? A man whose vows, whose very essence, forbade such feelings. He must be feeling incredibly guilty. And for that Julie was deeply sorry. She was not responsible for their embrace, because she had done nothing deliberately to cause it, but she cared for Father Gregory, and she was appalled by the idea that she had inadvertently caused him pain.

But he was a strong man. He, too, would deal with the incident and put it behind him. They both would, she assured herself as she got out of the tub. She rubbed herself briskly with a towel, slipped into a nightgown, and got into bed, hoping fervently that her dreams tonight would be about anything but Father Gregory.

GLITZ AND GLAMOUR, Julie thought as she observed the scene at Jack's party. His house, a striking contemporary decorated in black-and-white, which he had purchased after his recent divorce, was filled with Houston's moneyed set. If you lined up all the dollars Jack's guests controlled, they'd reach to the moon and beyond.

Women wore designer outfits tonight as comfortably as they'd wear jeans tomorrow morning; jewels vied with the chandeliers for sparkle. Every male arm boasted a Rolex, every male body a label suit.

Julie knew most of the guests. She saw Claire Mellon, swathed in emeralds, a state senator's wife with whom she occasionally played tennis, several board members from the Museum of Natural Science. Most of the guests were married, but there was also a contingent of singles, many of them recently divorced.

Jack came up behind her, put his arms around her waist, and bent to place a moist kiss on her neck. "Having a good time?"

Julie nodded. It was good to get out, even if she did have to put up with Jack's attentions. "I'm glad I came."

"So am I. I want to talk to you later...after everyone's gone. Will you stay?"

"I have to be at work early tomorrow, Jack."

"All work and no play—" he said in a teasing tone.

She could match him cliché for cliché. "Early to bed and early to rise—" she replied.

"Make tonight an exception," Jack cajoled.

Hadn't that been exactly what she'd been telling herself the other evening? "All right. I'll stay."

He smiled and kissed her cheek. "I'll see you later."

Julie wandered over to the buffet table. Loaded with sumptuous fare provided by Houston's current "in" caterer, it was a work of art. She stood for a moment, admiring the display, then piled her plate with warm pastry filled with Brie, boiled Gulf shrimp, rare roast beef with horse radish sauce, and fresh vegetables.

She strolled over to the contingent from the museum and joined in the conversation about future exhibits. Later she visited with an old friend from college and heard about her current diet and fitness program, then she found herself in the midst of a group bemoaning the state of the Houston economy.

She was glad she'd come, she really was, but her enthusiasm was fading. Maybe she was coming down with something. The smoke, the noise, and the wine were giving her a headache. The throbbing had begun at the base of her skull, and now she could feel the pain creeping upward toward her temple. She wished she hadn't told Jack she'd stay late. She wasn't up to enduring any more of his soggy kisses. Given a choice, she'd prefer Rett's. She'd find Jack, she decided, explain that she wasn't feeling well, and go home.

She looked around the room, but Jack wasn't in sight, so she searched for a bathroom instead. A cold cloth might help the headache. She started down the hall, glancing in various rooms. The guest bathroom was occupied so she continued until she found the master bedroom. Jack would probably have some aspirin in his own bathroom, and she needed two of them.

Julie walked through the darkened room, past the king size water bed and the massive armoire, entered the bathroom and flipped on the lights. She blinked. Her own bath was luxurious, but this one could only be described as opulent. The oversized sunken tub and twin sinks were of black marble, the fixtures of gold. An exercise room with a rowing machine, a treadmill, and weights opened off one side of the room; running the full length of the other wall was a closet, its door ajar. Julie was accustomed to affluence, but even she couldn't help staring around the room in amazement. It looked like it was designed for a sheikh, she thought, but then "ostentatious" was Jack Benton's style.

She turned on the cold water and wet a cloth. The lights in the room bothered her; she turned them off and sat down at the dressing table, shutting her eyes and holding the towel to her head. *Peace and quiet,* she thought with a grateful sigh. The stillness of the room, the coolness of the cloth were soothing, and she dozed, then pulled upright with a jerk as the sharp slam of the bedroom door startled her.

She heard footsteps and a low, angry voice. "In the bathroom, and hurry."

Julie got to her feet and fumbled for the light switch. She'd better turn the lights on and announce herself. Where was the switch? In the darkness, she couldn't locate it.

The footsteps came closer.

"Relax. No one can hear." She heard a slow, East Texas drawl, then a snicker.

The first voice, deep and harsh, broke in. "And no one better."

The greeting Julie had been about to call out died on her lips. She'd best not reveal her presence to the two men who were about to open the bathroom door. Whatever they were arguing about, they apparently didn't want a witness.

Glancing around the darkened room for a means of escape, she made out the door to Jack's closet. Without hesitation, she ducked inside and pulled at the door. It didn't close all the way. With trembling hands she reached for the knob to pull the door the rest of the way, but she was too late. The bathroom door opened, and the lights flashed on.

Julie blinked in the sudden illumination, then focused on the man who faced her a few feet away. Jack. She could see tension, even anger, in the lines of his face, the set of his jaw.

"What is it?" he asked, his voice harsher and deeper than usual.

In contrast, Jack's companion, his back toward Julie, stood relaxed, leaning a hip against the counter. "Business," he replied.

"I don't have time for business tonight. I have friends here," Jack said shortly.

"Sorry to crash your party, but I don't think your buddies noticed."

Julie choked. In the crowd here tonight, this man was as noticeable as a country singer at the Met. From his brown polyester suit to his too-shiny shoes, he definitely stood out. Was that the reason Jack was angry, or was it the business he mentioned? The latter, she supposed. Probably the man was one of Jack's construction foremen. There could be trouble on a job.

"You have two minutes," Jack said, looking at his watch.

Unintimidated, the other man remained slouched against the counter. "Well now, I'll make it fast then. I'm a little short of cash."

"That's your problem," Jack said impatiently.

"I'm working under hazardous conditions. You're wanting the merchandise faster, plus we gotta get rid of the used goods."

Jack stared at him for a moment, then spread his hands. "How much do you need?"

"A thousand should do it."

"A thousand? I don't keep that much cash here."

"I can wait." His voice was lazy. "I got no plans for the evening. If you ain't got it, ask one of your friends."

With a muttered oath, Jack turned and left the room.

When Jack had gone, the man turned, giving Julie a clear view of his face. One glance told her she'd never forget it. His lips were thin, his nose looked as if it had been broken more than once, and his eyes were like a cat's—a strange, pale green with flecks of gold. His black hair was thinning, leaving a wide forehead marred by a small white scar above his left eyebrow. Julie shivered. He looked . . . not just unsavory . . . but dangerous.

He grinned, showing nicotine-stained teeth, and studied the room while he waited for Jack. After a moment, he turned back to the counter and examined the array of bottles, picked up one labeled Polo, and sprayed himself liberally, then coughed and waved his hand to disperse the fumes. Next he moved in Julie's direction. She shrank back, terrified that he might decide to look through the closet. Instead, he ambled into the exercise room, and she heard the sound of a switch and then the motor of the treadmill.

"Nice setup you got here," he drawled when Jack returned to the bathroom.

Jack ignored the comment. "Here's your thousand. The door over there will take you to the pool area. You can get out that way. And remember, the money comes off your pay when your work is finished."

"Sure," the man said. "An advance."

Julie heard the sound of a laugh, a door opening and shutting, and then silence.

Jack came back into the bathroom, took a deep breath, and peered at himself in the mirror. He took a comb from his pocket, ran it through his hair, then left he room, turning off the light.

Julie stood in the darkness, afraid to move, hardly daring to breathe. For the first time, she was aware of the faint smell of mothballs, the scratchiness of Jack's wool suits against her cheeks, the sound of her heart pounding in her ears. She told herself she was crazy to be upset. So what if a construction worker wanted to borrow money from his employer? It was probably a common occurrence. Yet she couldn't help feeling unnerved, as if she'd stumbled onto something that was best forgotten.

She wanted to get out of this closet, get out of Jack's room as quickly as possible without being seen. Stealthily she pushed Jack's suits aside, opened the door, and stepped into the bathroom. Her head was throbbing again, but she was no longer interested in aspirin. She just wanted to get out.

Julie tiptoed across the bathroom, opened the door slowly, and to her relief, found the bedroom empty. After hurrying through it, she checked the hallway, and saw no one there, either. She slipped out of the bedroom and hurried down the hall, welcoming the noise of the party, the sounds of laughter and music and normality.

She scanned the living room when she entered and saw Jack standing by the fireplace talking to several guests. The persona of charming, sophisticated host was securely back in place. Gone was the tense, impatient man she had observed only moments ago.

She caught Jack's eye, and when he came over to her, said quietly, "Jack, I won't be able to stay late to talk with you. I'm not feeling well, and I want to go home."

"But I really must talk with you tonight," he insisted. "If you're not well, you shouldn't be driving. Why don't you lie down in my room and I'll wake you when the party's over?"

Julie shook her head. "I'd rather go home."

"Then I'll come over later."

Good grief. What could be that important? she thought irritably. "Can't we talk tomorrow?"

"Tonight."

Julie took a step back, but Jack took her arm and said, "Let's talk now." His hand firmly on her arm, he led her out of the living room.

She might as well get this over with, Julie decided as Jack took her down the hall and into a paneled study furnished with a large rosewood desk, several leather chairs, and a love seat. He lead her to the love seat and sat down beside her.

"This isn't the setting I had in mind, sweetheart," he said, taking her hands in his.

"For what?" she mumbled. The headache was making her dizzy, and she was having trouble concentrating on his words.

"I've been wanting to talk to you for several days, and I decided I couldn't put it off any longer."

"What about?"

"I want you to marry me."

Julie blinked. Had she really heard him ask her to marry him? Of all the things she had imagined he might want to discuss with her, this was the last she would have thought of. "Wh-what did you say?"

"I said I want you to marry me. Surely you must have guessed how I feel about you."

Julie's headache pain receded, replaced by shock. Was the man crazy? For a moment, she fought the urge to giggle, then stifled it. This was no laughing matter. "Guessed how you...feel about me?" she repeated. "Why...no. We're friends, but—"

"Much more than friends. I've been crazy about you for years, and—"

"For *years*?"

"All the time you were married to Dirk. I wanted to give you time to get over the loss, but I can't wait any longer."

"Jack," Julie said in a slow, dazed voice, "I can't believe this. We've gone out a few times, but we hardly know each other."

"We can remedy that." He moved closer and took her in his arms.

Julie pushed against his chest and struggled away. "That wasn't what I meant," she said carefully. "I meant we don't know each other except in...in superficial ways...how we act at parties, what kind of clubs we belong to."

"We'll get to know each other after we're married."

Julie stood up and walked to the desk, then turned to face Jack. "No, Jack," she said quietly. "I'm flattered that you asked me, but I'm not ready to marry again."

He rose and came to her. "I'll change your mind, sweetheart."

She shook her head. "Don't try. I'm going home now. Good night, Jack."

Before he could stop her, she left the room, went down the hall to the living room, and hurried out of the house. She didn't breathe freely until she was in her car and on the way home.

CHAPTER EIGHT

AT HOUSTON POLICE HEADQUARTERS Greg sat down on a couch covered in cracking vinyl and waited for Captain Ferris to announce them to the receptionist at the front desk. He glanced at the Monday morning newspaper tossed carelessly on an end table then laid it aside and stared at the door across from him. *Harry Gorman, Jr., Chief of Police.* He was sorry Rudy hadn't been able to come along this morning. He'd have been impressed.

Ferris had mentioned on the telephone earlier that his superiors thought the information the priests had brought was important enough to be discussed with *their* superior, but Greg hadn't been prepared for the police chief himself. Apparently Benton's name sparked enough interest to take the matter all the way to the top. Good. Maybe now they'd get some action. He gave Ferris an approving smile as the police captain sat down on the other end of the couch.

They didn't have to wait long. Five minutes later the door opened and Harry Gorman came into the room. A large, ruddy-complexioned man, he looked like a cop. He had the kind of bulky body that cold easily have gone to flab once he'd moved behind a desk, but he obviously kept himself in shape.

Greg had heard he'd come up through the ranks. He'd started by walking a beat, then through hard work, determination, and shrewd political acumen he had progressed steadily until three years ago he'd reached the pinnacle—the dubious honor of police chief of one of America's largest and most crime-ridden cities.

Gorman nodded at Ferris and gave Greg a brief, firm handshake, then led them into his office. For a big man, he moved gracefully. He sat down behind a large metal desk and motioned Greg and Ferris to the two upright wooden chairs across from it. The city certainly didn't waste money furnishing offices, Greg thought as he sat down in the uncomfortable chair.

"Captain Ferris tells us you have a . . . theory about these Hispanic disappearances," Gorman began. "Tell me what you know . . . and what you think."

Greg grinned, liking the way Gorman put it. He related what he'd discovered about the kidnappings, the vehicles involved, and Benton's business problems.

When he finished, Gorman folded his hands and stared thoughtfully at a spot on the wall. "Whew," he said finally. "You know you're opening up a nasty can of worms, don't you, Father?"

Greg nodded. "Yes, sir, but it seems there's no choice."

The chief sighed. "Jack Benton," he said carefully, "is a force to be reckoned with. He's a successful businessman with, as far as anyone knows, clean hands up to now. He sits on the board of directors of one of Houston's largest banks. He has strong ties to the mayor's office. This is a . . . ah . . . delicate situation. I'm sure you understand."

Greg nodded. He understood very well. From his investigation into Benton's background, he was aware that the man had been a major contributor to the mayor's last two successful campaigns. He was also well aware that the police chief was appointed by the mayor. A delicate situation to be sure.

"However," Gorman continued, "it does bear looking into. Discreetly, of course."

"What did you have in mind?" Greg asked. He hoped that a "discreet" investigation didn't mean that Gorman was going to sweep this under the carpet because it was too "delicate" to get involved in.

"Of course," Gorman began, "we could notify the INS. They'd be out to raid Benton's Padre Island construction site sooner than you could say 'undocumented workers,' but I don't think that's the way to go with this." He sat silently, tapping his pen on the desk, apparently mulling over various options.

Greg was glad Gorman had vetoed the idea of raiding the construction site. They'd find the aliens, send them back across the border, extract some fines...but they'd never really touch Benton. What he'd like to do was—

Gorman looked up. "Let's take our time and see if we can catch someone in the act of kidnapping in our own jurisdiction. Then we'd have good reason to launch a full-scale investigation of Benton. If he's behind this and we want to nail him, we'll need every shred of evidence we can lay our hands on."

His opinion exactly, Greg thought. If Benton was as involved in this as Greg suspected he was, he damn well shouldn't get off with only a slap on the wrist for employing illegal immigrants. He should be prosecuted to the full extent of the law. Tying him to kidnappings would make that possible.

And if Benton wasn't involved himself, well, that needed to be cleared up, too. Regardless of how he felt about the man personally—and Greg realized that "personally" was the operative word here—he didn't want to see Benton falsely accused and his reputation ruined. He'd always believed in fair play; he wanted Benton to get a fair deal. Whether he deserved it or not.

"We have a few Hispanic officers we can spare for the next few days," the chief went on. "We'll use them as bait—wire them with microphones, let them get picked up and tossed in those vans, and see what happens."

Greg controlled the urge to jump up and cheer. This was more than he'd expected. "Sounds good," he said.

"Okay," Gorman said. "Let's figure out the most likely places to put these guys."

Together the three men studied a map of the city on which Greg had marked the kidnapping sites.

"Most of them are bus stops," Ferris remarked.

"Right. And most are within a few blocks of Canal Street." Gorman picked up his phone. "Eleanor, get me a list of all the bus stops within a two-mile radius of Canal and 75th."

When his secretary had brought the list, they chose four corners. "Brief your men and get them on those corners tomorrow," Gorman said to Ferris.

Ferris nodded.

"Frankly, Father," Gorman said, "I hope this idea about Jack Benton turns out to be a wild-goose chase."

"So do I," Greg agreed, "but the evidence suggests otherwise."

"Circumstantial evidence."

"True, but it mounts up."

"We'll see. I've enjoyed meeting you, Father." He rose and offered his hand.

"Thanks for your cooperation, Chief Gorman," Greg said.

The chief gave him a wry smile. "Put in a good word for me with the man upstairs, Father. If Jack Benton is as involved in this as you seem to think, I may need it."

GREG DROPPED Father Curry's keys off to him and strolled from the rectory to the church, whistling cheerfully. If luck was with him, the story should break this week. Things were going well...except with Julie. He'd seen her in the hall this morning, and they'd both been tense and uncomfortable. It was natural, he supposed, after their encounter on Friday. He'd thought about it all weekend, and it had made him more determined than ever to spend some time with her...as Greg Allen...after this was over.

The building was quiet. Everyone was out for lunch. He'd give Phil a call and let him know how this morning's appointment had gone, then he'd have a bite himself.

He left his office door open and sat down at the desk. He was about to punch in Phil's number when he heard a sound in the hall. Someone was running...and gasping for breath. Quickly he got up and went out to look.

"Father!"

"Teresa." He took in the Sanchez woman's heaving chest and frightened eyes. "What's wrong? Is Mario sick again?" he asked in Spanish.

She shook her head and put her hand to her breast. "I saw...I saw...a kidnapping."

Damn. Another kidnapping, and the police won't be out until tomorrow. "Come in my office and tell me what happened." The last thing he wanted was for Julie to overhear this conversation and get involved—

Too late.

The door at the end of the hall opened and Julie and Grace came in, obviously on their way back from lunch.

Greg took Teresa's arm to lead her quickly into his office, but she, too, had seen Julie, and predictably, she turned toward the person who had provided help and comfort in the past.

"Señora," she cried and ran straight into Julie's arms.

"Teresa. Is it Mario?"

"No, no. He is well, but I am so frightened. I saw—"

Greg strode down the hall. "She saw a kidnapping. She'll be all right. I'll talk to her."

"Oh, *señora*. There is more. I . . . I am afraid for my family."

Teresa clutched Julie's arm, and Greg could see there was no way he could pry her hands loose. With a sigh of resignation, he said, "Let's sit down, Teresa, and you can tell us what happened."

The three of them went into his office, but Teresa was too agitated to sit. In a rapid flood of Spanish, she told her story. "I was not working today—Señora Mellon is leaving this morning for a trip—so I took Mario to the little park near my house. My mother went, too. We were almost home—just at the corner near the house—when a green van pulled up. A man was at the bus stop. They . . . they dragged him into the van. My husband told me what you said the other night, Father, about the license numbers, so I have been carrying pencil and paper whenever I go out. I . . . I wrote down the license number."

"You did the right thing," Greg assured her. "You have nothing to be afraid of."

"Oh, but, Father . . . they . . . they saw me . . . the men in the van. My mother . . . she took Mario and ran to the house. They saw her go in. I ran the other way . . . to the church . . . to you. Father, *señora*, I am frightened. Those men . . . they know my house. They will come back. I am afraid for my family. I am afraid to go home. What shall I do?" She burst into tears.

Automatically Greg smoothed his collar. There was no question that Teresa's welfare was his responsibility. "I'll take you home," he soothed her. "I'll see that no one is around, and I'll stay until Arturo comes home if you like. We'll keep the door locked. Okay?"

"Yes, Father. I knew you would help."

Greg turned to Julie. "Give me your keys."

She shook her head and stood. "I'm going with you."

"There's no need," he said firmly.

"There is."

"If you're worried about your car," he said in English, "I can take care of it. I've driven it before."

"My *car*? My car has nothing to do with this." Her eyes flashed fire. "I want to be sure everything is all right there."

Hell, this was all he needed. She was going to dig in her heels and refuse to budge.

"Look, this is not your business."

"You made it my business. You asked for my cooperation, and you got it. Now I'm going." Her chin went up.

"Julie, this could be dangerous." He wanted to tell her that he wouldn't risk her safety, that he couldn't deal with the thought of anything happening to her, but he could only stand there in rage and frustration, his hands clenched to keep from grabbing her and shaking some sense into her. "Don't be an idiot," he said through his teeth. "Give me the keys."

"If you want the car, Father, I go with it."

"Forget it. I'll take Father Curry's car." He turned away.

"I'm still going," she said in a voice so determined he knew there was no way he could change her mind. He gave in. What else could he do? He couldn't take a chance of walking with Teresa; anyway, Julie would probably insist on walking along. "All right," he sighed. "Let's go. *Vamonos*," he said to Teresa.

Should he call the police? No, he decided. They might get to Teresa's house and find everything all right. No use crying wolf and antagonizing them just when they were beginning to cooperate. But, in case everything wasn't all right—

He stopped at Grace's office. "We're going to take Mrs. Sanchez home. She's witnessed a kidnapping, and she'd afraid the men may come back to her house. If we're not back in an hour, call this number. Ask for Captain Steven Ferris, and tell him what happened. Don't talk to anyone else."

In the parking lot, he turned to Julie. "Does she understand English?" he asked, gesturing toward Teresa.

"Very little."

"Good, then she won't hear me telling you what a stubborn, pigheaded woman you are."

"Save your breath, Father. I understand English, but I don't hear you, either."

They stood still, glaring at each other, the tension that had simmered between them since last week now erupting into anger.

"Come on, then," Greg said harshly. "We're wasting time."

Julie and Teresa got into the front seat of the car, and Greg sat in the back. He scanned the area as they drove down Teresa's block, but the green van wasn't there. His hand was on the door handle almost before they reached Teresa's house. "Stay in the car," he order Julie, but she was out and hurrying around to the other side before he could finish. "Great," he muttered, racing to catch up with her. "Keep back," he said as they reached the door.

Before he could knock, it opened...and Greg found himself staring at the barrel of a snub-nosed revolver.

The rangy, long-haired man who held it grinned. "Come in, Father, ladies. Join the party." A second man, short and pudgy, gestured them inside.

They had no choice. Greg positioned himself between Julie, who stood with her arm protectively around Teresa's shoulders, and the gun.

They entered the house to find Teresa's sister, Rosa, and another young woman cowering in a corner. A girl of about two years sat on the floor beside their chairs, and Mario slept in Rosa's lap. Carmela sat on a rickety chair, her head high, her eyes blazing at her two captors.

As soon as Teresa saw her family, she ran toward them with a cry. *"Mi niño."* She took Mario from her sister's arms and cradled him close. Julie started to follow Teresa, but the gun-wielding man stopped her. "You and him—over there on the couch."

As Greg followed Julie across the room, he glanced quickly around, looking for an escape route. There was none. Damn, why had Julie come? Why had he let her?

When they sat down, he hissed at Julie, "I told you to stay at the church. I told you it could be dangerous here."

"*You're* here."

"That's different."

"Male logic," she muttered under her breath, and Greg shot her an angry look.

Rosa had burst into tears upon seeing Teresa, and her cries awakened Mario, who now began to wail. The little girl, a ragged blanket in one hand, added her sobs to his.

"Can it," snarled the long-haired man, but the sobs continued. He turned to Julie. "You speak Spanish?"

She nodded. "Tell 'em to shut up," he ordered.

"Silencio, por favor," she told the group in the corner, and the sobs died away. Even Mario's howls softened to occasional snuffles.

Julie turned back to the two men standing in the doorway. "What are you going to do with us?"

Good question, Greg thought, watching the two eye each other. They didn't know, he realized. Good. The longer they waited to make a decision, the more likely it was that the police would come.

Perhaps he could delay them. "Where's your van?" he asked conversationally.

"Parked around the corner," the taller man replied.

"And the man you had . . . what happened to him?"

"Tied up in the van." He grinned slyly. "We can wait and take him where he's goin' later. But her—" he pointed at Teresa "—she took our license number. Now we couldn't let her get away with that. We hadta come back and take care of her. We're—"

His companion interrupted. He kept his back to the room as he talked, but Greg could hear him. "What're we gonna do with those two, Ray?" he asked, gesturing over his shoulder toward the couch.

"I don't know about him, but I got a few ideas for the lady."

Greg tensed. Just let them try anything. He edged closer to Julie.

"Yeah, well hold off on that. We gotta call Bud and find out what to do. I wasn't countin' on no Anglos in the group."

"You call him, Pete."

The man called Pete made a quick tour of the house and returned to the living room. "They don't have no phone."

"Go down to Canal Street and find one. And make it quick."

Pete, obviously the underling, scurried away.

Ray sat down to wait, and an uneasy silence fell. Greg checked his watch. Twenty minutes had passed since they'd left the church. Forty till Grace would call Ferris, maybe another ten to get someone here. He hoped Bud wasn't in the vicinity.

Ten minutes later, the kitchen door opened and Pete came in, carrying two cans of beer. "Found these in the refrigerator," he remarked. He handed one to his companion, then dragged a chair across the room and straddled it, popped the top of the can, and took a long swallow. "Bud's on his way," he announced.

Ray lounged in his chair, still holding the gun. He, too, took a healthy swig of beer. "Might as well enjoy ourselves while we're waitin', huh, lady?" he said, leering at Julie.

She regarded him stoically. *Scum,* she thought, watching him wipe his mouth with the back of his hand. She glanced sideways at Father Gregory, who was staring straight ahead. Wasn't he going to try to get them out of here? He seemed to be waiting for something. Then she remembered what he'd said to Grace. "If we're not back in an hour, call the police." And he'd given Grace someone's name. At the time Julie hadn't thought to question how he'd come by that name. Now she was just glad he had it.

The minutes ticked by.

Teresa and her family sat silently in the corner. Mario fell asleep, and the little girl sat sucking her thumb, blanket against her cheek. The three young women kept their eyes averted, not wanting to make contact with the men. Only Carmela seemed undaunted by the situation. She stared at their captors, as if by her eyes alone, she could bowl them over.

Outside Julie could hear children's voices. It must be after two...time for the lower grades to be dismissed from school. Somewhere a horn honked, and then there was the sound of a vehicle pulling up. A door slammed.

"That oughta be Bud. I'll go see." Pete went into the kitchen, and in a minute Julie heard the door open and close.

"What the hell's goin' on?" an angry voice said from the kitchen.

Julie frowned and leaned forward. There was something chillingly familiar about that voice. Where had she heard it before?

"We are pickin' up some merchandise—"

Merchandise, Julie thought. She'd heard that term somewhere else recently.

Pete was continuing, "—and we saw this Mexican gal and an old lady and a baby, and the gal was writin' down our license number. So we came back here."

"What the hell for?"

"To get 'em. Only, Bud," his tone betrayed nerves, "we got a couple of extras."

"Yeah. Who?"

"A...uh...lady and a priest."

"A what? You boneheads."

"Hey, calm down, Bud. You want a beer?"

"No! I wanna take a look at what you got. Then I gotta decide what the hell to do with 'em."

Pete returned to the living room, followed by a second man, taller, more wiry.

Julie stifled a gasp. "My God," she whispered, and Father Gregory glanced sharply at her as she put a trembling hand to her mouth.

That face. Hadn't she sworn she'd never forget it? The crooked nose, the scar above the left eyebrow, the gleaming cat's eyes. She'd seen Bud before—less than twenty-four hours ago. In Jack Benton's bathroom.

Merchandise. He'd used that word last night. *What—oh, no.* Merchandise was . . . was people! Could Jack—? *No.* It was unthinkable.

She had to do something. Without giving it a thought, she started to rise from the couch.

Ray noticed, and waved the revolver. "Sit down, lady. You ain't goin' nowhere."

Julie sat. Father Gregory turned to her. "What is it?" he mouthed.

Ray saw that, too. "Shut up, Father," he said, raising the gun to point it at the priest's head.

"Shut up, all of you," ordered Bud. "I gotta think. The Mexicans ain't a problem. We can get rid of 'em easy, but these two—" he gestured toward Julie and Father Gregory "—I gotta think about that."

Julie gasped. Until now, even when she'd recognized Bud, she hadn't been afraid. She'd been certain in some subconscious way, that Father Gregory would get them out of this. Now she was frightened, but not for herself. For Teresa and her family. She was aware of the truth of Bud's statement. She and Father Gregory presented a problem to him. If a priest and a wealthy widow turned up missing, the police would surely be called. But Teresa and her family could easily be disposed of. The men could take them anywhere, even kill them, and no one would lift a finger.

Ray suggested, "We can take this bunch and turn 'em in to Immigration. Ask 'em if they got papers, lady."

"They have papers," Julie informed him, her lips thin with fury. "And you won't get away with any of this."

"This ain't your business, lady," Bud said. His voice was menacing.

Too angry to be intimidated, Julie jumped up. "It is my business. I—"

"Lady, you're beginnin' to get on my nerves," Bud warned.

"Hey, Bud. Want me to quiet her down?" Pete offered.

"No I don't want you to 'quiet her down,'" Bud mimicked. "Hell, we're wastin' time here. What I want is to get rid of them Mexicans—" he raised his voice as Julie opened her mouth again "—and to get *her* off my back so I can think. Ray, get her outa here."

Ray gestured toward the bedroom with his revolver.

Did he think he could push her around? Gun or no gun, she wouldn't stand for it. "No!"

Father Gregory jumped to his feet. "Hush!" he commanded. He grabbed Julie's wrist.

"That's right, Father," Bud said. "Keep the little lady quiet. Ray, put both of 'em in that back room. And don't you two get any ideas about gettin' out," he added. "Try somethin' and Ray can put a bullet into one of your friends here quicker'n you know. Get 'em in there, Ray. I'm gonna call the boss."

Julie didn't want to think who "the boss" might be. She followed Father Gregory into the bedroom and listened to the sound of the door shutting behind her.

She waited a moment, then jiggled the doorknob experimentally. It wasn't locked, but a lot of good that would do them. They were directly across from the living room, where Ray was sitting with a gun.

Then she turned, to see Father Gregory surveying the windows.

"Someone put bars on them. Good protection, but there's no way out," he said. "Might as well sit down."

The room was empty save for half a dozen cots. He sat on one and motioned Julie to do the same. "All we can do is wait," he said in a low voice. "The police will be here soon."

Julie sat down on the cot across from him. "Father," she said in a strained whisper, "I know that man, the one who just came in."

He leaned forward to hear her better. "How?"

"I...I saw him last night. At Jack's party...Jack Benton's."

"You saw *that* man...Bud...at a party? At Jack Benton's?" Father Gregory sounded incredulous.

"He wasn't at the *party*. But he was at the house. I had a headache, so I went into Jack's bathroom to wash my face, and I heard two men arguing. I realized they didn't want to be seen, so I—I don't know why, but I hid in Jack's closet. They came into the bathroom and I listened to their conversation."

"Julie, are you absolutely certain it was Bud? Your mind can play tricks when you're upset."

"Father, I would swear in court that I saw Bud. It's the same man—same scar, same green eyes."

"Who was the other man?"

Julie looked away for a moment. When she turned back to Father Gregory, she had to fight to keep the tears back. "Jack Benton."

"And the argument?"

"I didn't hear anything specific. They were arguing about money. Bud said he was short on cash. And he talked about his job being dangerous. And about merchandise..."

"Aliens."

"I'm afraid so." A tear slipped down her cheek. "Jack gave Bud a thousand dollars. He didn't want to, but Bud seemed to have some hold on him. Then he sent Bud away."

"It must have been a shock for you. I'm sorry," Father Gregory murmured and sat silently while she struggled to pull herself together.

"We'll have to tell the police," she sighed at last.

"Yes."

"Will they be here soon?"

He glanced at his watch. "In ten minutes, if we're lucky."

They waited, Father Gregory watching her intently. Julie wondered what he was thinking. Was he skeptical of her story? Shocked? Had he come to the same conclusion that she had...that Jack might be involved in these kidnappings?

The outside door slammed. Bud was back. Father Gregory went and stood by the door, and Julie followed.

"Did you get through to the boss?" That was Pete.

"No, goddammit. He was out. Out with some of his bigtime pals—" Bud's voice dripped with sarcasm "—at the country club. While we take the heat."

"What're we gonna do?" Pete's voice again.

"Might as well get them Mexicans outa here. You two game for a ride down to the border tonight?"

At that Julie moved in front of the priest, closer to the door.

"Sure. Why not?" Ray replied. "We got three cute little Mexican *muchachas* for company. It might be fun."

"No!" Julie gasped, her hand on the doorknob.

Before she could turn it, Father Gregory jerked her hand away. "Don't be a fool," he whispered harshly.

"Let got of me." She pulled at her arm. "Are you going to sit here and let them take those people away? Didn't you hear what he said? They'll rape those girls. They'll—"

"There's nothing we can do but wait for the police." He grabbed her other arm. Eyes blazing, she struggled against his superior strength as he pulled her away from the door. "Do you want to go out there and get shot...or worse?"

A crash from the living room froze them in the middle of the room. They both turned toward the door. Julie pulled one arm away from Father Gregory's grasp and covered her mouth to stifle a cry.

"What was that?" she whispered.

"Sounded like a table."

She stared at him, rigid with horror. "What are they doing out there?" she breathed.

The priest sighed. "They're probably going to mess things up before they go. It's part of the game."

"How can we just stand here and let them do it?" She pushed at his arm with her free hand. "Let me go, Father!"

He grabbed her arm and pulled her against him. "I won't let you go," he whispered. "Do you think I'd let you go out there and get hurt?" She stared up at him blankly while tears coursed down her cheeks. "Listen to me," he said urgently. "There's nothing you can do. The police are on their way."

She shook her head but kept her eyes on his face. Her hands clutched his arms.

"That's right, love," he whispered. "Hold on to me. Don't listen to what's going on out there. Just hold on. It'll all be over. Soon."

She stood in a daze, her eyes fastened on his as if they were a lifeline. She couldn't move, couldn't think. "We have to go in there," she said at last, her voice high and breathless. "We have to—"

"Hush," he said thickly, and silenced her with his mouth. And then the noise from the other room receded, replaced by the pounding of her heart, the sounds of her ragged breath and his. All thought, all feeling was focused on the pressure of his chest against her breasts, the heat of his mouth on hers, the scrape of his teeth against her lips, the sweet roughness of his hands on her body. Her hands left his arms to twine around his neck, to pull him closer. Her mouth opened under his seeking tongue and invited it in. Her bones seemed to soften until her legs could hardly support her and the only solid things in her existence were his body and the strength of his arms.

Greg tightened his hold, wanting her closer still. His hands pushed aside the rough wool of her sweater and sought the soft skin of her back. His lips caressed her mouth, his tongue foraging for its inner sweetness. He was lost in her, drowning in her.

Then suddenly the contact was broken. She shrank back, pushing against his chest, her eyes wild with shock. "Father!" she gasped. "No!"

Greg stared at her dazedly. Her words made no sense to him. He'd forgotten his part in the masquerade, forgotten everything but Julie.

"Father, please," she whispered desperately, "let me go. We . . . we can't. It's . . . wrong."

"It's right," he said hoarsely, and bent to kiss her again.

"Please. We'll both regret this. Your vows—"

"Julie, things aren't what they seem. Believe me."

"No." She struggled out of his arms and stood, trembling, a few inches away.

It's over, Greg told himself. *The police will be here in a few minutes. Enough of this disguise. I can tell her. Now.* As she watched in shock, he reached up to remove his collar.

Shouts from outside stopped his hand in midair. Car engines. Sirens. Running feet.

"The police," Julie cried, turned, and ran for the door.

Greg reached it first. "Stay behind me," he ordered. "We don't know what will happen." He opened the door slowly.

The room they entered was in disarray. Puddles of beer dotted the floor. The chairs and table were overturned. Clay flowerpots were broken. A plant sat beside one, with clumps of dirt scattered around it; one lone leaf lay on the arm of the couch. The women and children were huddled together, too terrified to move.

From outside came the blare of an amplified voice. "This is the police. Drop your weapons, and come out with your hands up."

Pete stood at the window, peering out between the slats of the wooden blinds. "Six of 'em at least,' he reported nervously.

"Let 'em wait. Let 'em try to get us. We got the edge on 'em," Bud scoffed.

"I don't know, Bud. If we make 'em wait, they'll storm the house. I seen it on TV once."

"So go out. Give 'em an easy time. But don't expect someone to come and bail you out."

Pete looked at Ray.

"I think we should go," Ray said. "I ain't got a record. I've never had no trouble with the cops."

"Okay, you two yellow bastards go. Gimme your gun, Ray. You sure as hell won't need it out there."

Ray handed over the revolver, and he and Pete opened the door slowly. Hands up, they headed out.

Bud stood nonchalantly, twirling the gun. In a few minutes, the voice outside began again. "Come out. We've got the house surrounded. You have three minutes."

Bud went to the window and raised it a few inches. "Go to hell!" he shouted.

Greg put his hand on Julie's shoulder. "Let's get the others back in the bedroom so they'll be out of the way when the police come in."

"Will they... come in?"

"Through the kitchen, and soon."

Carefully he edged toward the Sanchez women, motioning them to move toward the bedroom. They backed away, one slow step at a time.

Bud remained at the window, paying no attention to the occupants of the room.

"Now you, too," Greg whispered to Julie.

But it was to late.

There was a crash, and he heard the kitchen door splinter. Bud heard it, too, and begun looking around for an escape route.

Before the police could enter the room, he bounded across it, his eyes on Julie. She had no chance to react. He grabbed her and jerked her in front of him as three uniformed police, guns at the ready, burst through the living-room door.

"Hands up!"

"No!" Greg yelled.

He started for Julie, but one of the policemen grabbed his arm. "Out of the way, Father. We'll take care of this."

"Don't bet on it," Bud drawled. "Now, I've got this little lady here, and her and me are gonna walk very slowly out that front door and get into my car. And you all ain't gonna do a damn thing about it." He grinned.

Don't you bet on it, Julie thought. She was angry, hot, searing angry, and nobody, *nobody* was going to use her this way. With a quick movement, she bent her head and sank her teeth into the arm that Bud had thrown across her chest. He gave a cry of surprise and pain, stumbled and shoved Julie violently aside. Before he could regain his balance, two men had him pinned.

Julie saw it all in slow motion as she fell sideways—Bud's shocked face, the quick, almost balletlike movements of the police as they grabbed him, and Father Gregory's stunned look of surprise.

And then she felt the pain as her head hit the corner of a table and she crumpled to the floor. A curtain of gray, speckled with little black pinpricks, descended before her eyes. From far away she heard Father Gregory's voice. "Call an ambulance. Hurry!" Through the slowly falling curtain, she saw him kneel beside her, felt his arms around her, and saw his eyes, clouded with fear and pain. Then the curtain finished its descent, and the world went black.

CHAPTER NINE

OBLIVIOUS TO THE NOISE and activity around him, Greg remained by Julie's side. She was as still as—no, he wouldn't think that. She wasn't dead, just unconscious. But that was bad enough. How long since they'd called for the ambulance? He didn't realize he'd spoken his thought aloud until the police officer behind him answered. "Only five minutes, Father. It should be here soon."

Only five minutes! They'd been the longest five minutes of his life. He took Julie's limp hand in his and began to rub it, as if his energy could revive her.

All of this was his fault. If he hadn't gotten her involved in his investigation, she'd be in her office where she belonged, safe at St. Martha's...

St. Martha's! Someone needed to call the church and tell them what had happened. The priests needed to know what was going on. And he had to call Julie's doctor. Damn! The house had no phone!

"Father. Father!"

He became aware of a voice calling him, a hand on his arm. He looked up and saw Carmela. The old woman knelt beside him and looked at Julie's white face. "She will be all right," Carmela said reassuringly.

"I hope you're right," he sighed. "We need to reach her doctor. Where's the nearest telephone?"

"At the grocery on the corner. Come. I will take you."

The police officer, who was still standing behind Greg, cut in. "I'll send one of my men with her, Father."

He didn't know the name of Julie's doctor, Greg realized, but surely they'd have that information at the church. He gave the policeman the number and told him to speak with Grace.

The officer gave the order, then turned back to Greg. "I'll need a statement from you, Father."

Reluctantly Greg moved from Julie's side and gave an account of the afternoon. Just as he finished, the policeman and Carmela returned with the name of Julie's physician. Then he heard the wail of a siren. The ambulance at last!

He watched the white-coated paramedic examine Julie and lift her onto the stretcher. He started after them, but the officer he'd been talking to restrained him. "Sorry, Father. You'll have to come with me."

Greg stared at him blankly.

"One of my men just talked to Captain Ferris. He wants to see you at headquarters."

Greg shook the man's hand off. "Later," he said.

"Now," the officer said. "You can go to the hospital later." He placed his hand on Greg's shoulder and led him firmly outside to the squad car.

The ride to police headquarters, the conversation with Ferris seemed endless. Greg observed what was going on around him—words, movements, reactions—like the trained reporter he was, but with only half his mind. The other half—and his heart—were in the ambulance, in the emergency room with the woman he'd held in his arms only moments ago.

He recounted again the events of the past few hours, watched Ferris's shocked expression when he reported that Julie had seen Bud at Jack Benton's home and listened carefully when a sergeant stepped into the room to tell Ferris the location of an isolated spot east of Harlingen where the kidnap victims had been taken.

As soon as the sergeant left, Ferris was on the phone to the INS in Harlingen. He related all the information he had, listened for a few moments, then said, "Look, can you hold off until morning on the raid? We'll send a couple of guys down to join you. The kidnappings are in our jurisdiction, and we'll want to question people at the construction site." He waited a moment, then said. "Good. I'll set that in motion and be back in touch."

He hung up and turned back to Greg. "Now, Father, where were we?"

By the time Ferris was finished questioning him, Greg's anxiety was at a fever pitch. In a few moments, he'd be a reporter again, no longer a priest, and he needed to get to Harlingen to cover the raid, but first and foremost, he had to find out about Julie. He strode out of Ferris's office, and ran headlong into Father Curry. "Tim! How's Julie? Have you heard?"

The priest ignored Greg's question. "We have to go," he said in a low, urgent voice.

"I have to call the hospital."

Father Curry grasped his arm. "You can call later. Come on."

Eyes narrowed, Greg shook off the priest's hand. "Now!" he growled and headed for the nearest phone. He grabbed a directory and rifled through the pages, searching for the *M*'s. Why was it when you were in a hurry you couldn't find the listing you needed? *P...J...N...* He flipped back a few more pages and found Methodist Hospital.

His hand shook as he punched in the number. "Emergency room," he said, surprised his voice wasn't shaking, too. "I want to know the condition of Mrs. Julie Whitaker. She was brought in about an hour ago."

He waited, his hand grasping the receiver so tightly his knuckles went white.

"Sorry. We can't give out that information," replied a robotlike voice.

"This is Father Gregory, her... her priest. I was with her when she was injured."

"Sorry," the voice said again. "Hospital regulations. She's been admitted. You might try to reach her doctor."

"Hospital regulations!" He slammed down the phone and turned back to Father Curry. "Let's go."

Phil Barnes was sitting in the priest's car. Greg got into the back seat. As the car pulled away from the police station, he gave Phil a succinct account of the day's events. "We're lucky they've delayed the raid until morning," he said. "I can take the last flight out to Harlingen."

"I figured you'd need to get to the construction site," Phil said. "I made a reservation. Your flight's at ten o'clock."

He should have known Phil would think ahead. Some of Greg's tension dissipated. "Good," he said. "Now let's go to the hospital."

"Can't," Phil said.

The tension returned full force. "The hell we can't."

Phil angled around so he could look at Greg. "Look, Allen. I know you're worried about her, but you can't take a chance of going over there now."

"Take a chance? What are you talking about? What's going on?"

"The hospital is crawling with press, with TV reporters. This story made the six o'clock news."

"Six o'clock?" For the first time Greg was aware that it was dark. He glanced at his watch. Seven-fifteen. He frowned at Phil. "Why should a news story keep us from going over there?"

"Think about it," Phil urged. "Whitman from Associated Press is there, Carmody from UPI. They'll recognize you and—"

Greg fingered his collar and looked at Father Curry. "You're right," he sighed. "They'll ask a thousand questions."

"Embarrassing questions," Father Curry murmured.

Greg nodded. Questions that, if answered, would end the careers of two good men. Men who had risked everything to save their people. How ironic if, just at the moment when they'd accomplished what they'd set out to do, their own lives were torn apart. No, of course Father Gregory couldn't go to the hospital. But Greg Allen "—*I'll* go. Greg Allen."

"Forget it," Phil ordered. "You have less than three hours to file your story, pack your bag and get to the airport."

"And," Father Curry added, "we must get you out before questions are asked at the church. There've already been calls from the press. Besides, we can't allow you to talk to Julie, to *anyone* here, as yourself until Rudy and I have seen the bishop."

Words of protest died on Greg's lips. If it had just been the news story, he'd have told Phil to go to hell, turned around and gone to the hospital. But he couldn't do that to the priests. He'd given his word. He wouldn't go back on it.

He spent the next two hours in the rectory, his stomach churning, as he typed his account of the day's events, threw his clothes into his suitcase, and cleaned out his office. He called the hospital again, learned that Julie had been moved from Emergency to a private room but that calls were not being put through. The floor nurse refused to give him any information. Another call, this time to the supervisor, was equally frustrating. He tried Julie's doctor, having gotten the name from Father Rudolfo, but was told by a bored answering service that Dr. Brenner wasn't on call tonight.

He tried the hospital once more while Phil stood glowering at him, pointing at his watch. No use. No one would tell him anything. Greg felt like strangling someone—the telephone operator, the doctor, the hospital administrator—anyone remotely connected with the medical profession. At last he gave up and went downstairs.

He stood in the hallway, suitcase in hand, facing the two priests. "What will you tell the staff?" he asked.

"For now, only that Father Gregory has been called back to Washington," Father Rudolfo said. "That is all we can do until we meet with the bishop and explain the situation." He gripped Greg's hand. "As soon as we have talked to the bishop, everyone will be told what you have done for our people."

Greg felt a lump rise in his throat. "What *you* have done," he said. He turned to Father Curry. "Thank you for the opportunity to be a part of St. Martha's."

The priest gave him one of his rare smiles. "Thank you for coming to us. God be with you."

"And with you. I'll be in touch," Greg murmured and followed Phil out the door.

He'd been in such a rush he hadn't even had time to change clothes. In the car, he took off his priest's clothing and pulled on a sport shirt. He buttoned it quickly, feeling incomplete without the now-familiar collar.

They reached Hobby Airport with only minutes to spare. Greg shouldered his bag, checked in at the almost-empty ticket counter and grabbed his boarding pass. He sprinted through the concourse and arrived at the gate just as the last passengers were heading into the jetway. With a last longing glance at the pay telephones near the gate, he handed his pass to the attendant and boarded the plane.

GREG PULLED HIS WINDBREAKER closer around him and waited. The predawn darkness was cold and eerily silent. Not a bird, not a rustle of wind broke the stillness. He felt as if the world were holding its breath, waiting.

Around him Immigration officers huddled in their jackets, their thoughts, like his, turned inward. What would they find down the road? Who would they find? They'd know soon, but for now, they waited.

They'd left Harlingen an hour ago and driven deep into the south Texas countryside, down farm roads, then down a dirt road that was little more than a trail. Half a mile from the spot where they'd been told the construction workers' camp was located, they parked and left their vehicles. Now they stood, surrounded by nothing but darkness, scrub, and a few mesquite trees. Above them, only a sliver of moon lit the sky.

No one spoke. Sound carried too easily out here, and their plan was to take the camp and whoever was guarding it by surprise.

They continued to wait.

At last, at a silent signal, they began to move forward.

Greg could see little beyond the bulky body of the man in front of him; he felt as though he were walking blindfolded. He could hear his heart pounding, feel the muscles in his jaw tense. Only a few minutes more.

As they walked, the black sky softened to gray. Far to the east, Greg could see a whisper of pink on the horizon. Now he could hear sounds that signaled daybreak—the call of birds, small animals scurrying through the brush.

They halted among some trees where they couldn't be seen, then the men ahead of him began to spread out, encircling the area. Greg edged slowly forward. And had his first sight of the camp.

Surrounded by barbed wire, in an area no more than a hundred feet across, were half a dozen tents, two portable toilets, and a construction trailer, this last apparently to house the guards. Nearby, several vans were parked.

The trailer door opened, and a beefy looking red-haired man came out, carrying a rifle. "Thought I heard something," he said over his shoulder.

"What is it?" came a sleepy drawl from inside.

The redhead scanned the compound. "It's nothin'. Prob'ly just one of the Mexicans up early."

The other man ambled to the doorway, rubbing his eyes. "Yeah, they just can't wait to get to work," he chuckled. "But we better check, just to be sure it's not—"

"Immigration! Drop your gun!"

The guard turned and gaped as a dozen officers moved out of the shadows. His rifle fell to the ground.

"Hands up! You in the trailer, get over here."

Now there was noise and activity all around. Immigration officers checked the trailer, cut the wire, searched the area. Men emerged from the tents, urged on by shouts from the officers. Confused, dazed, they huddled in small groups, shivering in the first light of dawn.

Would any of them make a break for it, Greg wondered. But no one moved, or even looked toward the woods. They stood, fatalistically, waiting for *la migra*, for Immigration, to herd them away.

Greg walked past the barbed wire and into the camp. Camp, he thought, was a euphemism. This was nothing more than a prison, one with conditions no organized system of criminal justice would tolerate.

Images crowded his mind. A rusty pan by the remains of a cooking fire. Mud. A gaping hole in the side of one tent.

And the men. A ragged crew in tattered, grimy clothes they'd obviously slept in, their eyes filled with despair as they watched the scene around them. One man—a boy, really—had an angry red gash along one arm; another wore a handkerchief as a makeshift bandage around his hand.

Sounds echoed in Greg's ears. Officers shouting, a clang and a curse as someone's foot connected with a stack of cooking pots, muttered words in Spanish, a deep hacking cough repeated over and over.

Smells assailed his nostrils. Garbage, filth, sweat.

Bile rose in Greg's throat. He'd seen conditions equally appalling at other times, in other countries. But this, *this* was the United States. And these people weren't nameless strangers. He remembered Mr. Salazar's tremulous voice as he described his son, and found himself searching the faces before him, wondering which was Esteban. Which was the young man who had been taken in front of the grocery store? These people were his neighbors. This time, what he saw hit him in the gut.

And he'd see to it that others felt the same way. In words as clear and vivid as he could, he'd paint a picture no one who read them would forget.

Greg heard the sound of engines. Officers had commandeered the vans parked nearby and were beginning to load what men they could accommodate. "The rest of you, follow me. *¡Sígame!*" came the brusque command.

Greg had seen enough. He fell into line beside one of the aliens.

"What was it like there?" Greg asked in Spanish as they trudged away.

The man said nothing.

"I'm a reporter with a news agency. I can tell your story."

"Tell them..." the man said hoarsely, "tell them we have been in hell."

"Yet you stayed."

"*Sí,* what could we do?"

"There were many of you, only two of them. You could have overpowered them." Greg pointed out.

The man behind them answered. "If we do that, there is no money. We wait for the money they promised us."

Of course. The promise of a salary had held them here, made them endure inhuman conditions while they waited for their payoff. These were people who'd left the poverty of their homeland for money. Not just for themselves, but to send to the families they left behind. "When were you to be paid?" Greg asked.

"When the job was finished," the man behind them said. "For now, we got only ten dollars a day."

Greg doubted they'd have seen a penny when their work was done. *Slave labor,* he thought, and wondered how Benton could sleep at night. "How many were in the camp?" he asked.

"Sometimes forty, sometimes more. They took some away, if they were sick, if they did not work hard."

"What happened to them?"

"*¿Quién sabe?*"

"Who knows?" echoed Greg, thinking he had a damn good idea. Dumped back across the border, that's where they were. He turned to his companion. "You're grateful it's over then?"

The man spat on the ground. "Grateful? To *la migra*? Will they be kinder to us than those men back there, those...animals, who fed us tortillas and beans three times a day and barely enough of that, who left us to sleep on the ground with flimsy blankets to cover us, who worked us from sunup to sunset? No, we will be taken to their headquarters, questioned, and then sent back across the river. Again."

But they would be back, Greg thought. Because the border was like a revolving door. Men came, were sent back, and doggedly came again, drawn like a magnet to *el norte*. The laws, the Border Patrol—nothing seemed to stop them. The dilemma was one that sharper minds than his had thus far been unable to solve.

At least he could tell the story of what he'd seen. And let others judge for themselves. He'd planned to spend some time in Houston, time with Julie, when his role as a priest was over. Now he knew his story wasn't over yet, but just beginning. And regardless of what happened with Julie...even if there'd been no Julie Whitaker...he had to go back to Houston. Because these people's story had to be told. And because he had to tell it.

WHEN JULIE WOKE, early-morning sunlight lit the room. For a moment, she stared blankly around her. Then she remembered. She was in the hospital. And her head hurt. What had happened?

She knew she'd wakened once during the night. Someone had been in the room—a nurse. Though she couldn't remember how she'd gotten here, she clearly recalled their conversation.

The nurse must have heard her moan because she'd leaned over the bed and asked, "Mrs. Whitaker, are you awake?"

"Where am I?"

"Methodist Hospital." Her tone was professionally soothing. Efficiently she placed a blood-pressure cuff around Julie's arm.

"Wh-what happened?"

"You hit your head. You have a concussion."

"I don't...remember."

"It's all right. You'll remember soon."

"I hurt all over."

"I imagine so. You have some bruises. Try to go back to sleep now. If you wake and need anything, I'll be right here. Your doctor wanted someone with you tonight. Now rest. You'll feel better in the morning."

"Morning," Julie had mumbled. She'd drifted toward sleep, then caught herself with an effort. She'd had a question to ask. "Father...Father Gregory?"

"Your father?"

"No. A priest."

The nurse shook her head. "I don't know anything about a Father Gregory."

Julie tried to sit up, then winced and lay down again. "I have to call the church," she said, reaching blindly toward the table where the telephone should be. "I have to see if he's okay."

"I'll call for you," the nurse offered. "Just lie still. What's the number?"

"Number?"

"The phone number."

"Phone number," Julie repeated. Her mind had gone blank. "I...can't remember." Forcing back alarm at this, she bit her lip.

"It's all right," the woman soothed her. "Just give me the name of the church."

That, at least, Julie remembered. "St. Martha's."

"I'll call from the hall so I won't disturb you."

The nurse left. Julie felt her eyes closing, but she forced herself to stay awake. Though she couldn't remember much about what had happened to her, she knew Father Gregory had been there.

The door opened.

"Did you reach him? Is...is he all right?" Julie asked anxiously.

"I reached one of the other priests. He's fine. Now, Mrs. Whitaker, you need to rest."

Obediently Julie had shut her eyes. Once she'd known Father Gregory was safe, she could rest easy.

Now the nurse smiled a good-morning, checked her temperature and pulse, then picked up a purse and jacket. "I'm leaving now. If you need anything or have any pain, just ring, and one of the floor nurses will take care of you. Your doctor will be in to see you shortly."

When the woman had gone, Julie lifted her hand and held it in front of her face. She could see only a round, fuzzy shape. Her head still hurt, too. She couldn't recall how she'd hit it, but slowly she began to remember little snatches of the previous day.

There'd been a kidnapping. She'd gone to Teresa's house. Men were there. And one—a cold, menacing face with feline eyes—he'd grabbed her, but why? And there was noise, confusion, and another face—worried blue eyes, gentle hands—that was all. Thinking hurt her head, and she gave up and dozed until the door opened and someone walked in.

She couldn't make out who he was until he reached her bedside. Then she recognized her physician, Dr. George Brenner.

"How do you feel?" He reached in his lab coat for a penlight and shined it in her eyes.

She tried to turn away, but that hurt her head. "Not my best," she mumbled. "How did you find me... or how did they find you?"

"The secretary at St. Martha's called me. Look this way... now that way. Vision blurry?"

"Uh-huh."

"It'll clear up soon. Hurt?"

"Feels like someone hit me over the head."

"From what I understand, that's about what happened."

"No...I...I fell." Suddenly she remembered everything with painful clarity. The man, the gun, the whole afternoon. "What...happened to everyone else?" she asked urgently. "Was anyone hurt? Did they get that man... Bud?" She pulled herself up to a sitting position, ignoring the pain that throbbed in her head.

"Easy now. The police will answer all that. There's an officer waiting to see you now. And when your vision is better, you can read about it in the newspaper. You're quite a celebrity this morning. You made the front page. The nurses tell me there were even a couple of reporters around here."

Julie lay down with a groan. *From Miranda's column to the front page.* "When can I go home?" she asked.

"This afternoon...provided you take it easy. I'll be back to check you after lunch." He patted her arm and left.

Almost immediately, there was a knock at her door. "Come in," she called, and a man wearing a blue suit entered. No, she realized as he came closer, he was wearing a policeman's uniform.

"Mrs. Whitaker, I'm Captain Steven Ferris, Houston Police Department. I'm sorry to bother you so soon after your...accident, but I need to ask you some questions."

Julie managed a weak smile. "Information first, please," she said. "What about the others? Is everybody all right?"

"They're all fine. I'm afraid you're the only one who was injured."

"That man...Bud—"

"In the city jail."

She let out a long breath. "I'd hate to think of him out walking around. The house? Those men tore it apart."

"I believe one of the priests from your church has contacted the owner and has gone over there this morning to see that everything is cleaned up or replaced."

"I think you've answered all my questions. What can I tell you?"

"The priest who was with you said you'd seen this Bud before."

Julie sighed. The whole situation seemed unreal. "Yes, at a party Sunday evening. He was arguing with the host."

"Jack Benton."

"Yes."

"We'll need you to come down to the station and make a statement, Mrs. Whitaker, as soon as you're feeling up to it."

"Of course."

"The three men also mentioned Benton. In fact, he was brought in earlier this morning for questioning."

Julie gasped. "Is . . . is he in jail?"

"No. It appears his company was involved in transporting illegal aliens. We don't have proof yet that he was personally involved, but I imagine the grand jury will look into it."

"I . . . I can't believe it. Why would he do something like that?"

"Money. Apparently he needed cheap labor to complete a project or face foreclosure."

"Foreclosure. Jack? It's not possible."

"I'm afraid it's true," he assured her.

Julie was silent. Of course it was true. She'd known it as soon as Bud had walked into the house yesterday. Yet she'd kept hoping it was all some bizarre nightmare, that she'd open her eyes and it would disappear. Now, hearing Captain Ferris say it in that clipped, official tone made it irrevocably real.

Ferris continued, "Mrs. Whitaker, whether you like it or not, you're involved in this—"

Shock waves spread through her. Julie turned toward him, ignoring the pain, letting her voice reflect her anger. "Involved? How? I would never involve myself in anything as . . . as despicable as transporting human beings."

"What I meant was, you've had contact with Benton. You identified one of the kidnappers as someone you saw at his home. I've arranged for you to have police protection, at least for the next two or three days."

"Why? What could possibly happen to me?"

"Hopefully nothing. But a man who is desperate enough to resort to kidnapping . . . well, anything could happen."

"I see." She controlled a shudder.

"This is just a precaution, you understand. There's an officer outside your door here, and we'll have someone at your home for a while."

"I'm not sure I like the idea."

"Well, accept it regardless, just to be safe. And if Benton tries to contact you for any reason, let us know."

Julie nodded.

Ferris stepped back. "Someone will drive you home when you're released. Thank you for your cooperation."

He left the room. When the door opened, Julie could see a uniformed man sitting in a chair. *My bodyguard,* she thought dismally.

She was overwhelmed. The events of the past day were almost too much to contend with . . . especially one event, which had been hovering at the fringes of her mind ever since she'd regained her memory—the moments in Father Gregory's arms. Just thinking about it, even in this isolated and sterile environment, brought a blush to her cheeks and, to her horror, a strange tingle to her body. How could it have happened? Of course they were both overwrought at the time, but that was no excuse. And this was the second time. The first incident, the one in the rain, had been mild compared to this...this almost desperate meeting of mouths and bodies.

How could they go on this way—working together, seeing each other every day? It would happen again, much as they might try to avoid it.

Perhaps she would quit her job. Even though she loved working at St. Martha's, that might be the only solution. She couldn't subject a priest—or herself—to this kind of temptation on a daily basis.

An attendant came in with breakfast, but Julie ate very little. Her head still hurt, though she tried to will the pain away by thinking of other things. She turned on the television, but her vision was still too blurry and she wasn't interested in the inane game show that was on anyhow. She wished she could read the newspaper—

Oh, God, the newspaper! Hadn't Dr. Brenner said she'd made the front page? What if the wire services picked up the story? What if her family read it? They'd be out of their minds with worry.

With trembling hands, she reached for the telephone and called her parents' home.

A sleepy voice answered. "Hello."

She should have remembered it was an hour earlier in Colorado, too early for them to have been alarmed by the newspaper, thank goodness. She made her voice strong. "Dad, it's Julie."

"Hi, honey. How are you?"

"I've... I've had a little excitement. Actually everything's fine, but I thought I'd let you know so you wouldn't worry in . . . in case you heard about it."

"Julie, what are you talking about? What kind of excitement? Wait a minute. Ellie, pick up the extension. It's Julie."

When her mother was on the line, Julie told them her story, trying to make light of her part in the events of the previous day. There was a moment of silence when she finished, then her father said, "We'll take the next plane down."

"Oh, Dad, please don't. I'm fine, really. Just a little headache. I need a day or two of rest and I'll be back to normal."

"You need someone to take care of you."

She could hear the sympathy, the concern in her father's voice, but she'd been taking care of herself now for well over a year, and it was important to her to rely on her own strength. Besides, she needed her privacy now, needed time to sort through the confusing emotions that pummeled her from every side. As gently as she could, she dissuaded her parents from rushing down. "If I'm not feeling fine in a couple of days, I'll call you. I promise."

They settled for that, said goodbye with promises to call that evening and assurances that they'd call her sister Kay in Minnesota and tell her what had happened.

Julie hung up and lay back weakly.

No, she couldn't be weak. If she gave in to pain and exhaustion, she'd be marooned in this bed for another day, and no way was she going to tolerate that. She concentrated on feeling better, and by early afternoon when Dr. Brenner arrived, she'd almost succeeded.

"I'm going to discharge you," he told her, "but I want you to take it easy. You'll have some pain and dizziness for a while, so don't overdo it. I want to see you in my office day after tomorrow."

She readily agreed, and the discharge procedure was begun. Though she protested, she was taken in a wheelchair to checkout. She tried to ignore passersby's stares at the policeman who hovered alongside the chair. *Why couldn't they send a plainclothesman?* she wondered.

Her car had been brought to the hospital. By whom, she didn't know, and she didn't bother asking. She was just glad she hadn't had to make arrangements herself. She asked the young policeman to get her a newspaper while the hospital attendant helped her into the back seat.

"If you'll give me your address, ma'am, I'll drive you right home," said the officer politely.

"I want to make a few stops first," she said, giving him Teresa's address.

She might submit to police protection, but she refused to act like an invalid, no matter how weak and dizzy she felt. She was anxious to find out how the Sanchez family was faring. And she wanted to stop at St. Martha's. She had to face Father Gregory, face the emotions his presence generated, talk to him about their situation. Best to get that over with as soon as possible, she decided.

She wondered why he hadn't called her. Was he embarrassed about what she was beginning to think of as The Incident? Even so, she'd expected to hear from him. He'd always seemed so concerned about her welfare.

Putting thoughts of Father Gregory out of her mind, she opened the newspaper. Her vision was clearer than it had been in the morning, and she could make out the headline easily: "Kidnappers Take Hostages." She'd get Grace to read her the rest of the article.

When she arrived at the Sanchez home, Carmela opened the door, and broke into a smile. "Come in," she cried, taking Julie's hands. "Rosa, Teresa, Señora Julie *esta aquí*."

The women clustered around her, asking how she was feeling, thanking her for her help the day before, offering food and drink. Julie assured them she was well and insisted thanks were unnecessary.

When Julie left, she was feeling better, buoyed by the women's loving reception.

Her next stop was St. Martha's. When Grace looked up and saw her, she let out a cry of surprise. "For heavens sake, Julie, what are you doing out of bed?"

"Going about my business as usual."

Grace clucked in disapproval. "Come sit down. Can I get you something? How's your head? What did the doctor say?"

"Hey, one question at a time. No, thanks, I don't need anything. My head is sore but improving. The doctor said it was too hard to break."

"Thank heavens. We've all been worried about you. When the police officer called and told us what happened and said you were being taken to the hospital, we couldn't believe it."

"Thanks for calling Dr. Brenner."

"No problem. By the way, you didn't drive here from the hospital, did you?"

"No, a police officer drove me. I'm...I'm being given police protection. They...they're afraid Jack Benton might try to reach me. They think he's behind these kidnappings." Though her voice was calm, her hands began to tremble.

"Jack Benton! Julie, are you certain?"

"A police captain told me this morning."

"Surely Jack couldn't be involved," Grace protested. "A nice man like that. Why, he sent us all those heaters."

"Grace, I saw one of the kidnappers at Jack's house Sunday night. They were having an argument over money and over the 'merchandise' this man was delivering." Every time she thought about it, she felt sick. She gripped the arms of her chair in an effort to control her emotions. She wouldn't allow herself to cry.

Grace's eyes widened. "And I thought he was such a wonderful man, a great catch. I guess you can't go by outward appearances."

"It's hard to imagine what would drive a man to do such things to other human beings," Julie mused.

Grace nodded. "You were the only one who saw through him. You said he wasn't the right man for you."

"I know. I wonder if there's anything about Jack in the newspaper story. Would you read it to me, Grace? I'm having trouble focusing."

Grace opened the paper and read a detailed account of the ordeal. Nothing was mentioned about Jack Benton, but there were descriptions of the three men, and mention of Julie's injury. "Whitaker was injured as she distracted the kidnapper, giving police the chance to overwhelm him.

"What did you do?" Grace inquired. "Try a karate chop?"

Julie smothered a giggle. "I bit him."

"You *what?*"

"I really bit him," Julie said and laughed out loud. Grace joined in and soon the two of them were laughing so hard that tears were running down their cheeks.

Though the laughter hurt her head, Julie was glad to express some emotion after keeping her feelings in check for the past day. Fear, desire, pain, shock—better to release them in laughter than in tears.

Finally Julie wiped her eyes. The time had come to attend to serious matters. She had to see Father Gregory, difficult though the meeting might be. With trepidation, she said, "I'd better tell Father Gregory I'm all right. Is he around?"

"Oh, gosh, with all the excitement over your accident, I forgot to tell you. He's gone."

"When will he be back?"

"No, I mean really gone. He won't be back."

Julie sat down abruptly. Shock waves radiated through her body. "What do you mean?" She whispered, hoping Grace would attribute her weak voice to the aftermath of her accident.

"I'm telling you exactly what I know, which is very little. Apparently he got a call late last night to return to Washington."

Her brain didn't seem capable of registering what she was hearing. And not because of the accident. She'd been perfectly lucid just a few minutes earlier. "I don't understand."

"Who does? I told you there was something strange about him. He packed his things, cleaned out his desk, and off he went."

Without even a phone call to tell me he was leaving? "I can't believe it," Julie mumbled. She stared into space, trying to digest the news, then looked up when Father Curry entered the room. *Pull yourself together,* she thought. "Hello, Father."

He took her hand. "Julie, we've all been worried about you, but I see you've come through like a trooper. What are you doing here, though? You should be home in bed."

She smiled wanly. The way she felt at this moment, she had to agree. "I stopped by to pick up some things. If you two will excuse me, I'll go down to my office."

She walked slowly down the hall and into her office. The familiar room seemed different now—the leaves of the plant less verdant, the pillows less colorful, the china cat's grin a travesty of a smile. He was gone. He'd touched her life so briefly—with his warmth, his sensitivity, his concern. In a few short weeks she'd come to look forward to their talks, to hearing his rich laughter and seeing his warm smile. And then he'd begun to touch her in a different way— She wished they'd had an opportunity to talk about what had happened between them, a chance to clear the air. Well, the chance would never come. She'd just have to accept that, to relegate him to memory. Perhaps eventually she'd put this experience in perspective, but now all she felt was shock and grief.

With a sigh, she opened her file cabinet and removed several folders. She hated to get behind in her work. She could write reports while she was at home, type them herself. That would keep her busy, keep her from dwelling too much on the upheaval of the last two days. She dropped the files into her briefcase, picked up her mail, and left the room.

As she went back down the hall, she passed the door—now shut—to Father Gregory's office. Her footsteps slowed. As if a magnet drew her, she walked a step closer, then another. She pulled the door open and went inside, shutting it gently behind her, then stared around the room. The desk, which yesterday had been covered with a haphazard assortment of papers, folders and pamphlets, was clear. The rusty typewriter was gone; even the map of Houston that had hung on the wall had been taken down. The only sign that someone had been here was the heaping wastebasket and a few sheets of half-wadded paper on the floor beside it.

Left without a trace, Julie thought, her finger rubbing the old wooden desk with a caressing motion. With her other hand, she touched the chair, as if she could coax some essence of its recent occupant out of the rough upholstery.

It was for the best, of course, she told herself, straightening her shoulders. Nothing had come of their attraction and for that she was grateful. Now she could remember him as a friend.

She turned to leave, then automatically bent to retrieve the papers he'd tossed on the floor. She smoothed them gently and glanced at the writing.

Through the blur she could tell that the first sheet was an invoice of some kind, the second a personal note, written in a large, freeflowing hand . . . big enough for her to see easily. Vaguely aware that looking at these remnants was a last effort to keep him there . . . or let him go . . . Julie began to read:

Dear Greg . . .

The handwriting was bold, but definitely feminine. Perhaps a note from his sister.

I'm enclosing the pictures from our weekend in the Berkshires. Lord, that was fun.

Julie knew she should stop reading now, but she couldn't. Filled with a sick kind of dread, she continued.

I miss you. Washington's cold without you around to keep things warm. Love you, Steph.

She squinted until she could make out the name printed at the top of the sheet. Stephanie Barrett. Certainly not his sister. This was not the kind of correspondence one had with a brother. It was meant for a friend. Or a lover.

She stared at the note again. The name was familiar. Stephanie Barrett . . . Barrett. Suddenly she remembered. She'd overheard Father Gregory talking on the phone. "Take it easy, Barrett," he'd said, his voice warm and husky. No, Stephanie Barrett was definitely not his sister.

Julie sat down stiffly in Father Gregory's chair. Shock, revulsion, disappointment: all coursed through her at once. This priest whom she had thought tender and caring . . . this man whom she'd come to admire and respect . . . was nothing but a . . . a womanizer. How many women had there been, in how many parishes? Was that why he was sent here . . . to get him away from his last— She couldn't form the word in her mind. She'd thought there'd been something between *them*, concerned herself about its effect on him, worried that he was experiencing guilt because of his dedication to the priesthood.

Guilt? That had never entered the picture, on his side at least. Vows? He probably didn't give them a passing thought. She covered her eyes with her hands and let the tears pour through them. Time passed as she sat there unable to move. With a superhuman effort, she was at last able to pull herself out of the chair and move toward the door. She started into the hall, then turned back and picked up the letter from the desk where she had left it. She couldn't leave it lying there in plain sight. *Why should I care?* she asked herself with a bitter laugh as she slipped the paper into her purse. But no, she couldn't leave the record of his indiscretions for anyone else to see. She'd take the letter home and burn it, she decided, and watch it turn to ashes, as her feelings for him had done.

She moved down the hall in a daze, and almost bumped into Father Curry.

"Julie, are you all right?" he asked.

"What? Yes, I . . . I guess I'm weaker than I thought."

Grace came into the hall. "Honey, what is it? You should sit down. You're as pale as a ghost."

Julie shook her head. "I just want to get home."

"Good idea," Father Curry agreed. "And I don't want to see you back here for at least a week...longer if you need the time. Come, I'll walk you to your car."

He took one arm, and Grace took the other. Passively Julie allowed them to lead her outside and help her into the car. On the way home she sat like a statue, staring into space. She'd had a lot more than a blow to her head, she thought. She'd had a blow to her heart as well.

GREG OPENED THE DOOR to his Harlingen motel room and looked longingly at the bed. He hadn't slept in a day and a half. After the predawn raid of the camp, he'd driven across the Queen Isabelle Causeway to Padre Island. He'd found the sight of Benton's elegant half-finished condos ludicrous. Lavish hideaways on white sand beaches kissed by the gentle Gulf breeze. Dream houses built with human misery. He watched the shocked faces of the construction supervisors when they were confronted by Immigration officers, when their records were impounded. They would receive their just punishment, and he only hoped Jack Benton would get his, too.

He'd returned to INS headquarters where the men from the camp were being questioned, talked to them, talked to officers, then filed his story.

Now it was late afternoon and his first opportunity to call Phil. He picked up the phone.

"I looked at your story when it came in," Barnes said. "It's a good one."

"Thanks, but I called about—"

"Mrs. Whitaker. She had a concussion, but she's fine. She was released from the hospital this afternoon. Father Curry tells me she's going to take a few days off."

Greg sighed, and relaxed for the first time in twenty-four hours. "Thanks, Phil," he said. "What else is going on? Did they question Benton?"

"Yeah, and let him go."

"Figures." He kicked off his shoes, a bit harder than necessary, thinking of Benton. "What else?"

"I had a call from *World Day*."

"The news show?"

"Yeah, they want to do an interview with you Thursday morning."

"No kidding?" he couldn't keep the pleasure out of his voice. Just as quickly, it was gone. "I can't do it. Tim and Rudy—it would ruin them."

"They have an appointment with the bishop tomorrow morning. I'll call you in the afternoon. Meantime, get some rest. You sound beat."

"Okay," Greg said. He hung up the phone and lay down. Phil was right. He was exhausted. He shut his eyes, but thoughts of Julie kept him awake.

He wanted to call her, but what could he say? "Hi, this is Father Gregory, only I'm not Father Gregory after all." Hell, this wasn't the sort of thing you could explain over the phone. Besides, his promise to the priests still held. He couldn't reveal his identity until they'd cleared themselves with the bishop.

Despite his exhaustion, he spent the night tossing and the next morning wondering what the bishop would say. In the afternoon he paced his room, waiting for the call. Ten paces from the door, past the double bed with its faded spread and lumpy mattress, the dresser littered with notes and papers, to the window that looked out on the half-empty parking lot. Ten paces back. Over and over.

To distract himself, Greg flipped on the television. A soap opera. He changed the channel. Cartoons. Disgusted, he turned it off and tried the radio. Country and western blared through the room, almost drowning out the sound of the telephone.

He turned off the radio and grabbed the phone. "Yeah."

"Greg, this is Rudy."

"How'd it go?" Muscles tensed, Greg waited.

"Very well, The associate bishop here is from Cuba, and he is very interested in the plight of immigrants. He not only absolved us of guilt for what we did, but he praised us. And you."

A burden seemed to fall from his chest. "Thank God."

"Yes. And now you are free to do your interview, and anything else you wish."

Phil called almost immediately after Greg hung up. "I've just talked to *World Day*. You're set for Thursday morning."

FOR THE NEXT DAY and a half, Julie did little. She was numb all over, and she had barely enough energy to move. She ate little, slept a great deal, and willed herself to forget what had happened.

Easier said than done, especially when every edition of the newspaper brought a new revelation. The evening she came home, the headlines screamed, "Land Developer Questioned in Kidnappings." The story alleged that Jack Benton was the mastermind behind a kidnapping ring. The next morning's paper indicated that the grand jury would be looking into Benton's affairs within the next ten days. Normally, the article went on to say, cases were brought before the grand jury in order of occurrence, but this case had already received so much publicity and the central figure was such a prominent member of the community that the grand jury was beginning its investigation immediately. Every time she read the paper, Julie felt her fragile control slipping just a bit more.

Friends who dropped by with food and comforting words told her it was natural after the trauma she'd experienced, but they didn't know the half of it. Within a week's time, all her illusions had been shattered. She'd seen her husband's friend for what he really was—a vicious, amoral man who would do anything to anyone if it suited his purposes. She'd seen a man for whom she'd cared deeply for what he was, too—a hypocrite. At times she wished fervently that she'd never picked up that damning letter; at least Father Gregory's image would have remained untarnished. At other times she told herself it was best she'd learned what he really was—it would be that much easier to get over him.

All this took its toll. She'd experienced so many strong emotions in the past few days—from raw passion to wrenching grief—that she could hardly feel at all anymore. Nothing but a dull, unending ache.

On Wednesday the evening paper contained an account of a "camp" outside of Harlingen near South Padre Island. It was here the kidnapping victims were transported, here to a compound surrounded by barbed wire, a virtual slave labor camp. The details were so clear Julie could see the camp, hear the voices of the men, smell the stench.

Terrible as the story was, she had to give the reporter credit for his incisive and realistic style. G. W. Allen. She found herself watching for his byline now, recognizing this continuing story as an exceptional piece of reporting.

Therefore, on Thursday morning she turned toward her television set expectantly when she heard his now-familiar name. She was at the breakfast table, a small TV on the shelf across from her, and she'd tuned in to *World Day*, a news program with a fifteen-minute segment each day on an issue of current interest. Today it was the immigration problem. As usual, individuals versed in the particular issue were to be interviewed. This morning G. W. Allen would appear on the show.

Julie poured cream into her coffee cup and reached for a spoon as the moderator introduced him. "Our first panel member is G. W. Allen, investigative reporter for World-wide Press. His byline is a familiar one to anyone who keeps up with Latin-American affairs. In recent weeks, Mr. Allen has been in Houston, covering a series of kidnappings in the Hispanic community in which the victims were forced into working for next to nothing. Mr. Allen."

Julie watched with interest as the camera zoomed in on...on a blond-haired man with piercing blue eyes.

The spoon fell out of her hand and dropped into the cup, sloshing scalding hot coffee onto the table and her arm. She felt nothing. She stared at the TV set, her mouth gaping, as reporter G. W. Allen, in a voice that was all too familiar, discussed the kidnappings.

"I understand you worked undercover in Houston," the moderator remarked. "Can you tell us in what capacity?"

"I'm not at liberty to discuss that," Allen answered pleasantly. His voice droned on, but it sounded to Julie like gibberish.

Not at liberty to discuss it. I guess not. Had the other priests known? But of course, they had to.

Oh, good grief, he wasn't a priest after all. She began to laugh. She laughed and laughed, unable to stop, knowing hysteria was taking over.

The blare of the telephone finally brought her to her senses. She took a weak breath and answered it.

"I told you he wasn't a priest."

"Score one for you, Grace. You were absolutely right." She wondered if Grace could hear the remnants of hysteria in her brittle, high-pitched voice.

Apparently Grace didn't notice, for she continued. "My goodness, who would believe it? A reporter in disguise. And in our own parish. Exciting, isn't it?"

"Very," Julie muttered.

"How are you feeling?" Grace inquired. "Is there anything I can do for you?"

"No thanks, Grace. I'll be back to work tomorrow."

Julie hung up the phone, suddenly aware of the stinging sensation on her arm. *Damn, I burned myself. Burned myself?* The urge to laugh came again, but she forced it down. *Yeah, I really got burned.*

She thought of her last encounter with Father Gregory—those moments in his arms. She remembered her anguished words to him, "No, Father. We mustn't. This is wrong." G. W. Allen must have gotten a kick out of that. He'd used her, used them all to get a story. He hadn't even bothered to come by the hospital to see her. Or taken five minutes to call her and explain. Five minutes. That's all it would have taken to assuage her guilt and pain. She squeezed her eyes shut to prevent tears of anger and humiliation. Damn him. The only consolation she had was that she would never, *ever*, have to see G. W. Allen, alias Father Gregory, again.

AS SOON AS THE TELEVISION interview was over, Greg headed for the airport and his return to Houston. He'd be following the investigation of Jack Benton, but more important, he'd be doing an in-depth series on the lives of immigrants. He wanted to show what these people were like, to chronicle both their misery and their courage.

He told himself this was clearly the best story of his career. At last the elusive Pulitzer might be within his grasp. He ought to be feeling fantastic.

Instead he was frustrated as hell. And all because of Julie Whitaker. By now, she must know who he was. She might have seen him on television or heard it from the priests. How did she feel? He wanted to talk to her, and he'd almost reached for the phone as soon as he stepped out of the TV studio, but he'd stopped himself. This was something that had to be handled in person. Soon he'd be back in Houston. Back to finish his story and to take care of other unfinished business. There was no doubt in his mind that he was going back to Julie.

CHAPTER TEN

JULIE RETURNED to their office on Friday. She drove her own car, having told Captain Ferris that she no longer wanted police protection. If Jack contacted her, she would inform the authorities, but she absolutely refused to have them hovering over her.

As it had been after Dirk's death, work was her lifeline and her solace. It was what she needed to fill her heart and mind until they healed.

She was engrossed in a brochure from a health clinic when someone knocked. She looked up with her usual smile. "Come in."

The smile died on her lips. "Fath—"

"Greg Allen. May I come in?"

"I believe you're already in."

His smile was a bit tentative but as infuriatingly appealing as ever as he crossed the room and dropped onto a chair.

How dare he come back and barge into her office like this . . . after all he'd done . . . and hadn't done. Freezing her emotions, adding a chill to her voice, she said, "What is it, Mr. Allen?"

"Greg."

She said nothing. The room seemed to have shrunk in size in the past ten seconds. His presence overpowered it.

Blue eyes studied her thoughtfully. "How are you feeling?" he asked.

"Better, thanks," she said stiffly and turned away. As if he cared, she thought. He hadn't bothered to check when she was ill.

"I wanted to go to the hospital with you, but—"

"It wasn't necessary." She wanted him out of here...out before her anger spilled over in full force. Pointedly she picked up the brochure on her desk.

He didn't move.

Julie was painfully aware of him—of his eyes appraising her, of his hands folded loosely in his lap, even of the tempo of his breathing.

Finally Greg broke the silence. "A lot has happened since I saw you last."

"An understatement if I ever heard one."

"I'm given to them."

"Yes. Or sometimes you say nothing at all."

"Julie," he said slowly, "I wanted to explain this whole situation before I left, but I couldn't." He leaned forward as if expecting a comment, but she didn't make one. "I suppose the priests told you who I was?" he said.

She fought to control her voice. "No, I saw you on TV before they had a chance. It was quite a shock."

Understanding and concern showed on his face. "Julie—"

"Don't . . . please." She turned away. Why did he have to come back? She'd been hoping to put this behind her. When she turned back, he was still staring at her intently.

"We need to talk," he said softly.

"No."

"Yes."

"There's nothing for us to talk about."

"If that's what you think, then we really need to talk."

She rose and went to the file cabinet, turned her back toward him, and opened the drawer. "My choice, Mr. Allen. It's no."

Almost before she realized it, he was out of the chair and across the room. Eyes narrowed, he faced her across the open drawer. The tiger again . . . and ready to pounce.

"*My* choice, Mrs. Whitaker. I vote yes."

Fury choked her voice. "Get out."

"I can leave, but I'll come back. As many times as it takes to get you to listen."

"In case you've forgotten, Mr. Allen, this is a busy office." She gestured toward the door, through which they could hear voices. "I have people to see. And this isn't the place to talk."

"Fine. I'll wait for you and we'll go to lunch."

"I'm not taking a lunch hour today."

"Dinner then."

Exasperated, she pushed the file drawer shut. "Don't you ever take no for an answer?"

He shook his head. "That's what makes me a good reporter."

"This isn't a story."

"No," he agreed, his voice serious. "It's much more important."

Puzzled, she stared at him. The sincerity in his eyes threatened to pierce her shield of anger. Abruptly, she forced it back into place and turned away. "I'm not interested."

"God, woman," he said in disgust, "what does it take to book a simple dinner with you? Twelve heaters? Twenty? How many?"

She whirled around, her hand raised to strike. "You bas—"

He grabbed her wrist and held it. "Listen to me. Here and now, or over dinner. I don't care which, but you're going to hear me out."

Julie stared at him, her chest heaving, every one of her nerve endings acutely aware of his grip on her arm. "Let go of me," she said in a strangled voice.

"Only if I can be sure you won't slap—" Amusement flashed across his face. "Or bite."

She stared at him, aghast. What had gotten into her? She'd never hit anyone in her life. Unable to speak, she nodded.

Greg dropped her arm but didn't move away. He was so close she could feel his body heat. "Julie," he said quietly, "I care about what happened between us. Let's talk about it."

She hesitated, and he pressed his advantage. "If you won't talk about us, you can at least let me tell you about the kidnap victims. Some of them are coming back. They've had a terrible experience. They'll have problems."

What he said was true. She owed it to those men and their families to find out everything she could to help them. So, if she had to spend an evening with Greg Allen, well she'd force herself. "All right," she said. "We'll talk. About the men."

"Truce?" Greg asked, his eyes hopeful.

"Truce," she agreed.

"Extending through dinner?"

In spite of herself, Julie felt the beginnings of a smile. "Through dinner," she repeated.

"We'll have a friendly dinner then. I'll pick you up at your house at seven o'clock. I know the way."

JULIE HAD DRESSED carefully in a forest-green silk blouse and dark paisley skirt that picked up the green and added russet, brown, and gold. A gold choker adorned her neck and matching earrings shone in her ears. She'd purposely chosen the outfit to give a clear message—not too dressy or seductive—but subdued and professional.

She paced her living room, touching objects absently—a crystal bird; the figure of a young girl, her porcelain face innocent; a deep blue pillow resting on a chair. Normally this room, with its soothing colors, relaxed her. But not tonight.

She was nervous about the evening. How was she to relate to a man with a whole new persona? A man who'd made her furious but who'd also made her blood sizzle.

A schizophrenic evening, Julie thought. She'd be trying to reconcile two distinct personalities—Father Gregory, the sensitive, caring priest and Greg Allen, cool, arrogant reporter.

Whatever happened, though, she'd keep her composure. She promised herself that.

The doorbell rang. Julie jumped. She grabbed her purse and hurried to answer it, but stopped and ordered her jangled nerves to calm. Then she forced herself to walk slowly to the door. She opened it to a clear, starry night and a man who immediately sent her emotions into overdrive.

Greg's lips curved into a smile that made the tiny laugh lines near his eyes crinkle. It was a smile she'd often seen on Father Gregory's face, but the look of frank male appreciation in his eyes was pure Greg Allen.

He pulled a handkerchief out of his jacket pocket and held it up. "I brought a white flag. Remember our truce."

"I remember. A 'friendly' evening." She kept her voice neutral.

As they walked toward the car, she felt the light pressure of his hand at her waist, and knew that her pulse rate was increasing. Damn. She was already beyond "friendly," and the evening hadn't begun.

She got into the car and willed herself to be calm. It galled her to see that Greg seemed perfectly at ease, his hands relaxed on the steering wheel, a half smile on his lips. Maybe he was accustomed to such situations, but she wasn't. She waited for him to speak.

When he did, he surprised her. "I had lunch with Carmela today."

"You did?"

"Mmm-hmm. I went by and introduced myself."

"She must have been shocked."

"Surprised, but she recovered quickly and invited me to lunch. Makes the best tamales I've ever eaten. The family seems to have survived the trauma," he added. "The house is back in order. They're going on with their lives." He waited a moment, then said, "Carmela said you'd been by."

"Yes, I went the next afternoon."

"Right out of the hospital? You should have been home in bed."

Julie glowered at him. "Since you weren't there to advise me, I made the decision to do what I thought best."

He held up a hand. "Whoa. Truce, remember?"

Julie didn't bother to respond. *Composure,* she reminded herself. She stared out the window at the quiet streets, reminding herself that she was here for a professional discussion, not for an altercation. Still, anger simmered below the surface. She longed to bare her claws and take on the tiger... but then he might devour her.

Greg broke into her thoughts. "Julie, about that night you were in the hospital—"

Oh, no. Although she usually preferred to air differences, she wasn't about to let him broach that subject, not now. Not while her nerves were still so raw. Quickly she interrupted. "Tell me about the men."

She saw him draw a frustrated breath but he let her have her way. "They've been in hell," he answered bluntly.

"Your article made that pretty clear."

"The articles couldn't begin to do justice to that camp." He turned onto the freeway, and Julie could see his face in the brighter light. His mouth was grim as he described the filth and squalor he'd seen. "One man contracted pneumonia after working three days in the same wet clothes. Several were so weak they could barely walk. The stench of the place was something I'll never forget, and this is still March. In summer heat, it would have been— Shall I go on?"

Julie's hands were clenched so tightly that her fingers ached. She'd read his stories, but hearing him actually say it, in a voice tight with controlled emotion, made it even more graphic. She knew many of the men who'd been in the camp... young men, bright with hope for a better life. She fought down a wave of nausea, thinking what they must have suffered. "I need to hear it," she said, her voice as controlled as Greg's.

"In the beginning men were simply approached on the streets, offered jobs. They had no idea where they were being taken. When they got to the camp, they were told there was big money at the end of the job, so they put up with the conditions. But, just to make sure they didn't escape, there was a guard at the gate."

"The kidnappings started later, when Benton got desperate. His thugs started grabbing men off the streets. And *they* stayed, too. Money was at the end of the rainbow. Only, like most pots of gold," he added bitterly, "it didn't exist."

He turned into the restaurant parking lot and cut the engine but made no move to get out of the car. "It was slave labor pure and simple. Your 'friend,'" his voice dripped with sarcasm now, "had a nice little operation going, a real cost cutter. He saved enough to donate...what?...twelve heaters to the church."

"How dare you!" Composure forgotten, Julie grabbed the door handle, shoved the door open, and jumped out, slamming it behind her. She heard another slam as she stumbled blindly across the parking lot, and in an instant, Greg was beside her. He caught her by the shoulders and held her still, his eyes blazing into hers.

Julie fought back tears. "He wasn't my 'friend' as you so nicely put it, Mr. Allen. He was an acquaintance, nothing more. Not that I owe you an explanation of my relationship with him." Her voice caught. "And how dare you, *how dare you* say what you did as if...as if I had some responsibility in this. You—"

"I know. Bastard. I'm sorry. I shouldn't have said that. It's just that, when I think about Benton, I—"

"You take your anger out on me. Well, let me tell you something, Mr. Allen," she choked, "I'm not responsible for Jack Benton's actions. No matter what you or anyone else may insinuate."

Greg's grip on her arms tightened. "What do you mean? Who insinuated?"

"That police captain—"

"Ferris?"

"He said I was 'involved.'"

"Ah, honey," he said, his voice gentle now, his hands moving up and down her arms in a soothing massage. "We've given you a hard time, me most of all. I'm sorry." She pulled away from his touch and took a breath. "Apology accepted," she said unsteadily. She stared up at him for a long moment, then broke eye contact. "Let's go inside."

They walked to the door in silence. Inside the restaurant, Julie excused herself and went into the ladies' room where she stood for a few moments, collecting herself.

Their exchange in the parking lot had unnerved her. She understood that Greg Allen would be disgusted by Jack. Anyone would. But Greg seemed angry beyond the bounds of reason. For a fleeting instant, when he'd berated her for her relationship with Jack, she'd thought he was jealous, and she'd experienced a little frisson of pleasure at the idea. Ridiculous, she told herself. Greg Allen was upset over the things Jack had done. As she herself was. Ridiculous to imagine his feelings were more personal. Ridiculous to still be feeling the imprint of his touch.

With a toss of her head, Julie willed herself to be cool. To concentrate on the discussion of the *men* instead of her reactions to one *man*.

With a deep, calming breath, she opened the door, crossed the dining room, and joined Greg at the table. He rose and pulled out her chair, searching her face as if to make sure she was under control.

"Interesting place," he said, obviously searching for a neutral subject.

Julie nodded. *La Tour d'Argent*, the restaurant he'd chosen, resembled a log cabin on the outside. Inside it was furnished with period pieces that were far too elegant to have any relationship to the outside structure. The menu, another break with the atmosphere, was in French. *How appropriate for the evening,* Julie thought. *A schizophrenic restaurant.* At least it was off Miranda's beat.

Relieved that she'd calmed down, Greg studied Julie as she read the menu. He seemed to have a talent for setting her off. His celebrated finesse with women had deserted him where Julie Whitaker was concerned.

He kept the conversation light, and Julie seemed relieved. But after they ordered their meal, she returned to the subject of the kidnap victims.

"Were all the men found?"

He was sorry she'd asked that because the news was not good. "No. Some were dumped on the other side of the Rio Grande when they weren't fit to work anymore. And others were passed on to businesses in other parts of the country, for a price. Bud and his cronies had a little side racket going."

Julie's eyes widened with horror. "Then who... who is coming back?"

"Mr. Salazar's son has been found, and several others from St. Martha's parish."

"Nanda's husband?"

"I'm afraid not. He could be in Mexico. Or Wyoming or Minnesota, or heaven knows where."

"Will they look for him, and the others?"

"It's doubtful. Those without papers would have been deported. The others... Well, the INS isn't in the business of locating stray aliens and returning them to their families."

"So much suffering," Julie murmured. "I wonder if I'll be able to help."

"You will. The families whose men are missing will need you most, but the others will, too." He leaned across the table and covered her hand with his. "These people are fortunate to have you. You're good with them, and for them."

Julie looked up at him and smiled, and for a moment Greg felt the kinship that had existed between them in the past. Then she seemed to pull herself back to the present. Her eyes frosted over, and she yanked her hand away. Greg let it go. A restaurant was too public to air their differences. He'd wait. But not much longer.

He concentrated on small talk during the remainder of the meal. Though the topics he chose were innocuous enough, tension continued to build.

On the way home they were both quiet. Greg's muscles were taut with frustration. The evening was turning out to be a disaster. He'd planned to explain his abrupt departure, woo Julie with good food and wine, and concentrate on the future. Instead she'd held the line, refusing to discuss anything but the kidnappings. Stubborn. He felt like slamming on the brakes, grabbing her and shaking her until her teeth rattled. Not true, he admitted to himself. What he really felt like doing was slamming on the brakes, grabbing her, and kissing that frosty smile off her face.

Julie sat stiffly beside him. She was exhausted from the effort of containing emotions that threatened to explode at any moment. The silence in the car heightened the strain. She broke it. "Are you going back to . . . to Washington, or wherever it is you live?"

"I do live in Washington, and no, I'm not going back yet. I'm going to cover the grand jury investigation of Benton and follow up on the men who were in the camp."

"Oh." Was that the purpose of this evening then? To ingratiate himself with her so she'd provide him information about Jack? Well, she couldn't give him any. She was as stunned as everyone else about Jack's activities. "When I gave my statement to the police, Captain Ferris said I might be subpoenaed as a witness. I can't imagine why. I won't be able to tell them anything."

"You can identify Bud and tell them you saw him at Benton's."

"Yes, but I can't tell them anything else." Her voice rose. "I can't tell *you* anything else, either."

He gave her an annoyed glance. "What makes you think I expect you to?"

"I don't know. I just assumed—"

"Don't assume. You're the last person I'd suspect of being involved in Benton's business affairs."

That made her feel better. "The police didn't seem so sure," she said. "They insisted on having an officer around in case Jack tried to contact me."

He looked puzzled. "I didn't see anyone at your house or at St. Martha's."

"I got rid of them."

"Got rid of... You refused police protection?" He was clearly angry. "How could you do such a stupid thing?"

"I told you," she snapped. "I make my own decisions. Stupid or not, I didn't want police protection. I don't need it."

He looked contrite. "Sorry. I understand how you feel, but I don't like knowing Benton's walking around loose and you're alone. I worry about you," he added softly.

Both of them lapsed into silence.

They turned into Julie's driveway. Only a few more minutes to spend with this exasperating man, she thought. Then she could put him out of her mind. Perhaps she should be polite and invite him in for coffee. But what would he make of that? Would he construe it as willingness to talk about what had happened or as a more personal invitation?

He took the decision out of her hands by continuing their conversation about Jack Benton. "I've uncovered some interesting facts about Benton's financial status." He took Julie's key and opened the door, then followed her inside, still talking. "He lost a lot of money in oil, and to top it off, he bought a large block of stock in a Texas bank just before the economy went bad. At the price he bought them, those stocks would have gotten him out of trouble with his construction loans, but their value is now about a third of what he paid for them."

"There must have been ways for Jack to raise money to pay off those loans," Julie protested. She walked to the bar. "Would you like a drink?" she asked.

"Scotch."

She fixed his drink, poured *creme de cacao* into a slender liqueur glass for herself, and without paying much attention to what she was doing, sat down beside Greg on the couch.

"Benton apparently tried every means of raising money he could think of without success," Greg went on. "So his only solution was to save money on construction . . . and on salaries."

"But why? I thought I knew Jack. He was a friend of ours. He didn't have the most sterling reputation, but to stoop to such . . . such—"

"Atrocities?"

"Yes."

Greg took off his jacket, leaned back, and stretched an arm along the back of the couch. "I'm sure he didn't start with those intentions. Until a few months ago he was a successful businessman. He was aggressive, even ruthless in some of his business dealings, but he wasn't a criminal."

"Then why?"

"Success is addictive. When he was about to lose everything, he realized he couldn't do without it—the big house, the Porsche, the fast-paced life—so he did the only thing he could think of to save himself."

"Becoming a kidnapper. That was his solution?"

"Yes, and Benton would say it was perfectly logical."

"But the *people*—"

"I doubt if he gave a minute's thought to the people. They hardly counted as human beings to him."

Julie sat silently. "I can't understand that kind of thinking."

"Because your mind doesn't work that way. People are important to you." He looked at her thoughtfully. "Are we going to talk about this all night?"

"No...yes. I...I want to ask you something."

"Go ahead."

Julie took a breath. "Why didn't you call me before you left?"

He stared at her, clearly surprised. After avoiding the subject he'd wanted to pursue all evening, she'd suddenly brought it up herself. She hadn't intended to. She'd told herself exactly what she'd told him...that this evening was to be strictly business. But she couldn't deny the questions, the wounds that had been festering these past days. He'd been right this morning. They needed to talk.

She turned to face him. She could see hints of tension in the set of his shoulders, but when he spoke, his voice was soft, almost a caress.

"I did call you." The deep blue eyes that stared into hers held nothing but sincerity.

"When?" she asked. "How?"

"I must have called the hospital a dozen times. You were still unconscious when I left town."

The anger that had begun to dissipate flared again, fiercer than before. "You left town to track down the next installment of your news story, and now you're back...with some meaningless apology. You used me, used the church to get your story—"

"Wait a minute!" Greg cut in. "That's an unfair accusation."

"No? You spent a month using St. Martha's as your base of operations. You used me to gain access to the people. You used the parishioners to gain information. You used Father Curry and Father Rudolfo to—"

Greg held up a hand to stop the flood of words. "And just where do you think the idea for all this originated?" His voice was deathly quiet, but Julie had all she could do to keep from flinching at the barely controlled anger.

"I suppose your news service gave you the assignment, so you feel you're blameless."

"Think about it," Greg said in the same level tone. "How could I have arranged all this without help from the church?"

Julie's eyes widened. "You mean the priests cooperated?"

"You got it. Not only did they cooperate, but they initiated the whole thing."

Julie sat silently, stunned.

"Now," Greg said quietly. "Can you understand why I didn't call you?"

Julie couldn't help it. The volcano she'd worked so hard to contain suddenly erupted. Words poured out of her like hot lava. "No, I can't. How do you think I felt . . . waking in the hospital not knowing what had happened to you? And then finding you'd left, with no word of explanation . . . not a visit to the hospital . . . not even a phone call."

He drew a ragged breath. "Damn!" he swore. "Don't you think I know that? Don't you think I'd have come to you if I could? Lord knows I tried. First the police dragged me to the station for a statement, then Worldwide hustled me out of town. It was like a comedy of errors . . . only it wasn't a comedy for us. It was a tragedy."

She could see he meant what he was saying. But it didn't matter. Now that her anger had been freed, there was no stopping it. "A tragedy that could easily have been averted," she snapped.

"No, dammit, it couldn't," he said, raising his voice. "There were press at the hospital, people who'd have recognized me. What do you think would have happened to Father Curry and Father Rudolfo if I'd been spotted? This was their attempt—a desperate one at that—to help their parishioners. No one in the Diocese knew about it. If anyone had found out, they'd have been censured for bringing an outsider into the church, having him pose as a priest.

"I gave the priests my word. And at one point I almost betrayed them...for you. That day at Teresa's...if the police hadn't come when they did, I'd have told you. Fortunately I didn't. Because no one... *no one* was to know who I was until the priests cleared themselves with the bishop. And by the time that happened, I was in Harlingen."

"You could have called me then."

"No, I couldn't."

"You asked me to trust you. Didn't you trust *me* enough to tell me what was going on, even at the end?"

"Dammit, Julie," he said, raking his fingers through his hair. "This wasn't something to discuss on the telephone. We're having enough trouble resolving it in person. You can be one difficult lady to talk to, you know that? You've been difficult all along."

"Difficult?" Julie's eyes flashed. "What do you mean by that?"

"You wouldn't cooperate. You even withheld information about Nanda's husband."

"Because I didn't know what you were up to."

He laughed harshly. "Well, it's damn hard to confide in someone who blocks you at every turn. Besides, you were spending all your free time in the company of my prime suspect."

"Ohh!" Rage jerked her from her seat. She began to pace the room. "Are you going to bring that up again?" She turned back toward the couch, her fists clenched. "Not five minutes ago you said you never thought I was involved in

Jack's business affairs, yet here you go bringing him up again.'' She spun away and marched toward the window. "You make me so angry I could—''

He'd moved across the room so quietly she didn't know he was behind her. "You *are* a little wildcat, aren't you Mrs. Whitaker?'' He took her by the shoulders and swung her around to face him. "You—'' He stopped in surprise when he saw the tears on her cheeks. "You're crying.''

"Of course I am. No, I'm not. Just let me go, please.''

"No.'' Instead he pulled her into his arms. "I wasn't suggesting you were involved in his business, or anything else,'' he said, looking into her eyes. "I kept information from you as much for your own protection as for my commitment to the priests. What if you'd said something to Benton inadvertently, let something slip? You could have been in danger. I couldn't take that chance. And that night when you were in the hospital, I was torn in two—having to protect the priests, wanting to be with you. Even though *I* wasn't with you, my thoughts were. I *cared* what happened to you. Believe me.'' He put his hand behind her head and guided it to his shoulder, then put his arms securely around her.

Julie stood in his embrace as he gently rocked her back and forth. The tears she hadn't shed before coursed down her cheeks.

"Come here,'' Greg said softly. With his arm around her shoulders, he led her back to the couch. When they were seated, he reached into his pocket, brought out his handkerchief, and gently wiped her face.

She started to pull away. "This isn't like me—''

"Hush,'' he said, urging her back against him. "It's okay,'' he whispered. "You've had a rough time these past few weeks.'' He stroked her hair, her shoulders, her back.

Julie stayed in his arms, her head against his chest. Warmth, comfort, understanding. She'd needed them so badly these past days, and now they were being given unstintingly. She shut her eyes and relaxed, listening to his heart's steady beat, to the soft murmur of his voice in her ear.

He shifted to accommodate her more comfortably, then whispered kisses across her forehead, light, gentle kisses that comforted rather than aroused. It seemed natural then to put her arms around his neck, to lift her mouth to his. His lips were firm and warm, his kisses tender and, when he lifted her into his lap, she went unhesitatingly.

As he stroked her, she returned his caresses, running her hands over his firm back, threading her fingers into the hair she'd always longed to touch. Thick and soft, it was just as she'd imagined it.

His mouth moved from hers and burrowed into the warmth of her neck, his lips moist against her heated skin. "Julie," he murmured. "Sweet, sweet Julie."

Hungry for his mouth, she urged it back to hers. He continued to kiss her, his arms pressing her closer. She wasn't sure just when the tempo of his breathing changed, when his kisses became more urgent. She slowly became aware of his hand moving to the buttons of her blouse and loosening them, of his arousal pressing against her body.

She put her hands against his chest where the thunder of his heart matched the rhythm of her own. That wasn't enough. She wanted to feel his naked skin. She undid his tie and let it fall to the floor, then reached for the button at his collar. As her fingers touched it, memories slammed into her mind—of who he was, of who he'd been. Only last week he'd worn the collar of a priest. Now he was a stranger. She didn't know him at all....

"No!" She struggled against him, pushing with all her might.

Dazed, Greg stared down at the woman in his arms. An instant before she'd been warm, pliant; now she was stiff and unyielding. "Wh-what?" he asked, bewildered as she jerked out of his lap, shoving him back against the couch.

Hands shaking, she pushed the hair back from her face. "Was this what you had in mind, Mr. Allen? A bedroom scene? Well, forget it. I won't . . . I'm not—"

"You're not that kind of girl," he said in a parody of what she'd intended. His heart was still pounding, his body still taut, God, he *hurt*. "Look," he said in as reasonable a tone as he could manage, "I didn't plan this, if that's what you're thinking."

She turned away. When she spoke, her voice trembled. "I thought . . ."

"Go on."

"It doesn't matter."

"It does matter." He went to her, touched her shoulder and felt her stiffen. "Tell me what you thought."

He had to lean forward to hear the words. "I thought you . . . you were . . . comforting me."

"I was."

"But then you—"

"Look, do you still see a collar around my neck?"

Julie shook her head and said, "A different collar."

Greg sighed in frustration. "Of course it's different. I'm not a priest anymore. I never was. I'm a normal man, with normal urges, and dammit, the message I was getting was that you felt those same urges."

She was silent.

Greg reached for her again, this time pulling her around to face him. Her eyes were wide, her face tearstained. "You did feel them, didn't you?" he said quietly.

She nodded, almost imperceptibly. "But I don't know you."

"Julie—"

"I don't . . . want to talk about it."

He chided her gently. "That's not the Julie Whitaker I know—the woman who faces anything, from a stubborn priest to a kidnapper."

She gave him a faint smile. "I'm too upset to talk about it now."

"Tomorrow then. I'll come back in the morning."

"Greg—"

"In the morning. Go upstairs, get some rest, and we'll talk this out tomorrow."

He rose and took her arm. In the entry hall, he turned her toward the stairs. "To bed now. I'll be back in the morning."

Before she could answer, he opened the door and stepped outside.

CHAPTER ELEVEN

JULIE SPENT THE NIGHT tossing and turning, feeling alternately embarrassed and angry. Of course he'd misread her signals. She'd fallen into his arms with very little provocation, and she'd kissed him as avidly as he had her. No wonder he'd expected the evening to end in bed. But she couldn't.

There was no denying she'd wanted to, but she was too confused. She'd been half in love with Father Gregory, but Greg Allen was an unknown entity. She could no more give herself to him than she could to a stranger she'd met at a party. She knew nothing about him. Whether he was married, if he was involved with someone—the letter from Stephanie Barrett flashed through her mind—whether he was the kind of man she could respect and trust. He'd been playing a role, but she had no idea if the qualities he'd projected as Father Gregory extended to the real Greg Allen.

She could understand and respect his promise to the priests to keep his identity a secret, even from her. She could accept his assurance that he would have come to the hospital if he could, even his explanation that he'd waited to talk to her until they could meet face-to-face. She could forgive him all those things, but for the moment, that was as far as she could go.

It was almost morning before she fell into a restless sleep, and then she woke almost as soon as the first light of day shone in her window. In her agitated state the night before, she'd neglected to draw the drapes. With a groan, she got out of bed, showered, and dressed in jeans, polo shirt, and sneakers. She brushed her hair and pulled it into a ponytail, then went downstairs.

"Coffee," she decided, but the sound of Rett scratching on the back door detained her. "Okay. Out you go," she said.

She opened the door to a misty, cool morning. Despite the temperature, it was clear that winter was almost over. As usual, spring was coming early to the Texas Gulf Coast, and the redbud trees on her lawn were already blooming, their limbs outlined in fuchsia blossoms. Azaleas were budding, too. Petals of pink, white, lavender, and salmon lent their springlike colors to the landscape. For a moment, Julie drank in the tender harbingers of spring, then with a tired sigh, she let the dog back inside and shut the door. Winter was more her mood this morning.

"Here you are, fella." She filled Rett's dish and added water to his bowl, then watched him dive in voraciously.

She measured extra coffee into the pot. She'd need more than one cup today. Soon coffee aroma filled the kitchen. "Should be ready in two minutes," she murmured, her eyes on the pot.

The doorbell chimed, startling her. With a longing glance at the coffeepot, she left the kitchen and started for the front door, wondering who would be ringing her bell this early. It was too early for a neighbor to drop by, and it *couldn't* be...

She opened the door to find Greg, dressed in a knit shirt and thigh-hugging jeans that left little to the imagination, standing on her front porch, a rolled-up newspaper in his hand.

Her heart began to pound. Because he'd startled her, of course. "Wh-what are you doing here?" she asked.

He grinned at her astonishment. "I told you I'd be back in the morning. It's seven-thirty. Late already. Here." He dropped the newspaper into her hand and stepped inside.

Though he kept his manner casual, Greg was tense, and he wondered if she could tell. This morning his mirror had revealed red-rimmed eyes and haggard lines around his mouth. And no wonder. He'd spent a restless night. His body, taut with unfulfilled desire, hadn't cooperated when he'd gone to bed and willed it to relax. So he'd dressed, gone down to the hotel lobby and ordered a stiff drink at the bar. No good. When he returned to his room, he still couldn't sleep.

He'd lain on the bed, hands behind his head, staring at the ceiling. What was it with Julie Whitaker? She'd admitted she'd been as turned on as he. Then why the sudden freeze? Was it an act? He didn't think so. He knew Julie well enough by now to be sure she didn't indulge in games. No, something was troubling her, something besides the subjects they'd already discussed. She'd made some comment about not knowing him, but that didn't make sense. He'd have to find out what was really bothering her. Well, he was good at that. Reporters knew how to ask the right questions.

The truth was, he liked Julie as well as desired her. He needed to clear the air between them, even if the result was nothing more than the restoration of their friendship.

So here he was, following her into her kitchen. He smiled as he walked behind her. She looked like a teenager in jeans and ponytail. A very different picture from the professional image she projected at work. But he liked her well-scrubbed look. She was cute. Adorable. In fact, he felt like pulling her into his arms and telling her so. But of course, he couldn't do that.

She wasn't showing him any reaction beyond her first startled question. Well, if she wanted to keep it casual, he could go along with that. For a while.

"Do I smell coffee?" he inquired.

"Mmm-hmm. Want some?"

"Thanks."

She and Father Gregory had often shared coffee. Yet she hesitated. "I suppose you still take it black?"

Greg smiled. "Of course. I only changed my habit, not my habits." He settled himself in a chair in the sunny yellow breakfast room, its cheerfulness accentuated by the green of English ivy, flowering kalanchoes, and feathery ferns.

Julie brought his coffee and sat down across the table. "I didn't really expect you back," she began.

"Why? I said I'd be back. I usually keep my word." When she didn't comment, he told himself, *To hell with casual*. "Okay," he said briskly. "Let's talk."

"All right." Julie raised her eyes and faced him squarely.

He ignored the sparks of anger in her gaze and plunged in. "I didn't imagine your feelings last night, did I?"

"No, you didn't, but—"

"Then what happened? Why the sudden turnabout?"

"I don't believe in one-night stands," she answered seriously.

"As a matter of fact, neither do I." It was true. He wasn't the type to pick up a nameless face at a bar or a party, take her home to bed, and bid her goodbye the next morning. His relationships, whether they lasted six weeks or six months, went deeper than that.

"Look," he added, "I'm only going to be in Houston a short time. That's true. But *you* know you can't predict how long somebody will be around." He meant her to think of her husband, and when she nodded thoughtfully, he knew he'd scored a point. "Well, then?" he asked, pressing his advantage.

She looked at him for a long moment, then said hesitantly, "You've been living as a priest for weeks now. Maybe you just want a woman...and I'm conveniently available."

If she hadn't been so solemn, he'd have burst out laughing. If he'd just wanted "a woman," he'd have found one. But he wanted...needed Julie. He shook his head. "I wanted you," he said softly.

She took a breath and said, "Who is Stephanie Barrett?"

Stephanie Barrett? That was the last thing he'd expected her to say. Where had she found out about Stephanie? Not that there was anything to "find out." But Julie evidently thought there was.

"Stephanie's a reporter with Worldwide Press. We've known each other a long time. We had a 'relationship' a few years ago, but it didn't last long. We weren't meant to be lovers, but we're great as friends. And that's all we are. Just friends."

He watched Julie's silent reaction...first an embarrassed flush, then a thoughtful appraisal of what he'd told her, and finally acceptance. "I see," she said.

"How did you hear about Stephanie anyway?" he asked.

"I went into your office after you left and saw some papers on the floor. One of them was a letter from Stephanie. I shouldn't have read it, but I did. I was shocked."

"I can see why," he said. "The reference to a 'weekend' must have sounded damning. Actually a group of us went together. It was all very innocent, not even any coed sleeping arrangements. But to you, I must have sounded like the prurient priest."

"It wasn't funny."

"No, I suppose not. It must have been devastating."

She nodded. "It was. Imagining that a priest I'd respected was unfaithful to his vows. I took the letter to prevent anyone else reading it and feeling the way I did."

"That was . . . loyal of you."

"I cared."

Cared. Did she intend that past tense? He promised himself he'd change her mind if she did.

As she rose and took their cups to refill them, she gave him an opening. "But that's all in the past," she said.

"My point exactly," he agreed. "And now, we can focus on the present. And the future."

She returned to the breakfast room and set his cup down beside him. "I'm not sure how I feel now," she said, taking her seat. "I hardly know you."

He was honestly taken aback. "Of course you know me."

"I knew a priest named Father Gregory. I don't know *you* at all."

"You can't mean that. Father Gregory and I are one and the same."

"Are you? How can I be certain?"

"All right. Maybe you aren't sure this morning. But spend some time with me—Greg Allen—getting to know me. Then decide."

"I—" she began hesitantly, but Greg interrupted.

"I won't try to drag you into bed if that's what you're worried about. I'll make a deal with you. Just friends, until you want to change things. We were friends before. Why not continue?"

"No pressure?"

"None."

"All right." Julie gave him a full smile, thinking she might just enjoy this experience. Why not take a chance, she asked herself. After all, she had to admit, it was what she'd been wanting anyway.

"We can start by spending the day together. I've hardly been out of the barrio, and I'd like to see some of the area."

"Let me fix some breakfast first, and we can talk about what you want to see," Julie suggested. "How do you like your eggs?"

"Scrambled." He followed her into the kitchen and leaned against the counter while she made bacon and eggs and heated blueberry muffins.

They discussed possible excursions and settled on Galveston. Greg also invited her to join him for dinner Sunday evening. "I'm meeting Phil Barnes and his wife. Phil is the head of Worldwide's Houston office."

"I believe I met him once at a reception."

"Yeah, he mentioned that. I know he'd like to have you along. He wants to congratulate the lady who disarmed a kidnapper with her teeth."

Julie giggled.

"You're turning red, Ma'am."

"Imagine how embarrassed I would've been if you'd put that in your story. Thank you for keeping my secret."

"I'm one of those reporters who's aware of his subject's feelings and careful not to tread on sensitive areas. I didn't want you getting a reputation as a vampire."

When they'd finished their meal and cleaned up the kitchen together, Greg suggested they leave.

"I'll run upstairs and comb my hair," Julie answered.

He tugged at her ponytail. "Leave it. I like you the way you are. Just grab a jacket and let's go."

She dashed up to get her windbreaker, feeling ridiculously pleased with his off hand compliment.

A few minutes later, they were in Greg's rented Toyota, heading for Galveston. There they spent the morning exploring the Strand, an old warehouse area that had been restored and now boasted shops and restaurants. They stopped for hamburgers, then drove through Galveston's older neighborhoods, looking at gingerbread Victorian houses, and finally headed for the beach. Greg parked the car, and they descended a flight of steps to the sand.

A brisk wind was blowing, and Julie zipped up her jacket. The sand was tightly packed and damp from a recent rainstorm. She breathed in the salty smell of the gulf and watched the wind toss the spray into the air. A flock of gulls swooped down to the shore and soared away, their white wings bright against the blue sky. She bent to pick up a clam shell, inspected it, then tossed it away. "Not many pretty shells along this part of the gulf," she complained.

Greg slipped an arm about her shoulder. "I found some beauties near Cozumel a couple of years ago when I stopped to scuba on my way back from Panama. The water's beautiful—clear and warm—and the marine life is spectacular."

"I'd like to learn to scuba," Julie remarked.

"There's nothing to compare to it, except skiing."

"You *are* an outdoors person."

"Not exclusively. I like indoor sports as well."

Julie glanced up to find him grinning, and elbowed him in the ribs.

They turned back, now heading into the wind, and he pulled her closer. She liked the feel of his arm around her, the faint scent of his cologne that blended with the smell of sand and sea. She was sorry when they reached the car.

They had dinner at Gaido's Seafood Restaurant. The decor wasn't spectacular but Julie assured Greg that the place was a Galveston tradition. As they waited for their order, they fell into an easy conversation.

"How did you feel, being a priest?" Julie asked him curiously.

"Restricted," he answered promptly, giving her a suggestive grin.

Julie blushed, then grinned back. "I'm *sure* you did, Mr. Allen. Any other problems?"

He chuckled. "I felt I was walking a tight rope. One false step and I'd be a goner. And so would the priests. The morning Rudy got sick and couldn't say Mass, I thought the whole scheme would fall apart."

"Your absence didn't go unnoticed."

"Grace?" he asked.

"Right. You gave her enough intrigue to keep her occupied for days."

"And you?" His voice deepened. "Did you wonder about me, too?" As he had last night, he reached for her hand.

Feelings poured through her, feelings that had been inappropriate a week ago or even last night, but which now could surface without guilt or shame. She felt the heat from his hand spread through her body, flushing her face, speeding her heart rate.

"I wondered," she admitted, staring into his eyes. "But that's ended now."

Both of them jumped at a discreet cough. "Your wine, sir," the waiter announced. He uncorked the bottle, poured, and waited for Greg to taste. Without taking his eyes from Julie's or removing his hand from hers, Greg fulfilled his part of the wine ritual. His voice was husky when he said, "Fine." The waiter filled their glasses and disappeared.

Greg raised his glass to her. "To endings," he murmured. "And beginnings."

For the rest of the meal, Julie wondered how this evening might end. She wasn't sure what she wanted. One minute she longed for Greg to make love to her. The next she remembered his deceptions and wondered how she could possibly trust him. The only thing she was sure of was her confusion.

Later, when they arrived at her house, Greg parked and came around to open her car door. The light from the porch blended with moonlight to cast velvety shadows that softened the planes of his face. His eyes captured hers and she saw in them such naked longing that her chest tightened and her breath caught in her throat. Tension thrummed through her body.

But, to her surprise, Greg said good-night on the front porch and left her with a chaste kiss on the cheek. He was keeping to the terms of their pact, Julie reflected as she climbed the stairs to her room. In fact, he was keeping them almost too well to suit her. She'd have been willing to tolerate a *slight* infraction.

She'd really enjoyed the day. It had been so long since she'd spent a carefree day with a man, so long since she'd shared fun and laughter. Today they'd chuckled over a pot-bellied fisherman dozing on the pier, over two towheaded youngsters tossing bread to sea gulls, over the conversation of the people at the next table at Gaido's. All in all a perfect day, she thought as she got ready for bed. They'd made plans for Sunday, too. First they'd only talked about going to dinner, but by the end of the evening Greg had asked her to join him for a morning run and breakfast afterward. The anticipation of the day to come sent Julie to sleep with a smile on her lips.

THE NEXT MORNING Greg arrived early, dressed for running, and they set off for Memorial Park. Julie ran beside him for a while, then slowed to a walk. "I'll catch up with you on my second round," Greg called to her over his shoulder.

She strolled along, enjoying the sounds of birds, the greetings of the walkers and joggers, the fresh, cool air. Hazy memories of her dream about Father Gregory reminded her that her fantasy had magically come true. Well, part of it.

She'd almost completed the three-mile circle when Greg came abreast of her. He slowed to a walk, wiping his forehead with his sleeve. "The temperature couldn't be more than seventy degrees, but it sure feels warmer," he remarked.

"It's the humidity."

"Yeah. Coming from Arizona, it's a shock."

"You really are from Arizona then," Julie said in surprise.

"Of course. I told you that once."

"You told me you were a priest once, too."

"Touché," he laughed. "But everything else I told you was the truth. As for the priesthood... Well, during my stint as altar boy, I did have notions of becoming a priest, for about a week. Then I fell in love with journalism, and it's been a lifelong commitment." He wiped his face again. "Whew, that humidity must be ninety percent."

"But you must've spent time in humid places," Julie said.

"Jungles. I've been in Central America a lot lately, but I've never gotten used to the kind of heat that soaks through you."

They showered, changed, and drove to the Rainbow Lodge, a nearby restaurant, for brunch. "Tell me about your Central American assignments," Julie asked as they ate.

"I've covered the Contras and the Sandanistas, political unrest in El Salvador, and the invasion of Panama."

Julie shivered. "Sounds like a dangerous job."

Greg shrugged. "Anyplace can be dangerous. Houston, for instance. I hear a social worker in a church was held hostage last week."

Julie laughed at his remark, but her concern about the dangers of his work lingered. She'd feel that way about anyone, she told herself, not just about Greg.

After brunch, they returned to Julie's where they spent a lazy, pleasant hour sharing the Sunday paper. Rett wandered into the family room, decided Greg was a friend, and curled up at his feet.

Greg and Julie sat side by side on the couch, heads bent over the paper. They chuckled over the comics, argued over the relative merits of their cities' basketball teams, and shared articles of interest. She learned that he was a Doonesbury fan, that he read the Travel section as well as the news from cover to cover, and that he got a kick out of reading the ads in the Personals column and imagining what sort of people placed them. As they read, he put his arm around her, and for a moment the newsprint faded into a blur as Julie concentrated on the feel of his fingers lazily stroking her shoulder.

She was sorry when Greg rose and said he had some work to do at his hotel. "I'll be back for you at seven o'clock."

She was ready and waiting when he arrived. It wasn't the first time she'd seen him in a suit, but Friday night she'd been too nervous to look at him closely. Tonight, with the nervousness gone, she indulged herself in a thorough examination. The jacket showed off his broad shoulders, and the navy-blue fabric made his eyes look as deep as the ocean. He smiled at her perusal and returned the favor.

The way he looked her over made her blood quicken. His eyes traveled leisurely from her hair, down her soft sleeveless gray wool dress with a quick stop at breast level, and on down to her legs. "Nice," he murmured, then helped her on with her jacket and led the way to his car.

At the downtown Hyatt, he headed for the elevator. "We're meeting Phil and Sylvia in the dining room, but I have to stop in my room first to pick up some papers." He pushed the button for the eighth floor.

The first thing Julie noticed when they walked into his room was an arrangement of red and silver balloons placed incongruously between a stack of news magazines and a clock radio on the crowded dresser. "What's this?" she inquired.

"Birthday greetings from my sister and brother."

"Today's your birthday?"

"Yeah."

"Well, Happy Birthday! You should have told me."

He grinned sheepishly. "No way. At my advanced age, I'm trying to forget birthdays."

"How advanced is that?"

"Thirty-six."

Julie laughed and turned her attention to the room as Greg gathered his papers. *Except for the balloons, a typical man's room, even in a hotel,* she thought, enjoying the male clutter that she'd missed these past months. The windbreaker he'd worn yesterday was tossed carelessly over the back of a chair. A tie he'd apparently considered and discarded hung beside it. On the dresser were a half filled bottle of Brut cologne, a comb, and a scattering of loose change. The desk was strewn with tools of the journalist's trade—notebooks, pens, a small computer, and several books on immigration issues.

While Julie studied his belongings, Greg slipped the papers he'd come for into a folder, glanced at her, and set the folder down. He came up behind her and touched her bare shoulders lightly, fingertips only. She shivered.

"Cold?" he murmured. He covered her shoulders with his hands, and pulled her back against him. She felt his warm breath on her neck.

Their eyes met in the mirror. Fascinated, Julie watched his darken from azure to indigo. Breathing became difficult, as he turned her slowly in his arms until they were face to face. She couldn't take her eyes from his, couldn't control her shallow, quivering breaths. Her lips parted expectantly as his came nearer...nearer. When his lips closed over hers, she gave a little gasp of pleasure. He pulled her tightly against him. Mouth to mouth. Heart to heart.

She wanted the kiss to last forever. She wanted it to end so he could devour every part of her...

She felt Greg draw away and, confused, opened her eyes.

"Dinner," he mumbled.

Julie stared at him, dazed. He traced a finger around her lips. "Dinner," he repeated.

Unable to speak, she simply nodded. He took her hand, picked up his folder, and led her from the room. The elevator reached the lobby before she recovered her equilibrium.

The Barneses were waiting for them. Julie liked both of them immediately. Sylvia was a svelte contrast to her rotund husband. Phil was genial, Sylvia charming. Phil's wit was sharp, Sylvia's more subtle. They were a perfect balance for each other.

Sylvia was an architect who specialized in energy-efficient buildings. Phil was clearly proud of her accomplishments and she of his.

Conversation ranged from the prospects of the Houston Astros this season to the latest arms reduction proposal. Under the cover of chatter, Julie whispered to Sylvia that it was Greg's birthday.

"I'll take care of it," Sylvia whispered back. She excused herself, and Julie noticed her corner their waiter on her way to the ladies' room. When the main course was finished, the waiter appeared carrying a cake topped with three lighted candles, which he placed before Greg with a flourish. He then led them in a spirited rendition of "Happy Birthday."

"I'll get you for this," Greg muttered darkly to Julie.

She fluttered her lashes innocently. "I had nothing to do with it," she lied. "Sylvia made the arrangements."

"Make a wish," Sylvia instructed.

Greg cocked his head, then grinned wickedly. "Okay," he agreed. "I've made it." He gave Julie a glance that caused her to redden and stare down at her plate. Then he blew out the candles.

When the birthday festivities were over and the four of them were lingering over coffee, Sylvia turned to Greg and said, "I've been impressed by your coverage of the kidnappings."

"Thanks. Coming from you, that's a real compliment."

"Did you find the story interesting to write?"

"On a scale of one to ten, it's been a ten all the way."

"How so?"

"What made this one special was my perspective. It started as an ordinary story about anonymous people, then I got caught up in it. Acting as a priest, seeing these people firsthand, sharing in their lives in a way a reporter never does, made me aware of what they were going through. A reporter's supposed to stay objective, but I couldn't. These were neighbors, real people I'd seen at Mass, broken bread with. My focus changed."

"Your writing showed it. I've read most of your columns, and this is cleary the best work you've ever done," Sylvia said.

Julie had been silent during this exchange, her eyes riveted on Greg's face. *He really feels it,* she thought in surprise. She felt as if she'd been seeing two slightly different views of the same man through a stereoscope. Over the weekend they'd gradually moved closer, until now they suddenly came together into one clear, coherent picture. Of course Greg Allen and Father Gregory were one and the same, just as he'd maintained. The masquerade had been only a superficial one. The real man had never been obliterated, only obscured. Why had she taken so long to realize it?

She stared at Greg with such intensity that he noticed and raised a brow in question. Julie shook her head and smiled at him.

Greg wondered what she was thinking. There was something different in the way she was gazing at him, something in her smile that hadn't been there before. He watched her during coffee and conversation and found her watching him.

When they had finished, Phil and Sylvia headed for the parking garage and Julie would have followed, but Greg took her hand. "It's early. Want to have a drink upstairs at the Spindletop?"

"All right."

They said goodbye to the Barneses and took the elevator to the top floor where a revolving restaurant provided a spectacular view of the city. There were no tables for two available, so they accepted one for four by the window and sat side by side. They ordered brandy and turned toward the panorama before them.

"Look," Julie pointed. "There's the Ship Channel. St. Martha's would be just west of it, nearer downtown."

As Greg leaned over her shoulder to see, she turned toward him. Their mouths were only inches apart, but she only gave him a soft smile and returned her gaze to the window. His eyes traveled in the direction she had pointed, but he couldn't concentrate on the view. Her hair was silky and fragrant, her cheek baby-smooth next to his, her lashes long and thick. Good God, he thought, how long would he be able to contain himself? She was driving him mad. And the look in her eyes this evening—wonder, budding passion—was having its effect on his body as well as his mind.

Their brandy arrived, and Julie turned back to him. Behind her, Greg could see the lights of the city far below, the night sky and a sliver of moon above. Stars glittered, but Julie's eyes outshone them. Wide and luminous, they stared into his.

He reached for her hand. She nestled it in his. He turned it palm up, lifted it, and traced the fine lines with his fingertip. "I see a handsome stranger," he began.

"In the future or the past?"

"About six weeks past. He is not as he seems, but better by far."

"A silver-tongued devil," she commented, peering at her hand.

"A mild-mannered reporter," he contradicted, "committed to truth, justice, and the American way."

"I've heard that before somewhere."

"Have you? I thought I was being original."

They fell silent. He kept her hand in his, absently toying with her fingers, continuing to search her face for some clue to what was going through her mind.

Their waiter returned, offering more brandy, but Julie declined and said reluctantly that they'd better start home.

In the elevator Greg helped Julie on with her jacket and fastened it at her neck. "To keep you warm," he murmured and let his hands remain. Julie put her hands lightly on his wrists. They stood still, gazing raptly at each other, their bodies reacting less to the downward rush of the elevator than to the nearness of each other.

The elevator reached the lobby, the doors opened, but neither of them noticed. Finally the sound of laughter intruded. Greg looked around as if emerging from a trance and said, "Time to get out."

Julie glanced briefly at the open doors, then shook her head and reached around him. She pushed the button marked eight, and the doors slid closed.

Greg caught his breath. "Are you sure?" he asked huskily.

Julie nodded.

His lips curved in a tender smile. "I think I got my birthday wish," he whispered.

The elevator gave a slight lurch and started up.

CHAPTER TWELVE

GREG OPENED THE DOOR and led Julie into his room. A lamp by the bedside was turned on low, casting soft shadows over the bed, its covers turned down invitingly.

Greg shoved the door shut with his shoulder, shrugged out of his jacket and tossed it on a chair, then without a word, turned to Julie. She lifted her face, seeking his mouth and the pleasures she knew it would bring. His lips touched hers, then moved slowly over them, eliciting soft sighs. His hands tunneled through her hair, exploring its texture.

He touched nowhere but her face and hair; but they stood body to body, and every contact point was a caress. The thunder of his heart against hers, the pressure of his chest against her breasts, the firm strength of his thighs. She pressed closer and felt his arousal, felt the heat through the layers of cloth that separated them.

His tongue outlined her mouth. She parted her lips, inviting him in, then sucked gently. His taste, sharp with brandy, filled her mouth; his softly satisfied "Mmm," filled her ears, and she thought if she never heard or tasted again, this would be enough. All the dreams she'd ever had, of love, of him, seemed to come together, to mesh in this one intoxicating moment.

Impatient for more, she wrapped her arms around his neck and urged him closer. "Hold me," she whispered.

He drew back to look at her. "Shh," he murmured. "This is my birthday, and I like to open my presents...very slowly."

With feather-soft touches, his fingers moved over her face tracing her eyebrows, her cheekbones, the soft rounding of her chin. His tongue brushed her eyelids and trailed over to her ear. "I like to touch and taste first," he breathed.

His hands moved to her breasts, cupping them gently, his thumbs rubbing over the already distended nipples. "I like to feel."

Time melted away as she stood, her hands on his shoulders, her eyes fastened on him, hypnotized.

At last he raised a hand to the top button of her dress. "And now for the unwrapping," he whispered, "a little at a time."

Hours might have passed as he undid each button and parted the fabric with exquisite patience. Eons might have gone unnoticed as he kissed each exposed bit of skin. At last he slipped the garment from her. He kissed her neck, ran his tongue across her shoulder, then unfastened the front clasp of her bra. He was still for a moment, caressing her with eyes only. "The wrapping was lovely," he said smiling into her eyes, "but what's underneath is perfection."

He bent to her breast and took the peak in his mouth, his tongue teasing it, his hair soft against her shoulder. She buried her face in his hair, filling her nostrils with the scent.

Greg moved from her breast and bent lower, to gently slide her panty hose down her legs, his lips leaving moist kisses on the way. Julie felt her knees give way and clung to him. He straightened and lifted her easily, carrying her to the bed. He laid her on the cool sheets and sat beside her, continuing his tender assault.

Julie's eyes closed. Behind her lids she sensed a universe of colored lights, of glittering stars, of silvery moonbeams.

Was this real? It had to be, because no dream had ever evoked such sweet sensations. She felt a gush of warmth from deep inside her and knew her body was readying itself for his. But first . . . first she wanted to bring him the same pleasure he was giving her.

She opened her eyes and sat up. "Let me undress you now," she whispered.

He gazed at her, his eyes heavy-lidded. "Oh, yes."

She undid his tie, and slowly unbuttoned his shirt. She spread it apart and ran her hands over his broad chest. The hair was silky soft, and she rubbed her cheek against it, tasted it with lips and tongue, then quickly unfastened his trousers and lowered them, taking her lips on a journey down his thighs that left the muscles quivering. Now his briefs and her lacy panties were the only barriers between them.

Greg gently pushed her back on the bed and knelt above her. He kissed her again, from her forehead to her ankles, following his lips with his hands, tarrying along the way to tease and tantalize. He lay full-length over her, fitting himself to her, moving in preview of what was to come. She heard herself moan, heard the roaring of his breath in her ear, felt her heart racing out of control. Passion. Had she ever felt with such intensity? Urgency. Had she ever wanted with such desperation? Love. The reality of it, sharper than any dream, burst upon her mind, upon her heart, like a shower of stars.

Greg quickly removed their remaining clothing and turned back to her. "Now. My birthday gift," he whispered hoarsely.

Julie's arms reached out to embrace him; her body opened to receive him; her heart knew she was his.

Their bodies joined, they moved as one. They were one, moving ever upward to the place where dreams become reality, until they reached it together, and crested in a shattering rush of sensation.

Mine, Greg thought, tightening his arms about her.

Yours, Julie thought, holding him close.

The aftershocks of passion died away, and they lay facing each other, legs entwined, letting their heartbeats slow, their bodies calm.

Earlier Julie had wondered if she would feel awkward after making love to Greg, but she didn't. She felt lazy and languid, like a contented cat. She trailed her hand across his cheek.

Greg caught it and took it to his lips, nibbling gently at her fingers. "Mmm. I liked my birthday present."

Julie cuddled closer. She planted soft kisses on his shoulder, his chest. "Happy Birthday, then," she murmured, angling her face so she could touch her lips to his. As she did, she felt him heat and harden against her thigh. She glanced up at him. "Greg?" she asked.

"Yes!" He pulled her beneath him. "You might add, 'many happy returns,'" he whispered, and slipped inside her again.

Several hours later Julie awoke. Her eyes still shut, she tried to sort out what had happened. For a moment she lay still, thoughts and emotions reeling, then she sat up and slid noiselessly out of bed. She found Greg's shirt and slipped it on. She lifted the edge of it and rubbed the soft material against her cheek, inhaling the scent of him.

She padded barefoot to the window and looked outside. Below her the streets were deserted; above, the sky was velvet black. She leaned her forehead against the window, thinking.

This evening marked a turning point. Over a year and a half ago she'd said goodbye to Dirk in body. She stood silently, remembering times of love and laughter. Memories she would always treasure, but which could be no more than memories. Dirk would always be special to her, as first loves always are, but tonight she would bid him farewell in heart as well. Yesterday Greg had spoken of endings and beginnings. Tonight she would end her identity as Mrs. Dirk Whitaker and begin a new life on her own. Tonight she could finally accept the fact that Dirk was gone.

And Greg was here. Not that she deluded herself into expecting something permanent between them. He was an adventurer who lived in the present. So she would take what happiness she could and give no thought to tomorrow. When he left her, as he would, she would manage. She was strong, a survivor. She would make it.

Greg opened his eyes and saw her at the window. Moonlight washed over her, making her seem as fragile as porcelain. His shirt, far too large for her slender frame, hung almost to her knees. Seeing her in his clothes gave him a deep sense of pleasure.

She stood absolutely still, her head against the glass, one hand slightly raised and touching the window. What was she thinking, he wondered. Was she sorry they'd made love? He hoped not. The thought was painful.

He got up and went to stand behind her, putting his hands on her shoulders. "Are you all right?"

Without turning, she nodded. "Just thinking."

"It was the first time since your husband, wasn't it?"

"Yes."

"Regrets?"

"No." She turned to him and put her arms around his neck. "No," she repeated firmly. "I know who you are."

Moved, he pulled her into his arms. He understood what she was telling him. Father Gregory was no longer a separate individual but a part of Greg Allen. With a sigh, he bent his head to her lips. The kiss was long and satisfying, but he wanted more. He drew away and unbuttoned the shirt. "Come back to bed," he murmured.

Love was slow and sweet this time. They savored each other, experiencing every nuance, every movement to the fullest. Slowly and surely they came together. Gradually their heartbeats accelerated until they reached the peak and floated lazily back to earth again.

Julie fell asleep, a smile on her lips, but Greg remained awake, his head propped on his hand, watching her. So lovely, he thought. Once he'd imagined he could walk away from her after one night of loving. Now he knew it would take more than that to get her out of his head.

Of course, he wasn't looking for anything permanent. That wasn't his style, he reminded himself. But then, she wasn't seeking a permanent arrangement, either. She'd told him herself she wasn't planning to get married again. They were perfect for each other, each wanting the same thing— an affair, a passionate one, like a shooting star that rockets across the sky briefly but intensely, and disappears.

"Right," he told himself. "Right," he repeated and wondered why the idea seemed so wrong.

JULIE WOKE AT DAWN, sat up on the edge of the bed, and peered at the clock radio. Six o'clock. She leaned over and kissed Greg's cheek.

"Mmmm," he mumbled.

She shook him gently. "I have to go."

He turned on his back, opened his eyes, and focused on her slim, still-naked body. "What for?"

"It's Monday. I have to go home, dress, and get to work."

He hoisted himself up to a sitting position. "I've got a better idea. I'll drive you to work and pick you up afterward. That way you won't have to rush, and we can...sleep a little longer." With a wicked grin, he grabbed her arm and toppled her back onto the bed.

A half hour later they reluctantly got out of bed. Julie watched Greg as he dressed, noticing things she'd missed in the darkness—the bronze of his skin, the pattern of his chest hair, a ridge of tissue along his shoulder. She'd felt it last night but hadn't paid much attention. Now she saw it was a scar.

"What's this?" she asked, her fingers probing gently.

"Gunshot wound. I stepped in front of a bullet in Nicaragua."

She froze. Quickly she turned her face away. She didn't want him to see the horror in her eyes, or the fear. She had no right to be afraid for him.

Instead she made herself think of other things. She called her maid and told her to feed Rett, made a mental list of things to do when she reached her office. By the time they were both ready to leave, she had put the fear out of her mind.

They stopped and had sweet rolls at the little bakery across from the church. The young clerk greeted them warmly, not at all discomfited by Father Gregory's new identity.

When they sat down to eat, Julie remarked, "She didn't seem surprised to see you out of 'uniform.'"

"No," Greg explained, taking a sip of coffee. "The priests have explained who I am and why I was posing as a priest. Rudy tells me the response has been pretty positive. In fact," he added, looking a bit embarrassed, "I'm afraid they've made me into something of a parish hero."

Julie laughed. "Are you blushing, Mr. Allen? You shouldn't be. You deserve the title."

After breakfast, they returned to the parking lot. "I'll be back for you at five-thirty," Greg said. He made no move to kiss her, simply squeezed her hand. She was glad. The entrance of St. Martha's was not the place for passion.

"Have a good day," he said, and got into the car.

If the day were half as good as its beginning, it would be terrific, Julie thought. She strolled into the building and down the hall, a dreamy smile on her lips, and ran smack into Grace who was returning to her office with the coffee-pot. Water spilled on both of them.

"Oops, sorry," Julie said.

Grace looked her over thoroughly. "Were you still asleep or just daydreaming?"

"Both, I guess."

"Well, come in, and I'll put the coffee on. A good strong shot of it should wake you up."

Julie followed Grace into her office and sat down. The room looked different this morning, she thought, noticing details she usually overlooked. *Everything* looked different this morning.

"Busy weekend?" Grace inquired with undisguised curiosity.

"I spent some time with Greg Allen," Julie admitted. She wondered what the older woman, born in a less liberated generation, would think of that.

"I know," Grace said without censure. "I saw you getting out of his car."

Julie blushed.

Grace laughed good-naturedly. "So you spent more than time with him. It's nothing to be embarrassed about."

Pleased at Grace's easy acceptance, Julie confided, "I like him."

"I don't blame you. He's *very* attractive. In fact, I like him much better as a reporter than I did as a priest. But be careful, honey. Don't get in over your head."

"Grace, that's just the opposite from what you advised me with Jack Benton."

"So I was wrong about that one. But the difference is that Jack was right here in Houston, and Greg Allen is just passing through."

"I know that." Julie felt defensive. She didn't need a lecture on the perils of getting involved with Greg. She'd already recounted them to herself... and blithely ignored them. "I'm not counting on anything lasting," she added. "I'm going into this with my eyes open."

"That's what they all say," Grace muttered dourly.

Julie laughed, half-amused, half-exasperated. "I mean it."

"Okay. I guess you know what you're doing. I just don't want to see you hurt."

"I won't be."

"Well then, enjoy yourself. Enjoy him. He *is* a sexy devil, isn't he?"

Julie smiled with remembered pleasure. "Grace, you're absolutely right." Picking up her coffee mug, she gave Grace another dreamy smile and left the room.

As she neared her office, she heard the telephone and hurried in to answer it. "Julie Whitaker."

"Julie." The silky voice was all too familiar.

"Jack!" Just saying his name made her feel slightly sick.

"How are you, sweet?" he asked, as if nothing had happened.

How was she! Thanks to him, she and many others weren't well at all. She wanted to tell him that, but she knew she would be foolish to vent her rage. Instead she said, "Jack, I can't talk to you. I don't *want* to talk to you." She hung up the phone, aware that her hands were trembling, whether from anger or fear, she wasn't sure.

She sat down at her desk, then jumped when she heard a knock. She took a deep breath and promised herself she wouldn't allow Jack to affect her life this way. She opened her door and found Mr. Salazar and his son, Esteban.

Julie ushered them in, looking at Esteban in alarm. His steps were slow, he had lost weight, and his eyes had a haunted look. She'd like to show Jack Benton the results of his handiwork, she thought angrily.

When they were seated, Mr. Salazar spoke. "I give thanks every day to all the saints who brought my Esteban back, but I am worried about him. He is not well."

"Papa, it is nothing. I am only—" Esteban broke off in a fit of coughing—deep, racking coughs that continued until he was nearly out of breath.

"You see," his father said.

"Esteban, when did this begin?" Julie asked.

"At the camp. It rained, I think for days and I caught a cold. Many of the others did also. But mine stays with me—" Again, he coughed. He reached in his pocket for a rumpled handkerchief and put it to his mouth.

When the coughing spell was over, his father said to Julie, "There is blood on the handkerchief."

"Esteban?"

"Yes, there is blood. But not always. I will get over this soon. I must go back to work."

"Esteban," Julie said. "You must see a doctor. You are sick." She touched his shoulder to make her point and gasped when she saw his forearm, covered with festering sores.

"What is this?" she demanded.

"Bites of an ant, or of tics perhaps. I don't know."

"They're infected."

"In . . . fected? I don't understand."

"They are filled with poison." Julie stood up. "Mr. Salazar, you were right to bring your son here. Now, Esteban we are going to the health clinic."

"It is not necessary," he responded weakly.

"It is necessary. In fact, it is an emergency. Put on your jacket."

Julie found Father Curry and asked for his car. She ushered Esteban and his father out of the building. They spent most of the day waiting at the health clinic. A doctor examined Esteban, X rays were taken, and they waited again for the results.

"He has a massive bronchial infection and blood poisoning from the bites on his arm. I'm prescribing antibiotics, and he must stay in bed. Will you tell him that?" The doctor said.

Julie translated. Esteban nodded, until she mentioned bed rest, then he protested loudly. "I must find a job. I cannot stay in the bed."

"Esteban," Julie said patiently. "If you do not follow the doctor's orders, you will be too sick to find a job for a long time. You may even die."

Mr. Salazar, who had been listening quietly, began to wail. "Esteban, listen. God has not brought you back from the dead so that you should die again. Do as the doctor tells you."

"But I need to bring money home. I must work."

"*I* will find work," Mr. Salazar said.

Julie looked at the frail old man and knew he could not find a job. "The church will help you," she promised. *Or I will.*

On the way home Esteban sat with his eyes closed, his head thrown back against the seat. He seemed to doze off. Then a horn honked beside them. Esteban jerked upright,

his eyes flew open and he stared around him uncompre-
hendingly.

Julie was alarmed at his behavior. "What is it?" she
asked him.

"He is frightened by noises," Mr. Salazar explained.
"There were gunshots in the camp at night."

Oh, my God! Julie thought. "As soon as he's better, we'll
have to schedule counseling for him."

"What is counseling?" Mr. Salazar asked.

"He must talk with someone who will help him get over
these fears."

"Ah, as I did with you and when I came. That would be
good."

"Yes, but first we must get him well."

She dropped the men off at their house and returned to
the church just as Greg was pulling in. They met in the
middle of the parking lot.

"Hi." Greg's smile was the special kind that lovers give
one another.

Julie responded in kind. "Let me give Father Curry his
keys, and I'll be right back."

"Make it fast. I want to get someplace where we can say
hello properly."

She winked at him. "So do I."

On the way home, she told him about Esteban.

"That's the sort of information I want for my series on
immigrants, " he said earnestly. "I want to show what this
camp did to people, but more important, I want my readers
to understand why these people face incredible hardships to
cross the border and why they sat passively in insufferable
conditions in that camp instead of overpowering the guards
and breaking out. Will you help me?"

Without hesitation, Julie answered, "Yes."

He squeezed her hand. "Thank you."

"What can I do?" she asked.

"Convince these people to talk to me. Tell them I won't reveal anything that'll get them in trouble with the INS. I want to talk to the families whose men didn't come back as well as those who did. And I need to talk to others—to get an overall picture of the lives of both legals and undocumented workers."

"That's a lot to cover, but you'll have a wonderful series," Julie said.

"With your help," Greg smiled.

Julie smiled back, feeling the bond between them grow. "I'm going to talk to the Coalition," she said, "and ask them to set up a fund for the survivors of that camp. If the men are coming home sick, they won't be able to work. Something has to be done."

"My stories should help," Greg said. "Believe me, when the members of the Coalition read more about what these men went through, they'll be eager to help. But, if you like, I'll go with you to talk to them."

"Would you? I think that will convince them. And while we're there, we can set up some appointments with people you should talk to."

She settled back, shut her eyes and slept until Greg kissed her awake.

"Home, sleepyhead."

Inside, she checked her answering machine and heard a message from Jack. "Julie—" his tone was coaxing "—I want to talk to you. I'll call this evening."

Greg swore. "Has he been calling?"

"Today was the first time."

"And you refused police protection!"

"I doubt Jack would do anything but talk to me. Besides, I told you, I don't want someone hanging around, hovering over me."

He put his hands on her shoulders. "And I don't like Benton calling you. Let *me* hover, will you?" he urged. "I want to take care of you."

"I'm used to taking care of myself. I don't go for 'hovering,' but I will consider your 'hanging around.' Now let me see about dinner."

While they were eating, the telephone rang. Julie picked it up in the breakfast room. "Hello."

"Julie, I want to see you. I'm coming over."

"Jack, no! Don't come over. I don't—"

Greg got up and took the receiver from her hand. "Leave her alone, Benton," he said, his voice low and harsh. "Don't call again." He hung up and turned to Julie. "If that's hovering, you can learn to live with it. I won't have him harassing you."

Julie nodded. "It's okay." She hoped he couldn't see her hands trembling. Hearing from Jack again had unnerved her. She was glad Greg had stepped in.

Neither of them was hungry anymore, so she cleared the table and they talked more about Greg's articles. Julie gave him the name of a sociologist she knew who studied immigrant life-styles. She made a list of books she thought he should read. And she promised to introduce him to some activists in the Sanctuary movement.

Later they snuggled in her bed, watched the late news, and then made love. They fell asleep, curled in each other's arms.

This began a daily pattern. They would breakfast together, depart for their respective destinations, and meet again in the evening. Although Greg maintained his room at the Hyatt, they spent most nights at Julie's.

They spent hours talking about Greg's series, arguing over one point or another, discussing how a particular article should be slanted, making plans for Greg to see people who could give fresh perspectives on the issues.

Julie became as caught up in the project as Greg himself. She was positive the series would awaken readers to the plight of recent immigrants, was certain that no one could tell these people's stories as effectively as Greg. Of course, she admitted to herself, the fact that she had fallen in love with the man biased her.

After the discussions were over, every evening ended the same way—with passionate loving. In his bed or hers, lazy and lighthearted, or wild and urgent, it made no difference. For Julie, every night was heaven.

There were times, though, when she woke and lay in bed beside Greg, wondering. Thoughts would surface then, fears that Greg was more enamored with her expertise in working with immigrants and her numerous contacts in the Hispanic community than he was with her.

When these thoughts arose, she would push them aside, reminding herself that her relationship with Greg was a temporary one anyway, that by helping him with his stories she was helping her people, and that being with him made her blissfully happy.

Jack did not call again, but Julie still felt a faint sense of dread whenever the telephone rang, especially as the grand jury investigation approached. As expected, she received a summons to testify. Greg was more concerned than she was about her grand jury appearance.

She tried to reassure him. "I'm sorry to be dragged into this, but it was inevitable. Don't look so worried."

"Testifying will be rough on you."

"You're hovering again, Allen. I'll be fine."

"The press will be hanging around. I'm afraid they'll hound you. They'll see you as a 'love interest,' and they can be persistent."

"*You're* lecturing me about the evils of the press?"

"No, dammit. I'm being realistic."

She reached for his hand. "I appreciate your concern, but all I have to do is go in, testify, walk out, and avoid talking to anyone."

Greg mumbled something under his breath. "I'll drive you to the courthouse and pick you up afterward."

"If that'll make you happy." She pulled him close for a kiss.

As Julie had predicted, the grand jury questioning was strictly routine. At three-thirty, the jury foreman said, "We need to confer on a few points, Mrs. Whitaker. We'll take a fifteen-minute recess and you'll wind up your testimony shortly thereafter."

Julie went outside where her attorney was waiting since he was not permitted in the grand jury room.

"Everything okay?" he asked.

"Fine. We should be finished in a little while. I think I'll get something to drink. Can I bring you anything?"

"No thanks."

She strode down the hall, stopped to phone Greg and tell him she was almost ready to leave, then headed for the Coke machine she'd noticed earlier. As she rounded the corner, she swerved to avoid a tall man heading toward her, then saw that he was the one person in the world she least wanted to see. Jack Benton.

As nattily attired and confident as ever, he caught her arm. "Julie. We need to talk."

She gave him a cold stare. "We have nothing to talk about."

"Come on now. Surely you're not going to let this situation stand in the way of our friendship." He pulled her closer.

"We don't have a friendship, Jack. Or any kind of 'ship.' How can you even think of talking to me after all you've done?"

"Done?" He sounded genuinely puzzled.

"Why are you being investigated by the grand jury if you haven't 'done' anything?"

"Oh, that. Some of my employees got a little carried away. It was nothing."

"Nothing?" She couldn't believe the gall of the man. "Do you know how many lives were affected?"

"Julie, I didn't know what was happening on Padre. I gave orders to cut expenses, that's all. How they were cut, I didn't know." He shrugged.

Julie stared at him aghast. This man, standing here in his five-hundred-dollar suit talked as if the misery he had caused was nothing more than administrative oversight. "But those men. The camp. How did you think that happened?"

"Look, Julie. When I went down to Padre, I saw men working. Where they came from or where they lived wasn't my concern. I knew nothing about the camp until I saw it in the papers. And those stories were exaggerated. They were nothing but sensationalism. It's my understanding that the men in the so called 'camp' were well cared for and thoroughly compensated for their work."

Julie felt a blaze of anger, so intense she could literally see a red haze. "If that's what you think, Jack, then we certainly have nothing to talk about." She pulled her arm from his grasp and turned away.

His face changed then, from amiable to ugly. "It's all your fault, you know," he said in a low voice.

She stared at him, dumbfounded. "My fault? *My* fault? You're out of your mind."

"You heard me. Your fault. If you'd married me when I asked, I could have gotten out of this."

"What?"

"There'd have been enough money to pay off my loan. There was still time."

"You . . . you can't be serious," she gasped.

"Of course I'm serious." Like a chameleon, he changed his expression again, and his voice became cajoling. "It could still work out. Marry me, and we'll—"

"You . . . you despicable— Get out of my way," she choked.

Before he could answer, she was running down the hall. She saw a ladies' room, shoved the door open, and ran inside. Anger lashed at her like a tidal wave. Anger at what he'd done to his innocent victims, anger that he'd tried to use them *and* her for his own selfish ends. Tears flooded her eyes and poured down her cheeks. By the time her rage was spent, she was weak.

She turned on cool water and rinsed her tearstained cheeks. Then she squared her shoulders, combed her hair and put on fresh lipstick. If she ran into Jack Benton in the hall again she wouldn't give him the satisfaction of knowing he'd made her cry.

Her legs were shaky, but she made it back to the grand jury room, walked inside as if nothing had happened, and answered the remaining questions with her dignity intact.

Thank God, she thought when she was dismissed. Ignoring members of the press who were congregating outside the grand jury room she thanked her lawyer for accompanying her and bid him goodbye just as she spied Greg coming out of the elevator.

Greg saw Julie standing in the hallway. She looked . . . terrible. Chalk white. Eyes staring glassily. Alarmed, he sprinted across the hall to reach her. Standing so that he screened her from prying eyes, he asked in an undertone, "What's wrong?"

She shook her head. "Nothing. I'm fine."

"Like hell."

Hearing the murmur of voices behind him, he glanced over his shoulder. A throng of news people, both television and print reporters, clustered nearby. "I'm getting you out of here. Don't look at anyone, and don't say a word."

For the first time in his life, Greg mentally cursed the press. He took Julie's arm firmly and steered her across the hall, shielding her with his body from contact with the media. "No comment," he said tersely as questions were hurled at them. He ignored the baleful glances of his colleagues as he guided her toward the elevator. Fortunately no one tried to get in with them.

As the elevator moved to the first floor, he scrutinized Julie. She held her head high, but her hands were shaking. What the hell had happened in there, he wondered. The door opened, and he put his arm around her shoulders and hurried her outside.

He'd parked in a No Parking zone and had a ticket on his windshield, but that was the least of his worries. He stuffed the ticket into his pocket and helped Julie into the car.

He glanced at her anxiously as he started the engine. She still hadn't said a word. He made a quick decision and started for his hotel. When he turned into the garage, Julie spoke for the first time. "Why are we stopping here?"

"Because you're exhausted. You don't need an hour's drive home. I'm taking you upstairs and putting you to bed."

"Greg, please. I'm fine." She gave him a forced smile.

"You don't look fine," He pulled into a parking space, cut the engine, and turned to her. He tilted her chin up and looked into her eyes. "Listen to me," he said roughly. "You don't need to be strong 365 days a year. You're entitled to time off now and then." He put his arms around her and held her close. "Let me take care of you," he said against her hair.

She sighed and leaned against his chest. "Okay," she whispered.

He got out and came around to open her door. She looked so fragile he was tempted to lift her into his arms, but he knew she'd never tolerate being carried through the lobby. So he contented himself with putting an arm around her for support. When they reached his room, he led her to the bed, sat beside her, and took her hands in his.

"All right. What happened? What the hell did they ask you to get you this upset?"

"Nothing."

"Then why are you trembling? Why are you as pale as a ghost?"

"It wasn't the grand jury. It was—"

"Go on."

"It was . . . oh, damn, it was Jack."

His hands tightened on her arms. "What happened?"

"I saw him in the hall, and he said—"

"Julie, why did you talk to him? The police told you no contact with him."

She sighed tiredly. "Greg, I couldn't avoid him. We literally bumped into each other. He said he didn't know anything about what happened on Padre."

"Of course he said that. What did you expect him to do—admit he's a criminal? You have to expect that, honey. You shouldn't let it get you so upset."

"It wasn't that. He . . . he said it was my fault, that if I'd married him when he asked me, he could have paid off all his debts."

Greg felt his blood freeze. "He asked you to marry him? When?"

"At his party, the night before we were taken hostage."

"And?"

"And I said no." Her voice rose. "What do you think?"

"Were you in love with him?" he asked quietly. The thought that she might have cared for Benton hurt, but he had to know.

"In love with him? With Jack Benton? How could you even think that? I went out with him a few times . . . he was Dirk's friend . . . and he donated the heaters . . . but, in love with him? I didn't even like him. But no matter how I felt about him, it hurts to know he was . . . using me." Her voice was choked with tears. "It . . . just . . . hurts."

Greg sighed and pulled her close. "I know. You've been bruised and battered, and today was the last straw." He stroked her hair. "You need to rest now."

He drew away and began to remove her clothes. She sat passively as he undressed her, leaving only her panties and silk teddy. She let him lay her down and pull the covers over her. Then she sighed and shut her eyes.

Greg frowned thoughtfully at her limp form, then stripped down to his shorts and got in bed beside her.

"Greg?" she mumbled.

"Hush, I'm just going to hold you. Go to sleep, love."

The endearment came to his lips so automatically that he wasn't aware of it until he heard himself say the word. *Love.* He'd never called another woman that. Funny. With Julie, it seemed natural.

He'd called her "love," Julie thought drowsily. Probably didn't mean anything. Probably called all his women that. Still, it was nice to hear, and so nice to have his arms around her . . .

She drifted off to sleep.

When he was sure she was sleeping soundly, Greg got up and went to his desk to work. As soon as she stirred, he turned. "Feel better?" he asked lightly, trying to hide his concern.

"Much. I'm hungry, though."

She looked so lovely, sitting there in nothing but ivory silk, her hair falling in soft ringlets around her shoulders. She might be hungry for food, but the sight of her made him crave other things. But he forced his thoughts away from his needs and onto hers. "Get dressed, and I'll treat you to the best steak the Hyatt has to offer."

SATURDAY NIGHT Julie and Greg were invited to dinner at the Barneses. Julie had been pleased, and now in the living room after a delicious meal, she was obviously having a good time. She'd bounced back quickly after Monday's trauma, Greg thought. But he expected nothing less of her. She was a strong woman.

He watched her across the room, talking animatedly with Sylvia. Her hair shone in the light from the chandelier. The soft folds of the turquoise silk dress she wore gave tantalizing hints of what was beneath them. But he knew. The contours of her body were as familiar to him as his own—

"—about his chances?"

He'd probably lost the last five minutes of conversation. "Uh, I—"

"Didn't hear me. Sightseeing, huh?" Phil chuckled, and Greg saw him glance across the room at the slim calves below the turquoise silk. "Nice view. What I said was, what do you think the chances are that Benton will be indicted?"

"Good. The net's closing in. Three guesses who owns the land where the workers were kept."

"Benton of course."

"Right the first time. Also," Greg lowered his voice, "I heard off the record that Bud has some pretty incriminating evidence against Benton. Looks like old Bud is smarter than anybody gave him credit for. Just to make sure he didn't take the rap if they got caught, he tape-recorded his conversations with Benton."

"Those probably won't be admissible in court," Phil pointed out.

"Yeah, but the grand jury heard them. Also, Bud kept records of all his 'transactions' with Benton and sent him copies."

"I'll lay you ten to one Benton destroyed them."

"No. Bud sent them to Jack's secretary. Since they appeared to be invoices for 'merchandise,' she filed them."

"And they were found?"

"When the D.A.'s office seized Benton's records, there they were sitting in the files, nice and neat as you please."

"Have you told Julie?"

"No. I haven't told anyone. Benton's got a hell of a smart lawyer. If this gets out, he'd say it prejudiced his client's chances for a fair trial."

"Right. By the way, Allen," he added, "you're doing an outstanding job on the immigrant series."

"Thanks."

"You know, I've followed your writing for some time, but there's something new and different in your style."

"Yeah, the change comes across, doesn't it?" Greg said thoughtfully.

Phil nodded. "Loud and clear. Your stories have always been good, but they're more...human now."

"It's Julie's doing," Greg said, glancing at her.

"Oh?"

"Yeah. In the past I've seen an assignment as a challenge to be met, a puzzle to be solved. Now I see an opportunity to tell someone's story, to let the public feel it the way the individual who experienced it did.'' Greg smiled, a slow, secret curving of his lips. "I guess the woman's touch makes the difference." His eyes drifted back to Julie. He didn't bother adding that he meant "a special woman," but he suspected Phil knew.

Phil leaned back and lit a cigar. "So, what do you think of Houston?" he asked, surprising Greg with the change of subject.

"It's a great city. It suffered a setback with the oil crisis, but it's coming back. I like Houston."

"Like it well enough to consider a move here?"

Greg stared at him in surprise.

"I'm impressed with your work, Allen. I'd like to see you move your base of operations to Houston."

Greg considered for a moment, then said, "I'm flattered, of course. But I've never thought of leaving Washington."

"Houston's closer to Latin America. Lots of action here, too, as you already know."

He was tempted. The thought of Julie on a long-term basis was more appealing than he cared to admit. But Worldwide's headquarters were in Washington. His career demanded that he be there, too. Besides, Julie wasn't considering a permanent arrangement, and neither was he...was he? He shook his head. "I appreciate the offer, but right now I can't justify a move."

Phil gave him an enigmatic smile. "Really?" He glanced across the room to where Julie sat, engrossed in conversation with his wife. He took another puff of his cigar and blew a smoke ring. "Well, in case you change your mind, the offer's always open."

THE FOLLOWING TUESDAY the grand jury indicted Jack Benton.

"I'm glad," Julie said when Greg told her. "He deserves to pay for what he did to all those people."

"He's got a top-flight attorney. They'll do everything they can to delay a trial."

"Yes."

"And when the trial does come up, you'll have to testify."

"I know."

That worried him. He wouldn't be around to act as a buffer between Julie and the press. Maybe he could talk Lowrey into letting him cover the trial.

"Testifying during the trial won't be as easy as it was for the grand jury. Benton'll have a defense attorney there trying to poke holes in your testimony."

"I don't care. I'll go through whatever's necessary to see he gets what he deserves."

"I know you will. You're one tough lady."

They sat quietly for a moment, then Julie said, "I had some news today, too. Nanda Morales came by to see me. You remember her, don't you?"

"How could I forget? Her husband was kidnapped, and you didn't tell Father Gregory."

"Well, Carlos has been found. She got word through a cousin that he was deported. He's in Matamoros, and he's trying to make it back across." She waited for Greg's reaction, expecting him to be as excited by the news as she was. Instead he sat staring thoughtfully into space.

"I'd like to talk to the cousin," he said finally.

"Why?"

"To get some information," he said vaguely. "Think you can arrange it?"

"Probably."

She managed to set up a meeting between Greg and Nanda's cousin for the next Monday.

Monday evening, she was in the kitchen when the doorbell rang three times. Greg's special ring. As soon as she opened the door, she was lifted off the ground and held for a long, thorough kiss.

When he put her down, she gave him an appraising look. "You're in a good mood. Your meeting must have gone well."

"Fantastic," he replied. "These people have an amazingly efficient grapevine. He's going to get word to Carlos, and next week I'll go down to Matamoros."

"Why?" She didn't like the look on his face—the reckless grin, the too-bright eyes. "Why do you need to go to Matamoros?" she repeated.

"Honey, I'm writing a story on immigration. When Carlos crosses the border, I'm going with him.

CHAPTER THIRTEEN

"WHAT!" Julie backed away from him so abruptly that she bumped into the table in the entry hall. "That's crazy," she said, stumbling into the living room and sitting on the couch. Her legs felt too weak to support her.

Greg sat beside her. "Border crossings are part of the immigrations picture, in fact the most important part."

"But . . . but they're illegal."

"Not for an American," he pointed out logically.

"Not if he walks the bridge the usual way. But that's not what you're planning to do. You're planning to swim the river."

"Yes."

"And that's dangerous . . . even for an American," she said, voicing her real concern. She couldn't bear the thought of anything happening to him. "You're not going to be wearing a U.S. flag or something, to identify yourself. What if you get shot?" She heard her voice rising in alarm and bit her lip. Forcing a calmer tone, she added, "What if you get picked up by Immigration?"

"I won't be." Again, the reckless, devil-may-care smile.

A little boy playing cowboys and Indians, she thought. He'd been cooped up in the city too long. Now he was ready for an adventure. Angry at him for being foolhardy, angry at herself for caring, she said vehemently, "I think it's a ridiculous idea."

"Hey, wait a minute," Greg told her, eyes narrowed. "This is *my* story, remember?"

"I'm just telling you what I think."

"Do that then. But don't try to dictate."

His words stung. What right did she have to try to influence him? She was just a passing fancy, a woman whose name he probably wouldn't remember a year from now. Lately she'd been daydreaming of more than a temporary affair—picturing herself and Greg strolling on the beach in summer, decorating a Christmas tree, maybe even furnishing a nursery. Suddenly she felt tired and sad. She stared down at her hands. "I'm sorry," she mumbled.

"Apology accepted." He smiled at her.

She watched the way his lips curved, looked into the deep blue eyes that had become so dear to her. She'd go crazy waiting, wondering, worrying while he was at the border— "Take me with you," she said suddenly.

"What?"

"I want to go along." Her voice was firmer now. She wouldn't let him leave her in Houston.

"Have you lost your mind? Border crossings are no place for a woman. The Rio Grande's not a swimming hole—the current's strong. It's far too dangerous."

"Exactly what I told *you*."

"Too rigorous then," he amended. "And don't get that stubborn look on your face," he added when her chin came up. "The last time you insisted on coming where you didn't belong, you were held at gunpoint and ended up in the hospital."

"Greg—"

"Besides," he went on, not giving her a chance to interrupt, "You'd slow us down, put all of us in jeopardy."

That gave her pause. "All right. I'll drive down with you and wait in Brownsville while you cross."

"Why do you want to do this?" He sounded both puzzled and frustrated.

Because I love you. Because I can't sit here while you're four hundred miles away and wonder if you've been beaten or robbed or worse. "I've been to Brownsville before, Matamoros, too. I could help you find your way around."

Greg laughed. "Honey, I spend my life finding my way around in unfamiliar places."

She bit her lip. "I just want to be with you," she said. She'd spoken the truth. His series was almost done, and soon he'd be leaving her permanently. Every moment was precious.

His expression softened. "I want to be with you, too." He touched her cheek. "Come with me then, but on two conditions."

"What?"

"One, you don't even think of crossing with me and two, we don't visit Benton's construction site or the camp. I don't want to rehash that situation."

She drew a breath of relief. "All right. Now, my condition. I want to go to Matamoros to see Carlos, to make sure he's okay."

"I can go along with that." He tipped her chin up with his finger. "A kiss to seal our agreement?" he coaxed. When she complied, he sighed and pulled her closer. "Let's go down a day early and just spend some time together."

She nestled against his chest, enjoying his warmth, his strength, the feeling that he was hers even if temporarily. "Let's do that," she murmured.

THEY LEFT HOUSTON early Friday morning and drove south toward the Rio Grande Valley. Half an hour out of the city they came upon a field of bluebonnets. At Julie's insistence, Greg pulled over and stopped. "No Texan can see bluebonnets like this and pass them by," she told him.

She got out of the car and waded into the sea of blue. She took a deep breath, drawing in the sweet scents of earth and grass and flowers—of spring—then turned to Greg and spread her arms, laughing. "Isn't this wonderful? Can anything in the East compare?"

"Only the cherry blossoms in Washington."

Her smile faded. This was the first time he'd mentioned Washington. He'd be going back soon. "I guess you miss being there," she said.

Greg laughed and pulled her into his arms, thinking he'd rather be here than anywhere else in the world. "How could I miss Washington and cherry blossoms when I have bluebonnets and you?"

She sighed and tightened her arms around him, wishing she could hold him here forever.

They returned to the car and drove on. As the hours went by, the bluebonnets disappeared. The terrain became more desertlike, with cactus, sage and yucca. Oak trees gave way to low, spreading mesquite, their feathery leaves waving in the light breeze, their branches twisting skyward. The landscape, unrelieved by hills, stretched endlessly before them, arid and desolate.

In Victoria they stopped at a grocery store and bought sandwich makings, then pulled into a roadside park, spread a blanket and picnicked under the open sky. Afterward, Greg lay with his head in Julie's lap and shut his eyes.

She sat quietly, just looking at him—his sandy tousled hair, his lean body, his mouth that knew so well how to please her. What she loved most were his eyes. They were a shade of blue that appeared light at first glance but could darken to smoky sapphire in the space of heartbeats. *I love you,* she thought, and wished she could tell him. But she

wouldn't spoil their time together by confessing to feelings
he wouldn't want to hear, feelings he didn't reciprocate. So
she loved silently, glad his eyes were closed so he couldn't
read the message in hers.

He wasn't asleep, though. He reached for her hand and
held it to his cheek. "You have beautiful hands," he murmured drowsily, eyes still shut. "Beautiful skin, too. So soft.
And a beautiful name. Julie. Is that your full name or a
nickname?" he asked, opening his eyes and looking up at
her.

"Nickname."

"For what? Juliette, Julia?"

"Juliana."

"What's your middle name?"

"Christine. Why do you want to know?"

He brought her hand to his lips. "I want to know everything about you."

Julie's heart trembled at his words. Then she reminded
herself that he might have said the same thing to countless
women, countless times.

Greg realized, as he pressed soft kisses on her palm, that
he'd never said those words to a woman before. Why had he
chosen to say them to Julie? Perhaps it was the situation.
Lazy contentment on a day ripe with spring and the sight of
her—the soft breeze ruffling her hair, her lips curved in a
tender smile. Or perhaps it was something else—an emotion he wasn't ready to name.

He lay still a while longer, letting himself doze, then got
to his feet and pulled Julie up beside him. "Onward," he
said.

As the afternoon wore on and they neared their destination, they saw palm trees and citrus orchards. Greg felt as
if they were entering a tropical paradise.

He wanted to pretend that was all there was to this trip. A lovely woman, the balmy climate, a brief excursion to enjoy the delights of a foreign country—shopping for souvenirs, eating an exotic meal, then returning to their hotel to make love.

But both of them knew their real purpose in coming here. As each road sign told them they were getting closer to Brownsville, he felt the tension build. His fingers tightened on Julie's, and he felt her grip his hand in return.

He didn't want to face reality, not yet. Maybe because, for the first time in his career, he was acutely aware of the dangers that might lie ahead of him. Oh, he'd always known. But he'd accepted them, even relished them. Now they weren't so appealing. Perhaps because he knew how they affected Julie. *Putting a woman before your career, Allen? That's a new one for you. Danger is part of your life.* He'd have to think about that . . . later.

Now he resolved to push thoughts and fears aside for one more night, to give himself . . . and Julie . . . one evening of fantasy before reality set in.

In Brownsville they checked in at the Fort Brown Hotel. Surrounded by palm trees and lagoons, or *resacas*, the hotel was a quiet oasis in the midst of the bustle of downtown traffic, a perfect setting for fantasy.

In their room Greg made dinner reservations while Julie went into the shower. Then he shucked off his clothes and strolled naked into the bathroom.

He could see Julie's silhouette through the frosted glass of the shower door—slender legs, trim buttocks, softly rounded breasts. Her head was thrown back as she lathered herself with soap, and above the sound of the water he could hear her singing a Mexican ballad. His loins tightened.

He walked toward the shower, enjoying the sight of her. Then he opened the door and stepped inside.

Julie gasped. "You scared me to death. You . . . oh!"

He pressed her against him and muffled her words with his mouth. Water sluiced over them, but he hardly noticed. His hands began to move in sensuous circles over the soapy skin of her back and buttocks. "You were saying?" he murmured.

"I . . . just wondered . . . what you were doing here." Her breathing was shallow, her eyes already dark with passion.

He chuckled softly. "Saving time. We have a dinner reservation, remember?"

"Mmm."

"In fact, I think we should cut this shower short."

He reached behind her and turned off the faucets, then drew her out of the shower stall. Taking the bath towel from the rack behind him, he wrapped it around her, blotting droplets of water from her back. She clung to him, her eyes closed, her lips parted.

"Wrap your legs around me, baby," he whispered hoarsely as he lifted her. He carried her to the bed and lowered her to the mattress, his weight pressing her down. There was no waiting, no slow buildup. Passion was at its apex. He entered her swiftly, and within seconds they climaxed, shuddering. He heard her call his name, heard himself respond, then felt only dizzying pleasure. He collapsed on her, too spent to move for a moment, then rolled to his side, still joined with her, and clasped her against his heart.

They lay silently for a while, half dozing, until Julie whispered, "What about those dinner reservations?"

"Those? The Yacht Club has three seatings. I took the late one."

She laughed. "You devil."

He raised a brow. "A fall from grace?"

"Definitely." She kissed him thoroughly.

When they had regained sufficient energy, they got up and finished getting ready for dinner. Greg buttoned Julie's dress for her, enjoyed the sight of her slim legs as she fastened on silver high-heeled sandals, then leaned against the door and watched her put the final touches to her makeup. He'd never paid much attention to the ways in which a woman completed her toilette, but now he found himself engrossed in the way she put on lip gloss, fluffed her hair, straightened an earring. The intimacy of the scene touched something inside him, something even deeper than the passion they'd shared moments ago.

Thoughtfully, he turned and picked up his jacket. "Ready?"

She nodded, and they left the room.

The Yacht Club was in the tiny town of Port Isabel, across from the southern tip of Padre Island. The decor was Spanish, with dark beamed ceilings, white walls, and red carpets. They ordered seafood. Greg sat back, pleased that he'd picked this spot. Julie was enjoying herself, and most important, she was relaxed, tomorrow's business seemingly banished to the far recesses of her mind.

He smiled at her over his wineglass. "You look beautiful tonight."

"Thank you."

"I love you in blue," he continued. "You were wearing blue the first day I met you. I wanted you from the beginning."

Her lips curved. "Mmm. I wanted you, too."

He clucked his tongue. "In the church parlor? Hussy."

"No, I saw you before that."

"Where?"

"On the street. You were running that morning. I didn't know who you were, but I saw that sexy body in shorts, and

I was tempted to stop my car, drag you inside, and ravish you."

"Honey, anytime you want to ravish me, be my guest."

"I'll remember that later," she promised.

When they finished dinner and walked outside, arms around each other, to get their car, she paused and took a deep breath. "You can smell the Gulf," she sighed. She turned her face up. "Look at the moon. You feel like you can almost touch it. Isn't it beautiful?"

Greg pulled her closer. "*You're* beautiful," he said huskily and kissed her.

Her arms went to his shoulders, and she clung. He could have stood there kissing her forever, tasting her sweetness, but they were interrupted by the sound of voices.

"Greg," Julie laughed breathlessly, "we can't do this here. There're people around."

"Are there? I can't see anyone but you." He stared into her eyes, not caring who walked by, not wanting to move. Finally, he said, "Let's go home. I want to make love to you."

She laid her head on his shoulder for a moment. "Drive fast," she whispered.

But he didn't. He wanted to savor the anticipation of what was ahead. At the hotel, he took her arm. "Walk with me," he murmured. They strolled along the *resaca*, watching the moonlight play over the water. He stopped beneath a palm tree, pulled her close and kissed her deeply.

She drew back and traced her fingers over his lips. "Let's go in," she breathed.

In their room they made love slowly as befitted a fantasy. There were no words, no sounds but soft sighs. Only the sweet, flowery scent of her, the whisper of her fingers across his skin. Only the warm depths of her body as she took him deep within her. Then the fierce tide of pleasure, and finally, sleep.

THE FANTASY WAS OVER.

They rose early the next morning, ate a quick breakfast, and drove across the international bridge to Matamoros. The bright sunshine of the previous day had given way to clouds. Below them churned the muddy brown waters of the Rio Grande, swollen by spring rains.

The radio was turned to a Spanish rock station, the heavy beat of the music and the strident voice of the singer adding to the tension.

Hands clenched tightly in her lap, Julie stared out of the window. Near the bridge, on the town's main street, tourists were already thronging to shops, coming out laden with bags and boxes.

Along the street, sidewalk vendors hawked fake silver jewelry, papier mâché figures, cheaply woven blankets. She saw a middle-aged couple stop and haggle over a necklace, laughing as they bargained with the seller. Hard to believe that only a few blocks away life was deadly serious. Did these tourists imagine, as they casually crossed the bridge, how many men were waiting to cross in the other direction? How many men were willing to risk life and limb to reach *el norte*, the promised land?

Julie glanced at Greg. His face was set in somber lines as he turned off the avenue and maneuvered the car through narrow streets. They drove to an area of ramshackle huts and parked in front of one. She followed Greg through the weedy front yard and waited as he knocked on the door.

A man opened it. *"Buenos dias,"* he said. "I am Carlos Morales." He shook the hand Greg extended, then turned to Julie. *"Señora Whitaker, por favor*...please...come in. *Señora*, my cousin told me you would be in Brownsville, but

I did not expect you here." He spread his hands. "The house—I am sorry I cannot offer you better hospitality."

It was little more than a hovel. The living room held a couch whose springs were visible through the torn upholstery, a wooden bookshelf with a small TV, and nothing else. A stack of blankets piled in one corner attested to the fact that this place served as a way station for travelers on their way to the border.

But Julie cared little for the surroundings. She touched Carlos's arm. "I did not come to see the house," she assured him in Spanish. "I came to see for myself how *you* are."

"Sit down, *señora*, Señor Allen. I am well...strong... ready for work."

Julie wasn't certain of that. She studied him carefully. She hadn't met him before, but she knew he could be no more than twenty-five years old. Young and handsome, Nanda had described him. Yet the man before her bore the ravages of his ordeal in the camp. His face was gaunt, his eyes shadowed. True, there were vestiges of youthful good looks, but he seemed old before his time. Her heart ached for him.

"My wife," he asked eagerly as he sat down beside her on the couch. "She is well?"

"Nanda is fine. She is waiting for you, and the baby."

"Ah, he is not here yet."

Julie smiled at him. "No, he...or she...waits for you."

"I will be there." Then he turned to Greg, who had seated himself on the floor. "We cross tonight."

At his words Julie felt the first taste of real fear. It rammed into her stomach, then spread until it numbed her whole body. The room seemed suddenly much colder. Yet she forced herself to sit calmly and listen as Greg said, "Good. Where? When?"

Carlos gave him an indulgent look, the look of a professional confronting a novice. "We make plans only to go. How and where, we will arrange today. There is a park a mile from here. We will go there and find a *coyote*."

"Why?" Julie asked. "Why not just go yourselves?"

Carlos looked surprised. "That is the way it is done," he said, shaking his head as if that explained everything. Then, seeing Julie's puzzled frown, he tried to elaborate. "With a *coyote*, it is safer. They know the best ways. When the river is high, they have boats."

"How will you find a *coyote*?" Julie asked. She had heard stories of these smugglers of men. Some were benign, like the young man who had ferried Carmela Sanchez across the river on his back. Others were notorious for swindling *pollos*—chickens, as they called their human cargo. She suppressed a shiver.

Carlos laughed. "Do not worry, *señora*. There are *coyotes* everywhere. We will go to the park, and one will find us.

He offered them coffee, bringing a pot from the minuscule kitchen, which opened off the living room. Julie accepted a cup, although she wasn't certain she could force it down. But the warm, strong liquid melted away some of her fear.

As they drank, men began entering the house. Soon the small room was crowded with at least a dozen, all wearing an air of suppressed excitement. Carlos introduced Greg, explaining his purpose in accompanying them. Most of the men accepted the idea, several voicing their interest in having their story communicated to the *norteamericanos*. Two of them opposed the idea—one of these left; another grumbled sullenly but stayed.

At last one of the men rose. "It is time," he said, and the group crowded toward the door. Julie looked uncertainly at

Greg. She had expected the arrangements to be completed before they arrived. Should she go with them to the park or stay behind? He put out his hand. "Come," he said softly.

"Would you rather I wait?"

He shook his head. "I don't want to leave you here."

Relieved, because she didn't want to stay, she followed him out.

The temperature was warm, near eighty, and Julie felt a trickle of sweat between her breasts. Half an hour ago she had been shivering; now she was almost feverishly hot. Fear did that to you, she realized.

As they trooped along the narrow, dusty street they saw other men heading in the same direction, sometimes in twos and threes, sometimes in groups as large as theirs. She heard snatches of conversation:

"—near the bridge is too dangerous. It is better to cross by—"

"—a job in Chicago."

"The last time I crossed—"

"Once I was picked up in Phoenix—"

She realized that what was going on was a common occurrence for these men. How did they handle the uncertainty and danger with such stoicism? How did their women cope?

When they reached the park, they found it already crowded with men lounging on benches or sprawling on the grass. She saw only one or two other women. She sat down beside a palm tree, keeping in the background. Greg was involved in a conversation with one of their companions, a boy not more than eighteen who, she heard someone say, was making his second border crossing.

Carlos came and sat beside her. "By tomorrow night all these men will be gone."

There were easily fifty men in the park. "And others will take their places?" Julie asked.

"*Sí*. Mexico exports more *majados*, wetbacks, to the United States than anything else." He grinned at her, and she could see traces of the young man he must have been.

"When you get back, Carlos, I want you to come see me. You must have a medical examination."

"Ah, no." He brushed off the idea. "I am healthy, I told you."

"We must be sure of that. For your baby's sake."

"For the baby then."

Julie glanced around them. "Where are the *coyotes*?"

"All around you. See?" He gestured to a swarthy man in a black silk shirt who was talking to two men across the way.

Julie grimaced as the man made a dismissive gesture, turned and approached their group. He was a big man with a thin mustache and slicked-back hair. He looked like Hollywood's depiction of a small-time gangster.

Carlos left her and went to join the group's representatives, who were clustered around the smuggler. Julie heard their voices rise as they argued over price, then the *coyote* turned and walked away.

Carlos came back to her side. "Too much," he said. "He wanted four hundred dollars apiece. We can do better." He sat down again, and Greg joined them.

As the morning wore on, several more men approached them. Finally around noon a small, wiry fellow sidled up. "Thinking of making a trip?" he asked Carlos.

Carlos shrugged. "Maybe."

The man laughed, letting out a steam of whiskey-laced breath. "How many are you?"

"Eleven."

"For such a group, I will take you for one hundred in advance and another hundred when the trip is done. Two hundred each."

Carlos went to confer with his companions, then returned. "All right."

The man grinned, showing a gold tooth. "We go at nightfall."

Julie shivered. She hated the thought of entrusting Greg to the dubious protection of this vile-looking person.

The *coyote* moved from one traveler to another, collecting bills and coins. When he had received a wad of crumpled bills from Carlos, he turned to leave.

"Wait!" Carlos told him. He gestured to Greg. *"Otro"*

"Another?" The *coyote* stared at Greg. "He is a *gringo*.

"He is, but—"

"So let him walk across the bridge." He looked distrustfully at Greg.

"I can't," Greg said.

"No papers, hmm?" the man said providing his own explanation. "What did you do over there—kill someone, rob a bank?"

Greg shrugged as if to say that was his business.

The smuggler stared at him, considering for a moment, then said, "For you, three hundred."

Greg nodded and brought out a stack of bills.

The *coyote* counted and pocketed them, then suddenly looked at Julie. "This your woman?" he asked Greg.

"Yes." Greg moved closer to Julie and put a protective arm around her shoulder.

"I don't transport women," he said flatly.

"She does not go with us," Carlos put in quickly.

"Right," Greg said. "She will go back across the bridge and wait for me." His hand tightened on her shoulder, and she nodded.

The man seemed satisfied with the assurance that she would not accompany them. "All right," he said. "Be here at sundown. Someone will pick you up." He turned and left them.

The arrangements made, their group dispersed. Julie, Greg and Carlos walked back to the house together.

"Where will we cross?" Greg asked.

"Probably a mile or so this side of bridge, where there are trees along the river and we will not be seen so easily." When they reached the house, he drew Greg a crude map. "It is a good night for crossing," he remarked. "Cloudy."

"We'll go now to get ready," Greg told him. "I'll be back before sundown."

"Bring a bag to carry your clothes," Carlos instructed. "And wear boots if you have them. To protect from the snakes."

Julie cringed, but Greg merely nodded his assent.

"Goodbye, *señora*," Carlos said, turning to Julie.

She took his hands. "Take care," she said. "And remember, when you get back to Houston, come to see me."

Carlos walked with them to their car. Julie looked at him, at his tired face, at the shirt that hung loosely on is too-thin frame. The weeks in Jack's camp had taken their toll on his health. The crossing would not be easy for him. She glanced at the trunk of their car. How simple it would be to put Carlos there, cover him with a blanket, and just drive across the bridge. He would be spared a dangerous crossing . . . and so would Greg.

Greg followed her gaze. He took her arm and led firmly to the car. "No," he said, his tone unequivocal.

Inside the car Julie turned to him. "No, what?"

"No, we will not smuggle Carlos across the bridge in our car." He turned on the engine and pulled away from the curb.

"The river's so high. The current looks treacherous."

"Then there'll be a boat."

"But—"

"Drop it, Julie. I told you from the beginning, this is my story, and we'll do it my way."

She was furious. "I'm thinking about Carlos. *You're* thinking about your story."

Greg slammed on the brakes and pulled over. He looked as angry as she felt. "No, dammit. I'm thinking about you. Would you like to be charged with smuggling an alien? We're talking about a federal offense here. And don't ask me to do it, either. However I may feel, I'm not down here to break the law. I came as an observer, nothing else." His voice quieted and he reached for her hand. "Honey, I know you want to help Carlos. But you can't put all of us in jeopardy to do it. He'll be all right—"

"And you?" she asked in a small voice.

"So will I. Hey, let's not waste time arguing. We have things to do."

He started the car again, and they drove to a small grocery store where he bought a plastic net bag to carry his clothes. Then they returned to the American side of the border. They drove until they found the dirt road that paralleled the river and located the approximate spot where the men would cross.

Julie looked at the desolate area. They were a good five miles from their hotel. "I'll bring the car and pick you up."

"The hell you will," Greg muttered.

Julie raised her chin. "Try and stop me."

"I don't want you out here. Immigration patrols these roads."

"So? It's not a crime for an American to be here."

"You'll be alone—"

"I'll keep the car locked."

He groaned in frustration. "Julie—"

"Argue all you like, Greg. I'm coming. I'm not going to sit in a motel room twiddling my thumbs while you walk back."

They faced each other across the seat, an immovable object and an irresistible force.

"Stubborn—"

"Muleheaded—"

They spoke together, then Greg spread his hands in defeat. "Okay, you win. But don't come before eleven. And if anything happens to you, I swear I'll throttle you."

JULIE PARKED THE CAR at the rendezvous point and cut the engine. Darkness hung over the land like a vast black curtain. Clouds blotted out the moon and stars. At first she could see nothing. Then, as her eyes adjusted, she became aware of the dark silhouettes of trees.

From inside the car she could hear nothing but the pounding of her heart.

She glanced at the luminous dial of her watch. Eleven-fifteen. Six hours since she had dropped Greg off at Carlos's. When he was about to get out of the car, she'd felt a moment of pure panic. She'd wanted to grab him, plead with him not to go. Instead she'd made herself sound calm, almost casual. "Be careful," she'd told him. "I want you back in one piece."

He'd smiled at her and pulled her against him for a quick hard kiss. Then he was gone.

Where was he now? She pictured the men, waiting to cross the river, hiding in the shadows among the trees and rattler-infested brush. Then crossing the Rio Grande, fighting the river's swift current. What if they were seen, caught?

Even if they eluded the Border Patrol, there were other dangers. Snakes and scorpions, both animal and human.

She'd heard tales of men who lay in wait along the border, robbing and beating those who crossed.

She checked her watch again. Eleven-eighteen. How could time move so slowly? Maybe music would calm her nerves. She turned on a soft rock station but she couldn't concentrate. She picked up a pair of binoculars she'd brought and peered out the opposite window.

She saw nothing, though she knew somewhere out there men were moving through the darkness. Where was Greg? She strained to see, squinting into the glasses—

A sound came from behind her. Someone was knocking on the window. She gasped, dropped the binoculars, and turned to see a car parked alongside hers, blocking it. Two men were standing at her window, the other car's spotlight so bright she couldn't see who they were. Only that they were big. And here she was. Alone, miles from anyone, without a weapon.

One of them was saying something. She turned off the radio and rolled the window down an inch.

"Border Patrol, ma'am," the man said. "You having a problem?"

Were they Border Patrol? In the glare, she couldn't tell. "No...no problem...I—"

"What are you doing out here in the middle of nowhere?"

She'd rehearsed an answer should this happen. But it escaped her. "I'm...I'm...bird watching." She'd read somewhere that this area was in the migration path of waterfowl.

"Bird watching, that's a new one," he said over his shoulder to his partner. "Okay, lady. Out of the car."

Out of the car? No way. Border Patrol or not, there were two of them and one of her. Wasn't the best defense a good offense? "Let me see some identification first." She made her voice strong.

Obligingly, the man held his ID up to the window.

Stall. "Turn off your spotlight. I can't see."

He gestured to his companion. With only the headlights on, Julie could see the official insignia on the other car and the men's uniforms.

"Satisfied, lady?" the patrolman said impatiently.

She nodded and slid out.

"You're mighty close to the border, ma'am," the second officer said. "We're going to have to search your car." He turned on the spotlight again.

Julie gave him a haughty stare and hoped he couldn't see her knees shaking. "Is it against the law for me to be here?"

"No, ma'am, but the Rio Grande's just two hundred yards away," he said as he began methodically checking the front seat. "You shouldn't be out here alone. Too dangerous."

"I'm not alone," she said quickly. She wanted these men to think she had protection. And Greg was here... somewhere. "My friend's with me."

The officer turned and gave her a disbelieving stare. "Where's your friend?"

"He'll be right back." She felt a cold sweat. Where was he?

The men began on the back seat. "Sure he didn't get lost?" one of them asked.

"Of course not. He's...he's..."

"Right here," said a familiar voice behind them. Julie turned to see Greg ambling toward them, as nonchalantly as if he'd been to the corner grocery. He came up to the car and put an arm around Julie. She sagged against him, weak with relief.

"What's the problem, officer?" he asked.

"You her friend?"

Greg nodded.

"You 'bird watching,' too?"

Again, he nodded.

"Where've you been?"

Greg gave him an easy smile. "Out there," he said, gesturing vaguely toward the darkness. "No service stations around here."

"Yeah, well, we've got to look in your trunk."

"Certainly. Give him the keys, darling." Greg tightened his hold on Julie's arm. *Just a few more minutes,* his touch seemed to say.

Julie scanned the blackness around them. Once she thought she saw a movement in the trees to her left, but the two officers were so involved in going through the trunk that they were unaware of it. When they had satisfied themselves that the car held no drugs or illegals, they headed for their own vehicle.

"Wouldn't recommend this place for bird watching," one of them said. "You're asking for trouble out here." They got into their car and pulled away.

Julie and Greg stood immobile until the car's taillights disappeared, then Greg pulled her into his arms. She clutched him, relief buckling her legs, making her tremble uncontrollably. Greg held her close, stroking her hair. "It's all over," he murmured.

"I know," she choked, half laughing, half crying. "Carlos? Did he get across?"

"They all did. In fact, they passed right by us while the officers were distracting themselves with the car."

"I thought I saw someone." She narrowed her eyes and looked at him. "Are you all right?"

"I told you I'd be fine. And you, my little bird watcher, are you all right, too?"

"Now that you're back, yes."

"Good. Let's go back to the hotel and have a reunion."

They were silent on the drive back. In their room, they made love quickly, almost desperately. Then, wrapped in Greg's arms, Julie fell asleep.

She woke near dawn to find him at the desk, typing on his portable computer. She got up and went to look over his shoulder at the final paragraphs of his story:

We stripped to our shorts and stuffed our clothing into the bags we had brought. Then we waded into the Rio Grande. The current pulled at us, forcing us downstream. C— lost his footing and went under. The man beside him pulled him up. It was useless to go on. The water was too deep and the current too strong. We headed back for the Mexican shore.

The *coyote* sent his two young helpers for a boat, meanwhile motioning us to dress quickly and hide in a ditch some yards back from the riverbank. Here we crouched for half an hour, waiting, each of us deep in his own thoughts. A breeze came up, chilling our still-damp bodies. From above us came the drone of a Border Patrol surveillance helicopter. *"La migra"* someone whispered, but otherwise there was no talk.

At last our "boat" arrived—the overturned hood of an old car. C— and I and two others clambered in, seating ourselves on wooden planks. The two boys joined us and using planks for paddles, began ferrying us across. Balance was precarious. We threatened to capsize at least every thirty seconds. Debris swept by us—tree branches, grass, trash. The boys paddled furiously, and in less than ten minutes we were across. We jumped out, and I turned to watch them steer back across the river, but C— grabbed my arm. "Down," he snarled, and I saw that my three companions were crouched on the bank. I crouched, too, and we ran along, almost on all fours. Even in the dark, we took no chance of being spotted.

Our first obstacle was a barbed-wire fence. Carefully we crawled under it. We kept going, keeping low, hugging the shadows of trees. We had to stay alert for the dangers of the territory—Immigration, thorns, snakes, thieves who prey on the careless. Our group was lucky. We managed to avoid them all.

A hundred yards past the border, we halted, my companions to wait for the remainder of the group and me to meet my contact. I shook their hands and wished them luck, then turned and walked another hundred yards to the car that was waiting. For me there would be a shower, food if I was hungry, a bed with clean sheets. For my companions there would be hours of walking, hunger, thirst, and an uncertain future. For them, the journey is never ending.

Julie put her hands on Greg's shoulders, and he covered them with his. A special bond had been forged between them through their shared experience. She'd never felt so close to another human being.

ON MONDAY Greg's article ran in the morning paper. Now that she'd seen the whole story, she could appreciate the power with which he wrote.

Julie was filled with emotion—touched by the story, proud of the writer. But then she focused on the three words below the final paragraph—End of Series—and she felt unbearable sadness. There it was in black-and-white, the news that Greg's work here was done, that soon he would be leaving.

He told her the next night at dinner. "I have to be in Washington on Monday."

Though she'd expected them, planned for them, the words hit her with the force of a punch in the midsection. He was leaving. He had other worlds to conquer.

"Oh," she said, careful to keep her voice even. "When do you leave?"

"Sunday morning."

Julie struggled to speak normally. Her entire body had gone numb with shock. Her lips moved, but they felt as if they'd been deadened with novocaine. "I'll drive you to the airport."

"Fine."

They were as polite as two strangers, she thought. Perhaps that was the way to end a love affair. Had she really told Grace she wouldn't get hurt? That was eons ago. One thing was certain, she'd survive it. As Greg had said, she was one tough lady.

Later that night she lay awake as Greg slept beside her. How she'd miss the reassuring sound of breathing, deep and even; the way he rubbed his feet against hers to warm them; the way he reached for her in his sleep. Bedded bliss. Well, she hadn't bargained for wedded. She'd better be satisfied with what she'd had.

Damn him, she thought. Damn him for being who he was. *And damn you, Julie, for falling in love with him.* She wanted to beat the pillow, cry for the loss she was about to experience. Instead she shut her eyes and willed herself to fall asleep.

Saturday arrived. Julie felt the minutes ticking away, and knew that, as she had done all week, she was pretending. Pretending that his leaving didn't matter. Pretending that her life would go on without a ripple of regret. Pretending that she didn't want to cling to him and beg him to stay.

They had an early dinner, went up to her room, and spent the evening making love.

The last time, Julie thought, the idea so painful that she nearly gasped aloud.

The last time, Greg mused. Better for both of them. But as he held her close, he wondered why the future seemed so barren.

They overslept the next morning and dressed hurriedly, with no time to talk. They were quiet on the drive to the airport, too, Julie concentrating on her driving. Greg reached for her hand. "We'll make it," he said.

And they did, but barely. They pulled up to the terminal with only minutes to spare. Greg jumped out and pulled his bag from the back seat while Julie watched. In a way, she was glad this had happened. It prevented a long, lingering goodbye.

Greg dropped his bag on the sidewalk and got back into the car. He slid across the seat.

Julie put her hands on his shoulders. "Have a safe trip," she whispered.

"Take care. I'll be in touch." He gave her a brief, hard kiss, got out of the car and slammed the door.

She watched him as he grabbed his bag, stopped to check it in at curbside, and walked into the terminal and out of her life.

Julie didn't realize she was biting her lip until she tasted blood. Only then did she notice the pain. But the pain in her lip was minor compared to the pain in her heart. She'd deal with it, though. Carefully she relaxed the hand which had been tightly clenched. She wiped her lip with a tissue, then, with dry eyes, she turned on the engine and drove away from the airport without a backward glance.

GREG SPRINTED through the terminal and made it to his gate just as the boarding attendant was stepping away from the entrance to the jetway.

He strode through the passage and entered the plane. The tall blond stewardess gave him a radiant smile. "Just made it," she said, letting her gaze travel over him with undisguised interest.

Greg gave her a brief nod and made his way down the aisle. He had the window seat, and to his relief, the aisle seat was unoccupied. Good. He didn't feel like making conversation. He sat down, buckled his seat belt, and stared out the window.

"Seat belt fastened?" The blonde leaned across the empty seat.

Greg nodded.

"Good. I'll be back to see if you want anything." She gave him a look that indicated she was on the menu if he so desired. He didn't.

He turned back to the window and the cart bringing out a last load of baggage.

The engines started, the flight attendant gave the usual pre-takeoff safety spiel, and the plane taxied toward the runway. Greg kept his eyes on the window as they gained speed and lifted smoothly into the air.

Washington. Another assignment. A new challenge. He should feel content as he always did after an assignment was completed. But this time, he didn't. As he watched the last view of Houston recede in the distance, he had the nagging feeling that he'd left something precious behind.

CHAPTER FOURTEEN

SPRING ARRIVED in Washington. Leaves budded, new grass grew, and of course, the cherry trees bloomed. But to Greg the world was grim, wintry. He settled into a bleak depression. His apartment seemed drab and musty, though soft spring breezes wafted through the open windows. Work was boring. Tom Lowrey suggested he take the vacation he'd postponed, but there was nowhere he wanted to go. Instead he went to Florida to do an overview of the immigration situation there. When he returned, he was short-tempered and moody. After he'd snapped at one of the switchboard operators for misplacing a message, he heard her say, "Wow! What's gotten to him?"

Greg knew exactly what had "gotten to him." Julie Whitaker. She was responsible for the fact that he'd lost his appetite, wasn't sleeping well, and couldn't find anything he wanted to do. He neglected his usual morning run, refused an invitation to the ballet from a woman whose company he'd enjoyed in the past, and spent most evenings sprawled listlessly in front of the television.

He'd been home two weeks when he got word that he was a shoo-in for a Pulitzer nomination for his Houston series. His first thought was to call Julie and tell her the news, but he didn't. In fact, he'd had his hand on the phone a dozen times before, but he'd never made the calls. He was afraid if he heard her voice he'd be on the next plane to Houston. To Julie. To sharing morning coffee and evening brandy, to arguing over the latest news story, to falling asleep with her warm, sweet body pressed against his own.

Damn, he thought. Damn her for getting under his skin this way. He wasn't a man for settling down. But lately, just lately, the idea of someone to come home to...someone named Julie...was becoming more and more appealing.

Several days later he received a call from a publishing house in New York, asking if he would consider doing a book on the lives of immigrants. Even that didn't lift his spirits. Was it true, he wondered, that reaching the top in your profession wasn't all it was cracked up to be? Perhaps the climb was what gave you satisfaction, and everything afterward, award and all, was anticlimactic.

"What the hell is wrong with me?" he asked himself. Had he picked up some sort of bug? He doubted it; he didn't feel physically ill, just lethargic. But as he peered into his mirror while he shaved, he saw that he didn't look well. Of course, he couldn't expect to look so great after tossing and turning for the past eight hours. His bed seemed so empty. As he had every night since he'd returned, he'd wakened, reaching for Julie, and when he found himself alone, had been unable to go back to sleep.

This morning he sat at his desk, staring into space. Maybe he ought to call the New York editor back about the book. Or maybe he should take his vacation after all, go to Arizona to visit his folks. Maybe...

His ear caught the sound of a familiar voice. Stephanie Barrett was striding across the newsroom. She came up to him and threw her arms around his neck. "Is this the future Pulitzer nominee?"

"So I've heard."

She kissed his cheek. "Come on, Allen. I'm talking you to lunch to celebrate. Your choice."

He picked a popular lunching spot and followed Stephanie to her car. God, it was good to be with her. She was her usual exuberant self, talking rapidly over her shoulder, eyes sparkling.

After they'd given their luncheon orders, Stephanie stared across the table at him, her eyes narrowed. "You know, Allen, for a prize-winning journalist, you don't look so good. What's wrong? Pick up a tropical fever in Houston?"

He shrugged. "I don't know, Steph. I haven't felt well since I've been back."

"Have you seen a doctor?"

"No, I'm not sick really, just . . ."

"Just blah. What on earth happened to you in Houston?"

"Nothing. Houston was great."

"So tell me about it. How was life as a priest?"

When he finished his story, Stephanie sat back and nodded her head. "So the great Greg Allen finally succumbs. It's nice to know you're human after all."

"What does that mean?" he asked irritably.

"It means, my dear, that your illness is purely emotional. It's called falling in love."

Greg shoved his plate back and tossed his napkin on the table. "Thanks, Dr. Freud. What gives you such insight?"

Stephanie gave him a bubbling laugh. "Do you have any idea how many times you mentioned Julie What's-Her-Name during our conversation?"

"Whitaker. And I hardly mentioned her at all."

"Just every other sentence. Wake up, Allen. You're in love with the woman."

He toyed with his spoon. "So what if I am?" he muttered.

"Ah, so he admits it."

"Yeah, I admit it. I'm in love with her. So what?"

Stephanie looked surprised. "You mean you're not planning to do anything about it?"

"What would I do?" With the spoon handle he traced a pattern on the white linen tablecloth. He'd wanted a light-hearted lunch with Stephanie, not a heart-to-heart discussion that would leave him feeling more depressed than ever. He shot her a sour look.

But Stephanie, never one to be intimidated, smiled sweetly at him and continued. "For starters you might call the lady and ask her to move to Washington and live with you."

Greg stopped playing with his spoon and looked at Stephanie. "Ask her to give up her life and move here, without any kind of commitment? I couldn't do that."

"So make a commitment."

"Like what?"

Stephanie chuckled. "Ever hear of marriage?"

"Marriage," he repeated, rolling the word over his tongue as if it were a foreign term.

"Well, that idea obviously shocked you down to your toes. Yes, Mr. Allen, marriage. I hear it's catching on."

"Cute, Stephanie. For your information, I have heard of it, but I'm not the marrying kind."

"Oh, I see. Then what's the problem? Forget this woman. Listen, there's a new gal who just transferred here from London. Long blond hair, gorgeous legs . . . you ought to meet her."

Greg's answer was a grimace.

Stephanie began to laugh, and after a moment Greg joined in. "To be honest," he admitted, "I *have* thought of marriage a few times, but I don't think it would work."

"Why not?"

"I'd be away from home a lot, for one thing."

"Poor excuse, Allen."

"You know my job isn't the ordinary travel-a-few-days-and-come-home kind. I can be gone for weeks at a time."

"Absence makes the heart grow fonder." Stephanie gave him a teasing grin.

"It's more than traveling, Steph. It's the danger. Julie lost a husband once. I don't know if she could handle the situations I'm in on a routine basis."

"Ask her. At least give *her* the chance to decide. And maybe you'll travel less, and when you do, she'll learn to live with it, and the danger. You'll compromise. That's what marriage is all about."

"Julie said that once," Greg mused.

"You know, Allen, your writing on this last series shows so much insight into human emotions. Why are you so dense when it comes to your own?" She reached over and squeezed his hand.

Lacing his fingers with hers, he said, "I miss her, Steph. I wake up at night, wanting her, and she's not there. I think about her at the oddest times—when I hear certain songs, when something funny happens that I want to tell her about, when I'm eating dinner alone." He stared thoughtfully at the tablecloth. "It's driving me crazy."

Stephanie grinned at him. "Lo, how the mighty have fallen. So why are you running away from it?"

"Running? I've never run away from anything in my life."

"So what do you call this?"

Damn, she was right. "Walking maybe?" he asked sheepishly.

Stephanie shook her head. "Whatever you call it, you're leaving someone who obviously means a lot to you. Seriously, Greg, why don't you ask her to marry you?"

"She told me once she doesn't want to get married."

"People change their minds. And I hate to repeat myself, but why don't you try asking her if she's changed hers? Even if she says no, you won't let that stop you. Persistence is your middle name."

Greg grinned suddenly. "Damn right it is."

Stephanie signaled to the waiter. "I think our lunch is over."

"Yeah. I have a few things to do."

Back at Worldwide he told Tom Lowrey he'd take his vacation immediately, then went back to his desk and made two phone calls...the first one to an airline, and the second to Phil Barnes.

JULIE DEALT with Greg's departure stoically. She took up her usual routine, working hard as usual. Her suggestion to the Coalition about setting up a fund for returning kidnap victims and their families had been accepted enthusiastically and she was deeply involved in raising the money.

Although she was busy, she found work less than satisfying. There were reminders of Greg everywhere. Meetings with Mr. Salazar and Esteban, running into Teresa at the bakery, just passing Father Gregory's old office brought a pang. One weekend she drove with friends to their ranch in Central Texas. Wildflowers dotted the fields—a spring palette in yellow, blue, red, and pink. The sight of them brought poignant memories of the drive she and Greg had made to Brownsville.

In an effort to be logical she told herself everything had worked out for the best. She'd never make it as the wife of a journalist who routinely put his life on the line. But she knew that wasn't true. If she had an opportunity to make a life with Greg, she'd learn to deal with her fears.

Several times she thought of calling him but decided against it. He'd set the limits on their relationship at the beginning when he told her he'd only be in Houston a short time. And she had tacitly agreed to those limits. She had too much pride to call him and tell him she wanted more. Besides, what good would it do?

He'd used her, Julie thought. Used her knowledge, used her contacts, and then, when his story was finished, he'd left. With no talk of the future, only a laconic, "Take care." When she read his article on the immigration situation in Florida, she wondered bitterly if he'd had a woman there, too. Anger replaced her pain.

Only with Grace was Julie able to discuss her feelings. Never did Grace say, "I told you so," though Julie knew she was thinking it. Instead the older woman encouraged her to develop new interests. Grace was right, Julie decided. She did need something new and different to raise her spirits. Maybe she'd take a course during the summer, or brush up on her tennis, or . . .

This Friday evening, though, she didn't feel like doing much. She came home from work, ate dinner, and lay in bed watching television. After the news, she debated between the late show or a new best-seller she'd bought. She decided that neither appealed to her, turned off the light, and curled up on her side.

She still missed the warmth of Greg's body beside her, but she was slowly getting used to being alone. A light rain began to fall, and the gentle patter of raindrops against the window lulled her to sleep.

The shrill ring of the telephone intruded. She turned over and groped for the receiver, almost dropping it. "'Lo," she mumbled drowsily.

"Julie."

Her heart jumped. "Greg."

"How are you?"

"All right. And you?" *What inane conversation,* she thought.

"Fine. I want to see you."

She wanted to see him, too, ached to see him, to touch him. But she couldn't put herself through the agony of parting again. "When are you coming in?" She'd tell him she was going to be out of town, she decided.

"I'm here now."

Now! Suddenly she was wide-awake and furious. Did he think he could just drop in unannounced, give her a call, and she'd welcome him with open arms? What did he want? A weekend quickie, and then he'd be off to the next conquest without giving her a thought, while she...she would be left with emptiness and pain. Not this time.

"I was already asleep. By the time you'd get here it would be midnight," she answered tersely.

"I'm five minutes away, at the Stop-and-Go on Memorial."

"Greg," her voice turned icy, "I don't want you to come."

He paid no attention. "Five minutes," he said, and before she could protest, he hung up.

Julie jumped out of bed and pulled a skirt and blouse from her closet. She wasn't going to meet him in a nightgown, that was for sure. Her heart began to race as she dressed and pulled a brush through her hair, but she wasn't sure whether it was anger or excitement that set it pounding.

She ran down the stairs just as she heard his familiar three rings of the doorbell. She stopped, took a breath, and walked slowly to the door, steeling herself for the encounter ahead.

When she opened the door and saw him standing there in the soft April rain, her breath caught. Raindrops shimmered on his hair and on his lashes, and his eyes were alight with . . . with something she hadn't seen before.

"Hi," he said softly.

She wanted nothing more than to walk into his arms, but sensing that he was about to reach for her, she stepped back and answered him with a clipped, "Hello."

God, she was beautiful, Greg thought. Beautiful and sweet and everything that a man could ever want. And, like a fool, he'd walked out on her. Now her expression was cold, her manner distant. Though he'd dreamed on the plane of sweeping her into his arms and carrying her away, he realized he'd have to start all over with her. Well, he deserved it.

Julie led him into the living room, then turned and almost collided with him. Quickly she spun away and headed for the bar. "Would you like a drink?" she asked, positioning herself so the bar was between them.

Greg nodded. He gazed at her hungrily as she opened the cabinet. For the first time in his life, he felt unsure and vulnerable with a woman. Perhaps because this time the outcome really mattered. He wondered what he should say to her. He was an expert with words. Which ones could he use to tell her what was in his heart?

Julie occupied herself with the drink, getting a glass, filling it with ice—anything to keep busy and to keep from looking at him. "What brings you to Houston?" she asked.

"A problem."

"What is it? Something go wrong with a story and you want some help from me? Sorry. I'm not available."

Greg flinched at the sarcasm in her voice. He shook his head. "A personal problem."

"Oh? Your sex life a little slow? Sorry, I'm not available for that, either."

"No," Greg said quietly. "Another kind of problem. Much more serious. I don't know why I didn't recognize it before I left," he went on, leaning against the bar.

Julie had no idea what he was talking about. She reached for the Scotch and poured.

"The symptoms were there," he continued, "but I didn't notice them until I got back to Washington and they started to multiply." He knew he was rambling but he couldn't seem to stop. He moved around to her side of the bar.

What on earth was he talking about? she wondered, then focused on one word. *Symptoms.* For the first time since he'd arrived, she looked at him directly. He looked tired from the trip...no, he looked haggard. There were shadows under his eyes, lines around his mouth. He'd lost weight. Her heart constricted. Was he ill? And why would he come back here? Houston was a heart center, a cancer center...oh, God, no.

"What kind of symptoms?" she asked.

"I couldn't eat, couldn't sleep, walked around like a zombie for weeks. Then, all of a sudden, I realized what was causing it." He took a step closer.

"You're sick," she said. He nodded, and the glass she was holding fell from her hand and shattered on the counter. Scotch splashed onto her skirt, her shoes. She stared dumbly at the mess for a moment, then raised her eyes to his. She could barely get the words out. "Wh-what is it?"

"Love."

For a moment, the word didn't register. Then, suddenly, her eyes widened. Her gaze locked with his. "What...what are you saying?" she whispered.

"That I'm in love with you."

She stared at him, stunned.

When she neither moved nor spoke, he continued, the words tumbling out as he fought to tell her how he felt. "At first I wanted you. I thought once I had you it would be enough. But it wasn't. I didn't recognize my feelings. I've had experience with lovers," he said with a self-deprecating smile, "but not with love. I had to leave you to know what I really felt."

Julie stood transfixed. "And now?" she asked finally.

"Now I know I want you for the rest of my life. *Having* you wasn't the answer. I want to *give* you my love. I want to share a home, raise a family... with you."

"You're asking me to marry you?"

"Yes." He felt he was poised on the edge of a precipice. With one word she could send him headlong into oblivion... or pull him back to safety and love. He stood silently, waiting, praying.

At last she said softly, "I love you, too."

Neither moved for a moment, then they reached for each other. He pulled her against him. She clasped him tightly, holding on as if she were afraid he'd disappear.

He drew back and lifted her chin so he could see her eyes. "Say it again."

"I love you," she repeated.

"Julie." He kissed her hungrily, pulling her closer, starved for the taste of her. His hands and his lips rushed over her. He pulled her blouse up and found her breast, cupped it with his hand, and bent to suckle. His breath quickened.

Leaving a trail of clothing in their wake, they managed to make it as far as the couch, then fell onto it, their bodies joining, moving together in wild and joyous accord. Afterward, they lay curled together, warm and relaxed.

Running his hand lazily over the familiar contours of her body, Greg asked, "How long does it take to get a marriage license here?"

"Couple of days. Let's get married at St. Martha's."

"I'd like that. We'll go over tomorrow and talk to Tim and Rudy."

She frowned and punched his shoulder. "You idiot! You made me think you were sick."

"I think it's a lifelong illness."

"I hope so." She reached for his hand and kissed his fingers one by one.

He drew his hand away and regarded her seriously. "I'll still have to travel, and sometimes I'll be in danger. Will you be able to live with that?"

"Yes," she said quietly. "It won't be easy, but I'll manage it. I won't ask you to change who you are."

"For the first few months I'll be researching a book on immigration . . . and waiting to see if I win the Pulitzer."

"Oh, Greg. I know you'll win." She smiled radiantly, then said thoughtfully, "I'll have to give notice at the church. I want to find a job in a similar community in Washington. Perhaps Father Rudolfo can give me some leads." It would be hard to leave the people she cared so deeply about, but—

"You won't have to give notice. *I'm* going to make the move. We'll be staying here."

"Here? You haven't quit your job, have you?"

"No. Phil asked me to consider a transfer to Houston. I called him yesterday and told him I'd take it."

Julie propped herself up on an elbow and gave him an arch look. "Pretty sure of yourself, weren't you, Allen?"

"No," he said, surprising her with his seriousness. "You told me once you didn't plan to get married again."

She frowned, not remembering. "When was that?"

"The day your car broke down and I took you home."

Julie leaned down to kiss him, her eyes filled with love and laughter. "But, darling," she murmured, "I didn't know then that *you* were available."

Harlequin
Superromance®

COMING NEXT MONTH

#414 BETWEEN TWO MOONS • Eve Gladstone
The scion of black princes and robber barons, Tony
Campbell had a reputation for ruthlessness. But
when he took over her store—the most fashionable
woman's specialty shop in Manhattan—Kelly
Aldrich sensed another side to him. Could she tame
the British lion? She had to. Or be consumed by him.

#415 STARLIGHT, STAR BRIGHT • Kelly Walsh
Federal postal inspector Chris Laval knew Ivy
Austin's family meant everything to her. So when he
began to suspect Ivy's brother was involved in a mail
fraud scam, Chris had a problem: how could he win
Ivy's love when he might have to send her beloved
brother to jail?

#416 PLAYING BY THE RULES • Connie Bennett
Police lieutenant Alex Devane swore he'd never again
carry a gun. He'd seen and done too much to ever
want to be reassociated with violence. Ivy Kincaid
helped make Alex see he would only be helping
people by working on the Brauxton Strangler case.
She also brought Alex's passionate spirit to life
again, but Alex was determined not to endanger the
life of another loved one....

#417 STORMY WEATHER • Irma Walker
Stormy Todd was a troublesome tenant. When Guy
Harris evicted her from her home, she and her kids
showed up at his beach house! Guy found Stormy
hard to resist, but was there any future for an
unemployed single mother and one of San Jose's
most prominent citizens?

COMING SOON

In September, two worlds will collide in four very special romance titles. Somewhere between first meeting and happy ending, Dreamscape Romance will sweep you to the very edge of reality where everyday reason cannot conquer unlimited imagination—or the power of love. The timeless mysteries of reincarnation, telepathy, psychic visions and earthbound spirits intensify the modern lives and passion of ordinary men and women with an extraordinary alluring force.

Available in September!

EARTHBOUND—Rebecca Flanders
THIS TIME FOREVER—Margaret Chittenden
MOONSPELL—Regan Forest
PRINCE OF DREAMS—Carly Bishop

DRSC-RR